Stand Alone Novel

the WORLD Within

A Novel of Emily Brontë

JANE EAGLAND

ARTHUR A. LEVINE BOOKS
AN IMPRINT OF SCHOLASTIC INC.

All rights reserved. Published by Arthur A. Levine Books, an imprint of Scholastic Inc., *Publishers since 1920*. SCHOLASTIC, the LANTERN LOGO, and associated logos are trademarks and/or registered trademarks of Scholastic Inc.

Library of Congress Cataloging-in-Publication Data

Eagland, Jane, author.
  The world within : a novel of Emily Brontë / Jane Eagland. — First edition.
    pages cm
  Summary: Fourteen-year-old Emily would rather spend her days dreaming of adventures and wandering the moors, but when her father falls sick, and her sister Charlotte is sent away to school reality comes crashing in.
  ISBN 978-0-545-49295-9 (hardcover : alk. paper) 1. Brontë, Emily, 1818–1848 — Juvenile fiction. 2. Brontë family — Juvenile fiction. 3. Women authors, English — 19th century — Juvenile fiction. 4. Families — England — Haworth — Juvenile fiction. 5. Haworth (England) — Social life and customs — 19th century — Juvenile fiction. 6. Great Britain — History — 1800–1837 — Juvenile fiction. [1. Brontë, Emily, 1818–1848 — Fiction. 2. Brontë family — Fiction. 3. Authors — Fiction. 4. Family life — England — Haworth — Fiction. 5. Haworth (England) — Social life and customs — 19th century — Fiction. 6. Great Britain — History — 1800–1837 — Fiction.] I. Title.
  PZ7.E1155Wo 2015
  823.92 — dc23

                                                               2014004667

10 9 8 7 6 5 4 3 2 1   15 16 17 18 19

First edition, April 2015

Printed in the U.S.A.   23

Book design by Jeannine Riske

For Sheila and Lindsey

1

Though it is night, the sun casts an eerie light over these regions, forlorn indeed. The snow is so yielding that at every step I plunge up to my knees and can barely make any headway.

A cry from behind freezes my blood.

I turn to discover that Lieutenant Ross has sunk into the deadly white mass and cannot extricate himself. With immense difficulty I flail back to him.

"Parry," he says, with tears in his eyes, "I am done for. You must go on without me."

"Nonsense, my friend," I say. "Give me your hand. We will make it to the Pole yet."

"Emily!" Aunt's voice, sharp as a needle. "You are daydreaming again. Attend to your work."

Emily stabs the white calico in exasperation. She wasn't daydreaming — in her imagination she was her hero, Parry, the great explorer, and just at the critical moment Aunt came crashing in and broke the spell.

She sighs. Lucky Parry to be able to go off journeying in the wild wastes of the Arctic, unencumbered by annoying relatives making him do things he didn't want to do. *He* never had to sew nightshirts, for sure. Her back aches from sitting on the low stool, her fingers are cramped, and she's desperate to stand up and move about, to walk, to run. To escape this stuffy room. To be out of doors.

She wiggles her toes inside her boots.

There's a sudden movement at the window. Dropping her sewing, she dashes over and peers out just in time to see a flock of chaffinches disappearing over the mossy garden wall into the graveyard beyond.

Disappointed to have missed them, Emily lifts her eyes, gazing past the dark bulk of the church below her and the cluster of grey houses surrounding it that form the top of the village, across the smoke-filled valley to the distant hills. Their heather-clad slopes, glowing purple in the soft autumn light, look so inviting. Emily sighs again.

Resting her forehead against the glass, she squinnies down the lane past the Sunday school toward the bottom corner, where anyone approaching would appear between Mr. Brown the sexton's house and the church. But there's no sign of Branwell.

It's not fair. Their brother will be off somewhere, up to high jinks, probably, in all that lovely sunshine, while Aunt keeps her and her sisters shut up like prisoners. Every day apart from Sunday it's the same routine — an hour or more of sewing in Aunt's bedroom, a tedious ordeal that seems to last forever.

"Emily!" Aunt's voice cuts into her thoughts. "What are you doing now?"

"Looking at some birds."

"Birds! Much good will they do you. Have you finished that hem?"

"Almost."

"Show me."

Reluctantly Emily takes the crumpled nightshirt over for inspection. Up close, the rose water Aunt dabs on herself fails to mask the sickly-sweet whiff of perspiration and the sharp reek of snuff.

"How has this got so grubby, Emily? You must take more care." Aunt peers at the hem.

Awaiting her verdict, Emily stares at the familiar framed text on the wall. *The Lord is my Shepherd*, illustrated by a picture of a rather languid-looking Jesus leading a few sheep through a desert landscape with palm trees. She wonders, not for the first time, how, without a blade of grass or sprig of heather to eat, the sheep can be so unbelievably plump.

Aunt tuts. "No, no. This won't do at all. Your stitches are much too big and irregular." She holds the nightshirt out to Emily between her finger and thumb as if she can hardly bear to touch it. "You'll have to unpick them and start again." She looks closely at Emily and her expression of disapproval deepens. "Have you brushed your hair today?"

"Erm . . . I can't remember."

Aunt tuts again. "You really should take more pride in your appearance, Emily."

"Why?" Emily stares pointedly at the long hairs on Aunt's chin.

"Because it's natural for a girl to want to make the best of herself. It's ∴ . . . it's womanly."

Emily puts on an innocent look. "But I thought it says in the Bible that women shouldn't adorn themselves with 'broided hair' but with good works."

"Yes, of course it does." Aunt looks flustered. "But that's different. That's about not being vain — it doesn't mean you shouldn't brush your hair."

"But you said I should take more pride in my appearance. Isn't pride the same as vanity?"

Aunt thrusts the nightshirt at her. "That's enough, Emily. Take this and get on, do."

As Emily takes the offending article and slouches back to her stool, she mutters, "Branwell won't care if the stitches are big."

"But you should."

My stars, the old lady's ears are sharp.

Aunt goes on, "It is the mark of a lady to take care with her work. How often do I have to tell you? Regularity and neatness —"

"— are the sign of an orderly mind."

"Quite so." Aunt peers at her niece, suspecting "sauce."

Emily keeps her face straight. Out of the corner of her eye she sees Charlotte's lip curl with amusement.

As soon as Aunt's attention is off them, Emily winks at Anne, who is sitting on the stool next to hers. Her younger sister gives a brief, answering smile, but then she glances at Aunt and dutifully bends to her work again.

Poor Anne, she's having the worst of it today. Darning stockings is the most hateful thing.

Slowly Emily starts unpicking stitches. If Aunt had any idea what went on in their minds, she'd be shocked. *An orderly mind.* How dull that would be.

"Charlotte, keep still. This won't come out right if you fidget."

Poor Charlotte. She's been standing by the bed for ages while Aunt presses various pieces of material against her and marks the alterations. At sixteen — two years older than Emily — Charlotte's not getting any taller, but she's filling out, so she has to make herself a new dress. Only it isn't new, really — it's being concocted from an old one of Aunt's taken apart and cut down to fit.

The pieces of fabric lie spread out on Aunt's yellow quilt. For a wonder Aunt hasn't reminded them today, as she so often does, that when she first came to live with them she had to send all the way to Wales for this quilt, since only wool wadding was adequate to combat the rigors of Haworth winters.

Finally, after much prodding, Aunt puts down her chalk. "That will do well, I think."

It won't.

Charlotte's face is impassive, but she's fingering the dress pieces doubtfully and Emily knows what she's thinking. The dress is going to be a horror. Even turned inside out, you can tell the silk's been worn. And the material's such a dreary color, a peculiar rusty green. The heroines in Charlotte's stories wear elegant, beautiful gowns and they're always white.

Aunt has sat down on her stiff-backed chair, which is placed as close to the banked-up fire as she can get it. Spurred on by a sudden flare of antagonism, Emily lifts her chin. "Aunt, you know how you're always telling us about the lovely clothes you and Mama wore when you were young?"

Aunt pauses in her knitting and laughs, a trilling, almost girlish laugh. "Oh yes, all those pretty muslins and —"

Emily pounces, looking Aunt straight in the eye. "So why do we have to wear these plain, dull dresses?"

For herself she doesn't care at all, but she knows that Charlotte minds dreadfully. It's so unjust.

Aunt purses her lips.

Emily is aware of her sisters tensing as they wait for Aunt to erupt. But with a small nod of her head, the old lady says mildly, "That is a fair question, Emily."

She hesitates a moment and then says, "As you know, our papa, your grandfather, was a wealthy merchant. Penzance was a prosperous town and we moved in social circles where it was important that we dressed appropriately. Your mother and I were therefore fortunate that Papa could afford fine clothes for us. God, in His wisdom, has seen fit to place you in a different station in life. Different things are required of the daughters of a humble parson."

She sighs and looks out of the window.

Pulling a length of thread from the reel, Emily glances at Charlotte, who looks troubled. Perhaps it wasn't such a good idea to ask about the dresses.

After a moment Aunt turns back and her tone becomes brisk once again. "Now, Charlotte, what are you waiting for? Pin those bodice pieces together and then baste them. Emily, how many times must I tell you? Cut the thread with scissors, not your teeth."

They all resume their work.

With Aunt it always comes down to God in the end. As if there's no more argument to be had.

～

Later, released at last and out on the moors, Emily breathes in great lungfuls of air, as if she can't get enough of it. She wants to shout aloud with the relief of being free to move, of being away from Aunt's watchful eye. Striding along beside Tabby and Anne, she's enjoying the warmth of the sun on her face, the way the wind brings everything to life, making the grasses sway and sending the high white clouds scudding across the sky.

But Charlotte is lagging behind, looking miserable.

"Charlotte's out of sorts today," Emily observes to Tabby.

Tabby glances back. "Aye, she does seem a bit dowly."

Emily and Anne exchange looks. Tabby's expressions amuse them no end.

"But she's often 'dowly' these days and I don't know why." Emily kicks a stone.

"Nay, don't scuff thi boots like that, Miss Emily — they've got to last thee a good while yet. As for Miss Charlotte, it's just her age, I reckon. Nowt to fret about."

Emily looks back again. Maybe it *is* Charlotte's age. A few months ago she had an alarming experience — Aunt called it "the start of womanhood," making her sister blush. Perhaps that's what is disturbing Charlotte. Or maybe it's what Aunt said earlier about their station in life. And that was Emily's fault. She should never have raised the subject of fine dresses.

Suddenly contrite, Emily runs back and hops onto a rock in front of Charlotte, startling a scraggy sheep, who stares at her with its mad yellow eyes. Emily ignores the sheep and, flinging out her arms, she intones, "O Charles, God in His wisdom has seen fit to call thee to a glorious destiny. Thou wilt be great, esteemed amongst women." Then, dropping her arms and speaking in her normal voice, she adds, "And possibly even amongst men too."

Charlotte smiles, in spite of herself.

Emily, pleased at her sister's response, jumps down and links arms with her, and they walk on until they catch up with

Anne. Emily links arms with her as well and the three of them continue together, following Tabby, who by now is some way ahead.

"You know, you oughtn't to joke about God, Emily," Charlotte says after a few moments. She is serious now, looking up at Emily with a little frown wrinkling her brow.

"No, you shouldn't," chimes in Anne earnestly. "I think it might be considered blasphemy."

Emily gives an impatient shake of her head. These two can be so pious sometimes, especially Anne. It isn't as if she was saying anything dreadful about God.

Charlotte adds, "And you really shouldn't try to provoke Aunt. Fancy quoting the Bible at her. Poor Aunt."

"You thought it was funny," Emily points out. "And anyway, *she* is the provoking one, making us sew for hours. And it isn't fair. She would have hated wearing a dress like the one she's making you wear when she was young, but she doesn't care about our feelings."

Anne says, "I sometimes think she does feel sorry for us."

Emily turns to her, astonished. "Do you? She never shows any sign of it."

"When she says good night, she has a way of looking . . . so . . ." Anne makes a sad face.

"She might feel sorry for *you*," says Charlotte. "She likes you better than us." She suddenly sounds accusing.

Anne turns pink and her lip starts to tremble.

Charlotte really is out of sorts today. Pulling Anne closer, Emily leaps in before her sister says anything else. "You're probably right, Charlotte. But it isn't Anne's fault. Be glad it's not you that Aunt has chosen for a bedfellow. Does she not snore, Anne, and pass wind with a sound like a trumpet?"

Anne giggles, but then she looks serious. "Do you suppose if Mama were alive, we'd have to wear hand-me-downs?"

Emily exchanges a glance with Charlotte. They have a tacit understanding between them that they don't talk about Mama. But it's not surprising that Anne doesn't feel the same — she can't remember their mother at all.

Charlotte says quietly, "Even if Mama were here, we wouldn't have any more money. And Papa wouldn't approve of us wearing finery. Aunt was quite right about our situation. Living as we do here in Haworth, we've no need of fine dresses."

A silence falls. Emily chews her lip. This isn't good. If she doesn't say something, Charlotte will sink into gloom again.

"Listen." Emily comes to a sudden halt, causing the other two to stop as well. "Think how lucky we are not to be dressed up like dolls and have to mind we don't get marks on our gowns. Or tread daintily in our little satin slippers, the way Aunt would like us to." Emily puts her nose in the air and takes a few mincing steps. She's delighted when the other two laugh. "And just think — if we were the daughters of a wealthy merchant, we wouldn't have all this."

She gestures at the broad sweep of moorland, at the clear blue bowl of the sky. Overhead, unseen, a lark is singing his heart out. Emily, suddenly transfixed, listens with all her attention, her own heart swelling in sympathy with the joyous sound.

After a long moment, she comes back to herself and becomes aware of her sisters looking at her with bemused expressions.

She gives herself a shake. "Come on, it's much too nice a day for moping." She grabs their hands. "Let's run and catch up with Tabby."

And, with Charlotte half-protesting and Anne doing her best to keep up, she pulls them along.

⁋

Back home, breathless and windswept and on their way upstairs to wash their hands for tea, they meet Branwell in the hall. His hair is tousled, his shirt collar awry, and he has a smudge of dirt on his face.

"Where have you been?" Emily can't keep the envy out of her voice.

"Up at Marsh Farm. Some of the boys were ratting with terriers." Branwell's eyes glow at the thought of it. "Fred Harper's dog was the best. As quick as lightning. She grabbed a rat, like this, killed it with a shake of her head, and caught another before the first hit the ground." Branwell acts out the terrier's feat, overdoing it as usual and snarling and squealing so fiercely his face turns red. Then he bares his teeth at Anne, lunges, and pretends to bite her.

Shrinking away from him, giggling, she knocks against the hall stand, and the pewter plate with Papa's letters on it waiting to go to the post skitters off and hits the hard stone floor with a crash, scattering envelopes in every direction.

"Oh!" Anne's hand flies to her mouth and she freezes, looking petrified.

Emily stoops quickly to retrieve the plate. She examines it. "Don't worry, it's only a little bit dented. They probably won't even notice."

"Anyway, it's not your fault," says Charlotte. "It's Branwell's." She frowns at him. "You are a giddy goose sometimes."

Branwell looks the picture of injured innocence. "I was only —"

"What on earth is going on?" Aunt is standing on the first landing, glowering down at them. In her black dress and framed by the tall arched window behind her she reminds Emily of one of the four avenging angels of the apocalypse. Though the impression is somewhat spoiled by the outsized mobcap perched precariously on the top of her head.

Emily bites her lip to stop herself from giggling.

Aunt is in full spate. "How often have I told you? The hall is no place for your games. You're too old for such silliness, but if you must behave like barbarians, then at least do it outside. All this noise is disturbing your poor father."

"We didn't know he'd come home," says Charlotte. "Otherwise we'd have been quiet."

"Well, he has. And he's gone straight to bed."

Emily feels a prickle of alarm. Papa in bed so early? It's unheard of.

"I must go and see if he wants anything," says Aunt. "When you've put this shambles to rights and had your tea, I suggest you occupy yourselves quietly until it's time for prayers. Something useful, mind — not that foolish scribbling." Wagging her finger as a final warning, she disappears upstairs again.

There's a silence as they look at one another.

"Do you think Papa is ill?" Anne's voice is tremulous, her eyes wide.

Her question hangs in the air until finally Charlotte says, "I don't know."

"I'll go and ask Tabby. She'll tell us." Emily slips across the hall to the kitchen.

But Tabby, buttering bread for their tea, will only say, "There's nowt to worry thiselves about. Thi father's worn hisself out traipsing over to Trawden and back in the heat. He'll be right as ninepence in the morning, tha'll see."

2

But morning comes and their father doesn't appear, not at prayers, which Aunt leads, haltingly, or for breakfast.

"Your father is tired today," Aunt announces. "He'll be staying in his room for the time being. You can all carry on as usual, but you must be quiet. I don't want your father disturbed." She closes her lips tightly as if to forestall any further questions. But no one says a word.

Emily droops over her bowl. She was awake a long time worrying about Papa. Now she's tired and a lump like a heavy stone has lodged itself in her chest.

This morning the parlor seems cold, despite the fire Tabby has lit for Aunt. The peat flickers sullenly in the grate as if unwilling to burst into life. And in the shadowy light, the grey walls seem to press in upon her.

Emily looks across the table at the empty space where Papa normally sits.

She can't remember him ever missing breakfast before. He's often out for dinner and always has his tea by himself in his study, but he makes a point of joining them for the first meal of the day.

It's so strange without him there, his face animated, his eyes bright, as he entertains them with some tale or other of his boyhood in Ireland in the tiny village of Drumballyroney, or something he's heard in his parish rounds. Emily likes the thrillingly gruesome ones best — stories of violence, even murder — or the funny ones.

Only yesterday he was telling them about an old woman he'd heard of who asked for two holes to be put in her coffin lid. "When they asked her why, she said it was so that if the devil came in at one, she could slip out at the other!"

Aunt protested, as she often does. "Really, Mr. Brontë, do you think that's suitable for children's ears?"

But Papa just laughed and winked at them.

Dear Papa. He's like a whirlwind, bursting in on them from time to time and turning everything upside down. You never know what he's going to say or do next. He's so exuberant, full of energy and enthusiasm. So *alive*.

Emily picks up her spoon, looks at the porridge rapidly cooling and congealing in front of her, and puts the spoon down again. She glances covertly at Aunt. She's sipping her tea with a preoccupied air and restlessly crumbling a piece of bread on her plate. She's not even noticed that Emily hasn't eaten anything.

That means it must be serious. Aunt's normally as watchful as a hawk.

As soon as they're allowed to leave the table, Emily goes into the kitchen and empties her bowl into Tiger's dish. "There you are, puss," she says as the cat comes over to sniff at his breakfast. "You've got an extra-large helping today."

Then she seeks out Tabby in the back kitchen.

"Papa is ill, isn't he?"

Tabby pauses in her pan scouring and looks at Emily directly. "Aye, lass, he is."

Emily's heart starts to beat faster. "There was a pigeon tapping at the bedroom window this morning." The words come out in a rush.

Tabby gives her a look. "Now don't tha go believing that old nonsense."

"But you said it meant that someone was going to die. Remember?"

Tabby wipes her hands on her apron. "Listen, my lamb. I said that's what *some* folk believe, ignorant folk who don't know any better. What ails thi papa is nobbut a chill. He got caught in that heavy shower the other day, didn't he?" She clicks her tongue. "There's other parsons would look to their own comfort, but tha knows thi father — he thinks only of other folk. But he'll soon shake it off, so there's no need to grieve. Take this food to yon birds. Thi papa wouldn't want thee to forget them on his account."

She lays a work-roughened hand on Emily's cheek and it's this gentleness that alarms Emily the most.

൦൦

Having fed the birds in their makeshift cage in the yard — the doves, Rainbow, Diamond, and Snowflake, flutter down for the crumbs immediately, but Jasper the pheasant is being standoffish this morning — Emily goes upstairs to find Charlotte.

She tells her the news as they turn and shake their mattress.

"A chill?" Charlotte looks doubtful.

From Papa's room next door, they hear him coughing, a painful-sounding protracted spasm.

Charlotte's eyes meet Emily's across the striped ticking. "Let's not tell the others. Not unless we have to."

When they've completed their allotted tasks, out of habit the girls drift toward the study, where they find Branwell sitting at Papa's desk, sighing over his Latin translation of the New Testament.

A pang of annoyance shoots through Emily. He shouldn't be sitting in Papa's chair. But then she bites her tongue. With Papa lying ill upstairs, she mustn't start a row.

Branwell has brightened at the sight of them. "Aunt says we are to go on with whatever lessons Papa set us yesterday. But, I say, she won't know whether we have got further on or not. Shall we carry on with Glass Town?"

Charlotte shakes her head. "I think we should do some work first." She selects a book from the shelves under the window and takes a seat. Seeing that the others haven't moved, she says, "Papa would want us to, don't you think?" She's appealing to Emily and Anne.

Anne says, "Yes," at once and, finding her spelling book, she takes it over to the rocking chair by the fireplace. There's no fire, of course — the grate is empty and swept clean — but Anne still takes up her favorite position, with her feet on the fender.

Emily hesitates, torn. Branwell has a point. And she'd much rather spend the time writing about their imaginary world than studying the characters of the English monarchs. But she doesn't want to argue with Charlotte. Not today.

Sighing, she takes the history book from the shelf and perches on the windowsill. There's a cold draft whistling through the gap between the frame and the pane and rattling the shutters, but, knowing that Aunt is occupied with Papa, she's smuggled Tiger in with her — his warm weight in her lap is so comforting — and she'd rather sit here so she can look out.

The sky's overcast this morning, a uniform dull grey, and the wind's stirring the long damp grass and the nettles in the grave-yard. From the barn just up the lane comes the constant chink, chink of iron on stone — Mr. Brown, the sexton, must be cut-ting the lettering on a new headstone.

The existing headstones in the graveyard are hung with washing, looking as if a flock of geese has landed. Normally Aunt would complain about it to Papa and he would say what he always says — that it's doing no harm and where else can the villagers dry their wet linen? But today, Emily supposes, Aunt probably won't even notice. Everything is out of the ordinary.

She finds the right page, but she can't concentrate. She's lis-tening for sounds from Papa's room overhead. At one point she hears Aunt's iron-soled pattens clicking across the floor. Papa coughs occasionally, but it doesn't sound too bad. Maybe Tabby's telling the truth. Maybe he just needs a day's rest in bed and tomorrow he'll be up and about as usual.

Branwell starts humming a tune under his breath. He sounds too happy for Latin, so Emily cranes her head to see what he's doing. He's drawing something on the inside of the front cover of the New Testament. He becomes aware of her watching and holds it up so she can see: two muscular soldiers fighting with swords and shields. She smiles her admiration, then turns to see if Charlotte's noticed. But Charlotte, holding her geography book close to her face, is busy decorating its margins with her own sketches.

"Charlotte!"

Charlotte looks up and blushes.

"This is silly," says Emily. "We might just as well go on with our play."

Charlotte puts down her pencil. "All right. But we mustn't make too much noise."

Delighted, Emily jumps up and deposits Tiger on the floor. "I'll fetch the books." As stealthy as a cat herself, she runs upstairs to the room she shares with Charlotte, retrieves the old case from under the bed, and is back in a minute.

She kneels down on the worn rectangle of carpet in the middle of the floor and the others gather round. As soon as Emily raises the lid of the case, the miniature books with their blue or brown sugar paper covers spill out.

"We'll need somewhere else to keep them soon. This is getting full." Emily touches the battered leather case lightly, almost reverentially. It's the one Papa carried when he left Ireland for England, to take up his place at Cambridge University. She never sees it without thinking of how he came to this country with nothing, but was determined to make something of himself. It's just the right container for the little books.

Here is all their writing, scads and scads of it, the result of hours of playing and acting out their ideas and arguing about what should happen next, neatly printed in separate dated volumes, as if they were real authors. Just looking at them gives Emily a full, satisfied feeling. And she loves the fact that no one else apart from themselves, certainly no adult, can read the minute print they all use for their writings, so they're wonderfully secret.

"Right," says Charlotte, sitting back on her heels, "if you remember, the marquis, Arthur, has just met Lady Zenobia Ellrington."

"'A bluestocking of deepest dye,'" Emily quotes, earning the flash of a smile from Charlotte.

Branwell shifts restlessly. "He's not going to fall in love, is he? Because, if he is, why don't you go on with that by yourself, Charlotte, and I can start something else."

"Such as?"

"Well, I think my chief man, Alexander Rogue, should lead an expedition across the desert to suppress an uprising in the far west. Then we can have a great battle with cannon and muskets and heaps of corpses."

Charlotte groans and Emily looks at Anne and rolls her eyes.

"No, listen," says Branwell, waving his hands, "Arthur can go as well, if he can tear himself away from the alluring Lady Zenobia, and he can be horribly wounded in the battle, near death —"

"No!" Charlotte is distraught.

Branwell gives her a radiant smile. "But you, as Chief Genius Tallii, can appear and restore him with an incantation!"

Emily frowns. This has been happening too much lately — Branwell and Charlotte getting so caught up in the story that they forget they're not the only ones in this play. It's hateful of them to leave her and Anne out.

When they first started the plays, ages ago when they were small, they always made them up *together*. And it wasn't just that it was more exciting and fun that way, but it made her feel . . . what? Safe? Was that it? Yes. As if between them all they spun a web, a safety net that held her, and for a while at least she could be part of those worlds, could escape from the desperate feelings that had engulfed her after The Terrible Events — that's how she thinks of them now, shutting everything away in a box with a neat label on it and burying it deep inside her.

If they're not going to do this together anymore, she's afraid that the safety net might break, that the box might come open, letting all those feelings, those monsters, out again, and this time she'll have nowhere to hide. Her heart races at the thought.

There's only one answer — if Branwell and Charlotte are ignoring her, she'll have to push her way in.

"Listen, you two," she says, interrupting Charlotte and Branwell's conversation. "What about Parry? And Ross," she adds, on Anne's behalf. "You haven't mentioned them at all. One of them could lead the expedition."

"Parry!" Charlotte almost spits the word out. "The men will laugh at him." She pinches her nose between her first finger and thumb. "Coob od, lads," she says, sounding like Tabby with a cold. "Led de battle begid."

Emily recoils as if she's been stung. "That's not fair! Parry's just as heroic as the marquis! And far more noble than Rogue. But you're always leaving our men out. Aren't they, Anne? You write about each other's characters, but not ours."

Branwell turns on her. "That's because our men are compelling and do great deeds or ravish their listeners with the poetic outpourings of their souls. They're not weedy, like your men. And me and Charlotte have better ideas. Especially me."

Emily's opening her mouth to retort when the door opens and Aunt looks in. Her expression is so grim Emily feels her heart plummet.

But Aunt hasn't come to berate them for their raised voices and she doesn't even seem to notice Tiger. She beckons. "Branwell, run at once to Dr. Andrew with this." She hands him a note. "Wait for an answer and come straight back." Emily can hear the urgency in her voice.

Branwell leaps up and follows Aunt out of the room. The next minute they see his head go past the window. He's taking the shortcut through the churchyard.

In the silence Emily looks at her sisters. If the doctor is being consulted, it can only mean one thing. Papa must be very ill indeed.

3

Charlotte breaks the silence that follows Branwell's departure. "We'd better tidy up."

Anne immediately starts putting their lesson books away while Charlotte bends to pick up the little books from the floor. Emily goes to help her, but Charlotte waves her away, saying, "I'll do it."

How long will it be before Branwell returns? Emily wanders over to Papa's desk. There are all the familiar objects — Papa's spectacles case, his comical tobacco jar with its gargoyle face, his inkpot. He's left a pen out and she puts it back in the pen stand, arranging it tidily in line with the others. All the resentment and anguish that she felt a few minutes earlier has vanished. She can only think about Papa now.

She grips the back of his chair. Impossible to imagine him lying upstairs in his bed, pale and still.

Suddenly she notices that instead of putting the little books away in Papa's case, Charlotte has taken them all out and is arranging them in piles.

Emily drops to her knees next to her sister. "What are you doing?"

Charlotte's face is closed. "I'm getting my books out, separating them from everybody else's. I'm going to make a catalog of them. Then I'll store mine somewhere else and there'll be more space in here for yours."

Emily stares. Tiger comes up and butts his head against her, wanting her to stroke him, but she ignores him.

What does Charlotte mean — "my" books? They've always been "our" books. What's going on?

But there's no time to ask because the doctor's here now — Emily can hear his voice in the hall and Aunt greeting him.

Branwell comes in, leaving the door slightly ajar. He goes to say something, but Charlotte says, "Hush," and puts her finger to her lips. They all listen hard.

". . . complaining of a severe pain in his chest and he's somewhat feverish." Aunt's voice, slightly tighter than usual, but as crisp as ever. "I don't like to bother you, but I'm worried about him."

"You do right to send for me, ma'am. Shall we go up?"

The voices recede.

"Chest pain! And fever," says Branwell, tugging at his hair as he always does when he's agitated. "That could mean —"

"It could mean anything," says Charlotte hastily. "But Dr. Andrew will make Papa well again. That's why Aunt sent for him."

Emily blurts out, "He didn't cure Mama. Or Maria. Or Elizabeth. Papa sent for him then too." She bites the inside of her lip, aware of Anne's eyes flitting between them all, her hand flying to her mouth. Why did she say that?

Charlotte's face crumples, just for a second, and then she gathers herself. "We'd better do something quiet now. Branwell, will you read to us from *Blackwood's Magazine*? I don't think we finished that article Papa recommended, the one about the abolition of slavery, did we?"

That night, before she gets into bed, Emily rummages in the bottom of a drawer until she finds what she's looking for — the wooden lion Papa gave her for her sixth birthday. It's battered and scratched and it's lost its tail, but its splendid curly mane is intact and when she sets it on the chest of drawers its red painted mouth still roars in a fierce challenge.

Papa knew that this would please her far more than a doll or a pretty ornament. But then Emily's always felt that there was a special connection between them. He doesn't mind that she's a tomboy, outspoken at times and preferring to think things through for herself. And when Aunt complains to him that Emily's been climbing trees or fighting Branwell or challenging something he's said, he seems rather proud of her, if anything.

Charlotte's lying on her side, resting her head in her hand, her face solemn, watching without saying anything. In fact, she's barely said a word since the afternoon. Giving the lion a final pat, Emily climbs into bed and pulls the bedclothes up to her chin, creeping close to her sister. She's wanted to talk to her all day, but now that they've got the chance, Charlotte rolls over, presenting her back to Emily.

"Charlotte?"

No response.

"Charles? Won't you talk to me?"

Charlotte turns back, her voice full of fury. "You mustn't say those things. About Mama. And the others." There are tears in her eyes.

"I didn't mean to say it. You know what I'm like," Emily cries. "But it's true."

24

Charlotte blinks as if Emily has slapped her. After a moment she says, "It's not right. Think of Anne."

"She's not a baby anymore."

"Maybe not. But still, you know she's easily upset, you shouldn't risk alarming her by speaking of those things. It could bring on an asthma attack."

"But if Papa dies —"

Charlotte sits up, glaring at her. "He won't."

"But if he does . . . how will we bear it?"

Charlotte is quiet a moment, thinking. Then she says carefully, "If anything happened to Papa, we'd still have Aunt."

"Aunt?" What's Charlotte's talking about? Having Aunt won't help if they lose Papa.

"To look after us, I mean. Though I'm not sure that she'd want us. Or could afford to keep us."

Emily stares at her sister. She has never thought about what it would mean practically, if Papa died. She swallows hard and then says in a small voice, "We'd have to leave the parsonage, wouldn't we?" A shudder goes through her at the thought.

"Yes," Charlotte says tersely. "And Papa has no money to leave us. We'd have nothing at all. But let's not think about it. Because it won't happen. It *won't*." Charlotte shuffles rapidly down under the bedclothes.

Suddenly it dawns on Emily that it's not Anne whom Charlotte wants to protect from the truth — it's herself. But she can't blame her. She can feel it too — the box lid beginning to tremble as the monsters try to climb out. The Terrible Events pushing themselves back into her mind, insisting that she remember.

"Let's go to sleep now," Charlotte says firmly.

Emily turns on her side and Charlotte cuddles up to her back. This is how they like to sleep, facing the same way, curled up like spoons.

ᡀᠥ

Soon Charlotte's breathing deepens, but Emily goes on staring out of the window as she does every night, watching the light in the sky fade to darkness. When the stars begin to appear she shuts her eyes, but not to sleep.

There is something she must do, something she must face, because if she doesn't, her fear will grow and grow and swallow her up.

To give herself courage she thinks of the heroic Parry, bold, courageous, confronting the great unknown of the northern regions. Then in the darkness of the bedroom she says the word silently to herself, feeling the shape of it in her mouth.

Death.

She knows it. She has seen it everywhere. Out there on the moors where she has found stiff lambs with their empty eye sockets; heard the screams of a vole snatched by a kestrel. Out there in the churchyard where week after week, glancing from the windows, she has seen Papa standing by the dark grave holes, into which the coffins go, many of them tiny, but a good many adult-sized too.

But it's not just out there, keeping a safe distance. It can come inside too, in here, into the parsonage, their home. And though in their games and stories the four of them can make characters come alive again, she knows that really they are powerless against it. This is what she makes herself face now, with Charlotte sleeping next to her, concentrating on the shadowy memory buried inside her.

It comes with a sense of solemnity and hushed voices. She can remember a bed, too high for her to see the person lying there. Someone says, "Say good-bye to your mama."

Mama. Emily can't remember her face or her voice, but she occasionally has recollections of a sensation — of being safe, of arms tight around her.

Tonight, in this memory, there's no such comfort. What she sees is Papa, his head bent close to the pillow, with a look on his face so strange and terrible that Emily feels as if something is squeezing her heart.

She feels it now, as she makes herself remember. She's trembling, but she keeps hold of the feeling as long as she can, until she can't bear it a second longer.

That's enough.

She opens her eyes.

The rectangle of sky is there. She stares at it until her breath steadies, her heartbeat slows. She looks for the Great Bear and when she finds it she fixes her eyes on it, as if she wants to absorb its cold glitter.

4

"Emily, you're woolgathering again."

Emily comes to with a start. The forest where she's striding through the trees vanishes and she's back at the breakfast table in the parsonage with the others. Aunt's beady eyes are on her.

"Eat up your porridge, now, before it goes cold."

Obediently she ferries a laden spoonful to her mouth. She wonders how Papa is today.

It's been ages since he took to his bed. They know what his illness is now — pleurisy. After they heard Dr. Andrew say the word, Emily rushed to look it up in Papa's well-thumbed copy of *Modern Domestic Medicine*. When she read that it could be fatal, she shut the book fast.

Anne and Charlotte have been praying for Papa, but although she never discusses it, Emily hasn't been able to do that.

She's always accepted what Papa has taught her about God, but lately she's found herself questioning things. For example, the idea that God is watching over everyone. Jesus said that God even takes care of every sparrow, but she finds that hard to believe. Look at the terrible things that happen, to sparrows and to people. And if God was interested in Papa's health, why did He let him get ill in the first place? It makes no sense.

No, it's no good relying on God or expecting Him to answer their prayers. The only solution is to do what she can herself, so she has been concentrating on focusing her willpower, saying to herself over and over again, "Papa *will* get better. He *will*."

And then just the other day, after weeks of eating nothing more solid than toast, water, and gruel, Papa told Tabby that he had a fancy for a soft-boiled egg.

Emily's heart leaped when Tabby passed this news on. Perhaps it was a sign that her willpower was working — that Papa might get better after all.

A sudden loud report from upstairs makes them all jump.

"Papa?" asks Branwell, leaping to his feet. "That's the first time in weeks!"

Emily snorts. "Who else could it be? Papa's hardly going to ask Tabby to fire his pistol, is he?" She turns eagerly to Aunt. "Is Papa getting up today?"

For an answer, Aunt puts on a "wait-and-see" expression. But the next moment they hear slow footsteps on the stairs. Anne rushes to the door, flings it open, and peeps out. "It *is* Papa!" she exclaims.

As their father appears in the doorway, Emily and Charlotte jump up to greet him and Branwell lets out a great cheer.

"Gently now, children," Aunt admonishes. "Anne, let your father sit down." For Anne is hugging Papa's arm as if she never means to let him go. He pats her head and makes his way carefully to his chair.

Emily goes to hug him herself — it's such a relief to have him back among them again. But as he takes the cup of tea that Aunt has poured for him, she sees that his hand is shaking.

Sitting back down, she studies him carefully. He doesn't look as dreadful as when she last saw him — then his eyes had dark rings under them and his skin had an alarming bluish tinge. Even so, he doesn't seem very well. His face is pale and drawn, his cheekbones are jutting out more than ever, and he seems to have shrunk — his coat looks too big for him. He's wrapped yet another layer of white silk round his throat so now his cravat resembles a deep bandage supporting his chin.

In the space of a few weeks, Emily realizes with a small shock, Papa has turned into an old man. But he is alive.

He notices her looking and winks. "I missed the church tower this morning. Poor aim. Out of practice." A fit of coughing seizes him and they all watch anxiously.

When it subsides, Charlotte says, "Papa, are you sure you should be out of bed?"

He nods. "It's time enough. I can't be languishing up there or my parishioners will think I've forgotten them. Now tell me, what have you all been up to?"

ल๛

Life gradually returns to something like normal. Papa takes up most of his parish duties again, though he doesn't travel as far afield, and before long he's smoking his pipe in the evenings even though it makes him cough. Their usual routine resumes. They go back to having weekly piano lessons in Keighley with Mr. Sunderland and Papa teaches them in the mornings when he can spare the time.

But Emily can't relax. She's stopped being afraid that Papa might die at any moment, but she still feels anxious about him.

Because things aren't the same as they were before. Papa has changed.

He still tells them stories at breakfast, but his laughter seems forced, as if he's making an effort to be cheery. Often he has to break off because of a coughing fit. In the middle of their lessons Emily notices his attention wandering and sometimes when she goes into the study to fetch something or give him a message from Aunt she finds him just sitting, not doing anything at all. He rouses himself to speak to her, but she can tell that something's wrong — he seems weary and sad and distant. As if he hasn't quite returned to them.

Charlotte's aware of the change in Papa too — her eyes follow him anxiously whenever he's in the room — but she and Emily never talk about it.

The only thing Emily can do is what she always does — bury this worry along with all the others deep in the pit of her stomach. And because she's so desperate to be included, she stops arguing with Charlotte and Branwell about the course their play should take. Accepting whatever role they give Parry, she throws herself into it, scribbling away furiously. She even tries begging a candle stump from Tabby, intending to go on with her story after they're supposed to be asleep. Tabby refuses, of course, as Emily half-expected her to. "Tha'll not be wasting a candle on thi nonsense. And tha needs thi sleep, my lamb."

Emily doesn't think so. What she needs is to write. She can't change what might happen to Papa, or to any of them, but in the world of her stories she's in total control — she decides everything that happens and when and how. And while she's doing that, for the time being at least, she can forget everything outside her head and be comfortable and secure.

The safety net is still holding her.

ᏫᏓᎥ

One dark November morning Emily is passing through the hall on her way to brush the parlor carpet when she hears Aunt's voice coming from the study, saying something that stops her in her tracks.

"It's a pity about Emily . . ."

Holding her breath, Emily creeps closer to the door.

Aunt is still speaking. ". . . it would be ideal for her to mix with young ladies, to have some of her rough corners smoothed down."

Emily's heart starts to race. What is Aunt talking about? What is she planning?

"But if we can only manage it for one, I think it should be Charlotte. After all, she's sixteen now."

Papa sounds regretful, as if he doesn't like whatever it is they're talking about. What can it be?

"Very well."

From Aunt's tone Emily can easily visualize her tight-lipped expression — she doesn't agree with Papa, but she is giving way. Emily has seen this before, many times.

Aunt continues, "What Miss Wooler offers sounds as if it would suit Charlotte and she seems like a sensible sort of woman."

Who is Miss Wooler? Emily's never heard of her.

"The fees are more than I had counted on." Emily can imagine Papa's face, the burdened look that comes over him when money is in question.

Her mind is racing. Could it be art lessons? Since Mr. Bradley went away, Charlotte's often said she wishes they could have another art teacher. But would that involve other girls?

"As to that, Patrick," continues Aunt, "you know you can count on my help."

"Ah, Elizabeth. You have already given so much to this family. I can't —"

"Nonsense." Aunt's tone is brisk. "I have little else to spend my money on. It would please me to assist in any scheme that might secure the girls' future."

A chill runs down Emily's back. This isn't about art lessons. This is something far more ominous. And then she hears the words that send her running into the kitchen.

☙

The sight of Charlotte standing at the table calmly peeling apples pulls Emily up short. Such a tangle of feelings is burning in her chest that for a moment she can't speak.

Charlotte looks up and her expression changes. "Whatever is the matter?"

"I've just overheard Papa and Aunt talking." She swallows. "Oh, Charlotte, they're arranging to send you away to school! Aunt wanted it to be me, but Papa says that you must go."

Charlotte's face turns white, her hand jerks, and the curl of peel suspended from the apple she's holding drops into the bowl.

"Not back to —" She grips the knife like a dagger.

"No, it's a different one. Something Head? But still . . . a school . . ."

In silence the sisters look at each other and all the horror that Emily is feeling is reflected in Charlotte's face. But then a shutter seems to come down and Charlotte squares her shoulders. "Oh well."

"*Oh well!* Is that all you can say?" Emily skitters round the table and seizes her sister by the shoulders. "You can't go. Tell them you won't." She gives Charlotte a rough shake.

"Mind the knife!" Charlotte moves her hand out of the way. She looks into Emily's eyes and her expression is unreadable.

The back door opens and they swiftly move apart. Charlotte resumes work on her apple and Emily pretends to look for something in a drawer as Tabby comes bustling in with a basket of shopping.

"Hasn't tha done with yon apples yet, Charlotte? The dinner'll never be ready on time."

Tabby's eyes flick from one to the other. She's obviously aware that something's going on between them, but, being Tabby, she'll bide her time, at least for now.

෬෮

Later Papa calls Charlotte into the study. It seems an age until she emerges and joins the others in the parlor, but when she does, primed by Emily, they pounce and bombard her with questions.

Charlotte remains perfectly calm. Walking over to the table, she sits down and folds her hands on the cloth in front of her, the very model of composure. Speaking in a quiet voice, she tells them that she is to go to Miss Wooler's school, Roe Head, in Mirfield. Charlotte's godmother, Mrs. Atkinson, has recommended it. "She told Papa that her niece is a pupil at the school. And that she's very happy there."

Charlotte asserts this as if daring them to contradict her, but her eyes look anxious.

"Mirfield?" says Branwell. "Isn't that near Huddersfield?"

"Yes, it's only about twenty miles from here."

"Twenty miles!" To Emily this sounds as far away as the moon. "And when are you supposed to be going to this place?"

"When the new term starts, in January."

Only two months left, then. Emily is aghast.

Branwell too is beside himself. "But what about Glass Town? You can't just abandon it. How will we go on without you?" He tugs at his hair till it stands up like a wild coxcomb.

Charlotte's lip quivers and her hands tighten, but then she resumes her mask. "I'll be back in the holidays. I want to learn and this is a good opportunity."

Emily can't understand it. Charlotte can't want to go to school. Not after what happened last time. She must be putting on an act. But why?

There's only one thing to do. She'll talk to Charlotte and *make* her change her mind.

5

That night, as soon as they're in bed, she tackles Charlotte. "Why are you agreeing to go to this school?"

Charlotte fiddles with a button on her nightgown. "I haven't any choice." Her voice is flat.

"What do you mean? Of course you can choose. Papa would never make you go against your will."

Charlotte shakes her head impatiently. "You don't understand. Our position . . ." She stops, takes a deep breath, and starts again. "You know Papa isn't well-off."

"All the more reason not to waste money on school fees."

"It's not a waste, it's . . . like an investment."

Emily frowns. "An investment?"

"For the future. We have to think about the future. Especially with Papa . . ."

Charlotte doesn't finish the sentence, but she doesn't need to. Emily's stomach tightens. But Charlotte's wrong. They don't have to think about the future. Not until it happens.

"Anyway," Charlotte continues, "Branwell will be all right — he'll make a success of himself whatever he does. But we girls can't expect him to support us — we'll have to support ourselves. If I work hard at this school, I'll get the qualifications I need to be a teacher or a governess. It's what we'll all have to do."

Emily stares at her sister, appalled. *Teaching?* Is that really their only option?

"Do you *want* to be a teacher?"

Charlotte waves her arm dismissively. "What I want is irrelevant. It's what has to be."

Emily gives the blanket a fierce tug. She knows what Charlotte's doing — she's trying to be like Maria, their beloved elder sister. Even when she was being bullied by that hateful teacher Miss Andrews at Cowan Bridge, she would bear it patiently, declaring that what could not be avoided must be endured.

But Charlotte isn't Maria. She shouldn't be doing this.

She's about to tell her so when Charlotte turns to look at her. "But, Emily, I *do* want to learn as much as I can. Papa does his best, but he hasn't time to cover everything. And I think school will be good for me."

"*Good for you?* Charlotte, you can't mean that."

"I do. As Aunt says, it's time I got used to mixing with other girls."

"What on earth for?"

"Oh, Emily, don't be silly. We'll have to go out into society sooner or later. This will be good practice."

Emily is silenced, chilled by the very idea. They don't need "society." As long as the four of them have got one another and Papa and Tabby, they don't need anyone else. But maybe Charlotte doesn't feel the same.

Maybe she *wants* to meet new people.

Shaken by the thought, Emily stares at her sister. She remembers the way Charlotte separated her miniature books from theirs. This is yet another sign that she's preparing to move away from them.

Emily bites the inside of her lip. It's unbearable. Too much is changing. First Papa and now Charlotte. It can't happen. She won't let it.

She nudges Charlotte. "What if the school's like Cowan Bridge?" she hisses.

"It won't be." But Charlotte's voice wavers and Emily presses home her advantage.

"Remember that ugly purple uniform?"

"Yes!" Charlotte winces. "Of course I do! I hated everyone knowing we were charity children. But Aunt says there isn't a uniform at Roe Head. We can wear our own clothes."

Emily tries another tack. "But don't you remember how vile the food was? Burned porridge with bits of gristle and bone in it because the pan hadn't been washed properly."

Charlotte shudders. "And the grease floating in our milk."

"Exactly. And you can't have forgotten the bigger girls stealing our bread? What it felt like to always be hungry?"

Charlotte says nothing, but she looks thoughtful. Emily nudges her again. "Those frightful stories that Mr. Wilson wrote for *The Children's Friend* and made us read?"

"Don't," says Charlotte with a grimace.

" 'Edward, aged five, died of a mad dog bite,' " Emily intones. " 'But what a blessing it was as he was saved from sin and damnation, the fate that awaits all naughty children . . .' "

"Stop it." Charlotte puts her hands over her ears. "I don't expect Miss Wooler is anything like Mr. Wilson. And Papa wouldn't let me go if he thought anything bad might happen." Charlotte's voice cracks and she lets her hands drop. She turns to face Emily, her expression pleading. "I'd rather you stopped talking about it and just accepted the situation. Please."

Emily can see the tension in Charlotte's jaw. Another minute and she'll be crying.

Relenting, Emily lays her hand on her sister's arm. "I'm sure you're right. Papa will have looked into it all very carefully. He won't let anything happen to you."

She's only saying it to make Charlotte feel better — she doesn't believe it for a minute. But she doesn't dare go any further. She can't break the taboo and mention The Terrible Events, though Charlotte, she is sure, must be thinking about them too. And Papa was powerless to stop them, so it's not likely it would be any different this time.

Charlotte wriggles down under the bedclothes, the signal for sleep. As Emily snuggles herself against her sister, she shivers. And it's not just because the bed hasn't warmed up yet and the air in the bedroom has the chill of ice in it.

It's here . . . what she's done her best to shut away is here, and she can't avoid it.

ᏉᏆᏅ

Cowan Bridge. Where her older sisters suffered so much while she, enjoying her position as one of the "babies" and a favorite at that, petted and indulged by the teachers and the older girls, hadn't realized what was happening. First Maria, racked by a cough that would not go away, and getting thinner and thinner, until that day in the schoolroom when Emily saw her eldest sister bent over a page on which a bright red stain was spreading. Papa came in the carriage and took Maria away and they never saw her again.

She was told what had happened — Maria had died. But she found it so hard to believe . . .

And then Elizabeth, who the teachers said just had the fever, was sent home too, and the very next day Papa came for her and Charlotte.

She was so pleased to be going home, to be near Elizabeth. But they were all told to stay away from the old nursery where Elizabeth had been put to bed. She was not to be disturbed. Undeterred, Emily crept in when no one was watching. Surely her sister would want to see her? It was only when she saw Elizabeth lying in bed, her face white on the white pillow, her eyes dark and sunken, that Emily understood, with a shock, how ill her sister was.

But no one had told her Elizabeth was dying. No one had told her how little time was left for them to be together.

Blithely, stupidly, she'd gone about thinking that Elizabeth would get better and everything would be all right again. It would be sad, of course, because Maria wasn't there, but Emily would still have her own special protector and best friend.

But that wasn't what happened.

Emily shivers again. She can't go on . . . not just now.

She presses herself against Charlotte, who is sleeping now, her chest rising and falling in a regular, steady rhythm. Emily would like to be sleeping peacefully herself. But her thoughts won't stop — they come crowding in on her.

Everything had been all right until they had gone away from home, into the company of strangers. And she had liked them — the teachers who were kind to her — and she hadn't realized that she was being deceived. Because they weren't kind. How could they be when they had allowed her sisters to become mortally ill?

These were the lessons she had learned at Cowan Bridge. That strangers are not to be trusted. That if you go away from home, terrible things happen.

And here is Charlotte submitting herself meekly, voluntarily, to this risk.

Gently, so as not to wake her sister, Emily reaches behind her and pats Charlotte.

"Don't do it," she breathes. "Don't go away."

Then she closes her eyes, willing sleep to rescue her.

და

"Emileee."

Someone is calling her.

She climbs out of bed and patters along the landing to the old nursery. She pushes open the door and stops dead. The room is bright and there, sitting on the floor, are Maria and Elizabeth!

A warm feeling floods Emily's heart.

Maria has a book open on her lap. She holds it up so Emily can read the title: *Aesop's Fables.* Elizabeth pats the floor beside her and as Emily sits down, nestling close to her big sister, Maria begins to read. It's the story of the fox and the crow, one of Emily's favorites. She loves the way the wily fox flatters the crow and she laughs out loud when the crow drops the cheese and the fox gobbles it up.

"Do you want to hear another?" Elizabeth asks, smiling down at her.

She does, but she's wondering where Charlotte and Branwell and Anne are. She's bothered that they're missing the fun. Jumping up, she says, "I'm just going to fetch the others."

She runs downstairs, but there's no one in the parlor or Papa's study. She goes into the kitchen to ask Tabby, but she isn't there.

Emily begins to feel uneasy. "Hello?" she calls. No one answers.

For the first time she notices how dark it is.

She slowly begins to climb the stairs.

How high they are. It's such a long way between the step she's on and the next one. Her legs are getting tired.

When she reaches the landing halfway up, the pale face of the grandfather clock Papa winds every night looms out of the shadows.

She's passed it hundreds of times, but she's never noticed how tall it is, how loudly it ticks.

Emily shivers. She wants to curl up again with Charlotte under the warm blankets, but when she looks in their room, Charlotte isn't there.

She tries Papa's and Aunt's rooms. No one in there either.

That only leaves the nursery.

She opens the door, her heart beating fast. The room is empty.

Where are they? Maria and Elizabeth? And everyone else? Where are they?

Something raps on the window. A small white hand.

A child's voice cries, "Let me in. Emily! Let me in."

Gladly, Emily runs to the window and throws it wide. "Elizabeth?"

But there's no one there. Just the wailing wind, driving icy rain into her face.

Emily leans out into the blast. No one down in the churchyard moving among the gravestones. No light in the church, with its tall black tower.

For a moment she can't breathe. And then a feeling of horrible desolation sweeps over her and she howls into the night, into the darkness, the emptiness . . .

"Emily! Wake up!"

She comes to, sobbing, with Charlotte's arms round her.

"Shh. It's all right." Charlotte strokes her back. "You were dreaming, that's all."

Emily gulps. "It was that one, Charlotte. You know, about Maria and Elizabeth . . ."

Charlotte nods. "Don't think about it. It's over now."

When she's calmer, they settle down again. Charlotte is still holding her tight. "Go to sleep, now. I'm here. You're all right."

She is, but as the nightmare fades, the question pushes itself into her mind. What will she do if Charlotte isn't here?

She tells herself not to worry. She will not let Charlotte go away to school.

There's still time to talk her sister out of this.

6

The morning Charlotte leaves they all go out into the lane to wave her off. The sky is pressing down on them today, its dark clouds threatening snow.

Emily, shivering in the keen east wind, blows on her fingers and stamps her feet to try and warm them up. She can't believe this is happening.

Yesterday when her sister carried a traveling box down from the storeroom and asked her to help with the packing, of course she refused. And she wouldn't speak to Charlotte for the rest of the day, not even when they went to bed.

But it hasn't made any difference. Despite all her efforts to dissuade Charlotte — marshaling reasoned arguments, nagging, pleading with her to change her mind — her sister is leaving today. It will be five long months until they see her again. In that time anything could happen.

The rest of the family, including Aunt, give Charlotte a parting hug, but Emily refuses even to look at her. Instead she murmurs to Old Joey, the carter's horse, who snuffles her hand, hoping for something to eat, his breath leaving white clouds in the air. But out of the corner of her eye she can't help seeing Mr. Dowson helping Charlotte climb up onto the front seat of the cart. The box is already safely stowed in the back, where pigs and sacks of oats usually ride to market.

Aunt sniffs. "A pity the gig is hired out elsewhere today. She'll not create a very good impression arriving at Roe Head in a farm cart."

"Charlotte needs no outward show to sustain her," says Papa brusquely. "They'll see her true qualities soon enough."

Emily exchanges a glance with Branwell. It's not like Papa to be short with Aunt. Aunt is probably right about the impression Charlotte will make, but it's partly her fault. She's sending poor Charlotte off in that hideous cut-down dress and she even made her sleep in curl papers, so that now her hair is screwed up in a frizz of tight curls.

Emily hopes her sister hasn't heard what Aunt said. Charlotte's face is pinched, as if the cold has already entered her bones, but as Mr. Dowson cracks his whip and the wheels start to turn, she turns to her family and manages to force a smile.

Suddenly Emily's sorry. She shouldn't have been mean to Charlotte on her last day. And now Charlotte's going and she won't have a chance to make amends. As the cart moves off, she raises her hand to wave.

But it's too late — Charlotte has turned to face ahead and doesn't look back.

Watching her sister disappearing round the corner by the church, Emily feels an ache in her chest as though a thread connecting her to Charlotte is being tugged harder and harder as her sister is carried away.

What if it should snap?

"Come on in now, Emily," Papa calls from the gate.

Back in the house, they stand about in the hall, uncertain what to do next.

"Best get on," says Tabby, blowing her nose and moving quickly toward the kitchen.

Aunt takes herself off upstairs and Emily looks at Papa, expecting him to take them into the study for their lessons as usual, but, blinking behind his spectacles, he says, "I think, given the circumstances, we'll have a change this morning. I have some work I need to do. You children can amuse yourselves, can't you?" He doesn't wait for them to nod in reply, but shoots into the study and shuts the door.

They look at one another. Branwell shrugs and goes into the parlor. After a second, Emily and Anne follow him in and huddle near the fire. Emily wants its comforting warmth, but because the peat's damp it's giving off more smoke than heat.

She doesn't know what to do with herself. On any other day, they'd all be ecstatic at this unexpected holiday, but not today. Anne is scratching her chilblains and looking miserable. Branwell has thrown himself into a chair and is kicking its leg and scowling.

It must be hard for him too. When they're working on the Glass Town saga, he's so used to having Charlotte to spark ideas off. Even though he always claims the best ideas are his.

A sudden thought makes Emily sit up straight. Without Charlotte, Branwell will need her and Anne. They can go back to playing together, just like they did in the old days. Then when Charlotte comes back, she'll have missed them so much she'll want to join in again. It will be just as it used to be.

Emily puts her hand on her brother's shoulder. "Banny," she says, using their old pet name for him, "why don't we go on with Glass Town? It might cheer us up."

He shrugs her off irritably. "Don't call me that. I'm not a child anymore." He glares at her. "And what makes you think I'd want to play with you? It's the last thing I'd want to do."

For a moment Emily can't breathe. First Charlotte. Now Branwell. But she can't let him see how wounded she is. She narrows her eyes. "I see, Mr. Clever. You think you can manage on your own, do you?"

He snorts. "Of course. I don't need you."

A hot rush of anger floods her chest. "Go on, then. But you'll be sorry. Anne and I will keep our ideas to ourselves."

"Ideas? You two? Hah! The rubbish you two think of is enough to make the cat laugh."

Anne gets to her feet. "Branwell . . . Emily . . ."

Emily curls her hand into a fist, but before she can hit him, he says, "You're such silly babies, you don't understand anything about the things Charlotte and me want to write about. I'll do Glass Town by myself. I don't want you!" He flings himself out of the room and slams the door.

Emily smacks her fist down on the table, making Anne jump. "Damn you! Damn you to hell!"

Anne's staring at her with big eyes, but she doesn't care.

After a long silence Emily hears the melancholy sound of Branwell's flute floating down the stairs and all at once it's too much . . .

A knot forms in her throat, threatening to choke her. The room suddenly seems airless and she makes for the window. Pressing her hands and forehead against the cold pane, she looks out at the graveyard, where the black slabs of the upright head-stones stand forlorn, buffeted by wind-borne sleet.

She feels an arm slipping through hers and Anne says, "Never mind. Branwell might come round." She gives Emily's arm a squeeze. "And you don't need to worry about Charlotte; I'm sure she'll be all right. I'll pray for her especially hard."

Emily shakes her head, unable to speak.

Just at this moment she doesn't want consolation, she wants . . . oh, she wants everything to be as it was, tight and right . . . and safe.

She pulls away from Anne's clasp and heads for the door. But out in the hallway, she stops.

Where can she go? Where can she find a refuge?

⟳

The kitchen is what she chooses. Warm and full of comforting smells and with Tabby bustling about just as she always does.

When she comes in, Tabby, who's standing at the kitchen table weighing flour, looks up at her with a quizzical expression on her face.

Without a word, Emily flings herself onto a stool and picks up the book she left on the table before breakfast. After a second Tabby goes on with her work, clinking the metal weights onto the scales. Emily sighs and slams the book shut. She looks for Tiger, but he's nowhere to be seen. Listlessly she watches Tabby adding frothing yeast to the bowl of flour.

When she sighs for a second time Tabby looks over at her. "I daresay tha's finding it a mite strange without Miss Charlotte. We'll all miss her."

Emily doesn't answer.

"Pass salt box, lass."

Emily pushes it over. And suddenly she knows what she wants. Just as she used to do when she was little, she begs, "Tell me a story, Tabby."

"Well, now, let me think." Tabby ponders with the salt spoon in her hand. "Did tha ever hear tell of Captain Batt?"

Emily shakes her head.

"Well, then, here's a tale. One winter evening he comes home as usual, nowt appearing amiss, and up he goes to his room. But when it comes to be suppertime, he doesn't appear. His manservant, a bit puzzled like, takes it upon himself to knock at the maister's door. There's no answer. The man tries the door. It won't budge — it's locked fast. It takes two of them to break it down to get inside. And guess what?"

"What?"

"The room were empty. Not a trace of the maister to be seen. But there on the floor were summat that made them shudder . . ." Tabby pauses for dramatic effect and makes her eyes go big. "It were a bloody footprint."

Despite herself, Emily is entertained. "Did they ever find out what happened? To the captain, I mean?"

"The next day news came that the maister had been killed in a duel the afternoon before."

"So it was his ghost who came home?"

Tabby shrugs. "That's what folk say."

"Do you think it really happened?"

"I don't know, lass. There could be summat in it." Tabby pours some water into her mixing bowl. "There's many a tale of folk appearing to their kin at the very time they're dying somewhere else." She thumps the dough onto the table and starts kneading it.

Emily suddenly sits up straight. "Can I try that?"

"If tha likes. But wash thi hands first. And roll up thi sleeves."

Preparations accomplished to Tabby's satisfaction, Emily approaches the lump of dough cautiously.

"Nay, don't dibble-dabble at it, in that namby-pamby way. Push wi' the heel of thi palms and put thi weight behind it. The dough needs stretching else loaves'll be as hard as whinstone."

Emily, with sticky hands and flour up to her elbows, grapples with the elastic mass. As she wrestles it into submission, gradually the painful tangle inside her is soothed. By the time she's done, she feels much calmer. Her anger toward Branwell, her grief about Charlotte, all those feelings that have been tearing at her have subsided for the time being.

Once the dough is proofing next to the range, Tabby says, "Now then, I want thee to run down to Mrs. Grimshaw's for some sugar, for those blessed curates haven't left me a speck of it and thi Papa will be wanting some in his coffee."

Emily tenses. But Tabby doesn't seem to notice her dismay. She's too busy counting out coins from the old tea caddy. Shaking her head, she says, "It's all very well for thi Papa to invite yon fellows to tea, but they're like locusts. They'd eat us out of house and home if they could."

"Can't you ask one of the others?"

"Now tha knows Miss Anne can't go by herself, and besides it's far too cold out for the poor mite. And I think Maister Branwell'd best be let alone awhile."

Tabby has heard them rowing, then. Emily opens her mouth.

"Nay, don't make a fuss, my lass," says Tabby firmly, pushing the money into her hand. "I know tha likes a walk."

7

Emily fetches her cloak, grumbling to herself. Of course Tabby's right and if she'd suggested a ramble on the moors, Emily would have been off like a shot. But Tabby knows how much she hates going down into the village — it's mean of her to make her go.

Once she's out of the front door, Emily wishes even more that she *was* going for a proper walk. The cold is still biting, but the skies have cleared a little and above the church tower a pale sun is doing its best to shine through the veil of cloud. As she crosses the garden, where the twisted branches of the hawthorn and the bare stems of the fruit bushes are rimed with frost, her boots make a satisfying crunch on the frozen gravel path.

Passing through the wicket gate, she enters the churchyard. The dusting of snow on the gravestones crammed together on either side of her almost softens their oppressive presence. Almost, but not entirely. Whenever Emily sees these heavy grey slabs, she can't help thinking of Mama and Maria and Elizabeth, even though they're not buried here, but in the church. She tries to pass through the graveyard as quickly as possible, to not let herself dwell on them, but today she has to go more cautiously on the icy flagstones. By the time she reaches the corner by the church her mood is even darker. Casting one longing look along the track that would take her to the moors, she braces herself and passes through the archway into Kirkgate, Haworth's main street.

Luckily it's far too early for the bells that will release a stream of workers from the mills down in the valley, so she doesn't have to endure the brazen stares of the girls as they clatter up the cobbles in their clogs. But there are two men outside the Black Bull. Out of the corner of her eye, she's aware of their open curiosity and though they lower their voices as she goes by she hears them.

"Parson's lass."

"Miss Emily."

Emily grits her teeth. Just because Papa is the parson, and therefore a public figure, the villagers seem to think they somehow own the whole family. It's all very well for Charlotte to say, as she did once when Emily grumbled about it, that it's their keeping themselves to themselves that makes the cottagers even more curious. Why shouldn't they have a right to their privacy?

As she makes her way down the steep hill, the blackened stone cottages on either side of the narrow street seem to press toward her. Despite the cold, some doors are open to give light to the handloom weavers working inside. She imagines eyes watching her from within the dark interiors, but she looks to neither right nor left. She looks straight ahead, breathing through her mouth. Even so, she can still sense it, the smell rising from the open gutter beside her feet, which is choked with household waste, unrecognizable bits of rotting carcass, and the overflow from several privies.

Repressing a shudder, she makes herself keep going. Already she's regretting this morning's row with Branwell. She should have handled him differently. Instead of losing her temper, she should have buttered him up, and he might have agreed to let them help him. Charlotte would have known how to get him to do what she wanted.

Too late now. To take her mind off her failure she takes refuge in her favorite ploy. She isn't Emily going to buy sugar, but Parry, in disguise, and on a mission to bring back the vital elixir that will restore the life of the land's most revered sage. No obstacle will hinder her, no mire so foul nor enemy so hostile that she will not triumph.

Outside the grocer's there's a small knot of women passing the time of day. Charlotte would have forced herself to nod, to say, "Good morning." Emily is having none of it: As they step aside to let her pass she turns her head away. But one of the women, bolder than the rest, addresses her.

"Miss Emily, I hope thi father is keeping well."

She has to speak. She mutters, "Yes, he is, thank you," and makes a dive for the shop door. But there's no refuge inside. Mrs. Grimshaw saw Charlotte going past in the cart earlier and she can barely contain her inquisitiveness. Emily fends her off as best she can while Mrs. Grimshaw fetches a sugar loaf from the shelf. But even then the shopkeeper doesn't relinquish it, holding on to it while she asks further prying questions.

Emily's saved at last by the arrival of another customer. Mrs. Grimshaw turns to greet the newcomer and Emily slaps the money on the counter, snatches the sugar from her persecutor's hand, and rushes out.

Stomping furiously back up the hill, she invokes the most terrible afflictions she can think of on the odious shopkeeper. But by the time she's reached the church, she's calmer, and the familiar sight of the parsonage, with its serene grey stone frontage and its many small square windowpanes polished to a shine by Tabby, helps to soothe her even more.

At the front door, reluctant to leave the fresh air and go inside, she sits on the step for a moment, cradling the sugar loaf, swaddled in its blue paper, in her arms like a stiff baby. Not for the first time she thinks how lucky it is that the parsonage is built up here, isolated from its neighbors and far above the curious eyes of the villagers.

Charlotte once asked her why she minded so much being sent on errands by Tabby and all she could say was, "They know my name. The villagers."

She knew from the way Charlotte stared at her that her sister didn't understand, but she couldn't find the words for it, that sense of violation she experienced, out there among all those strangers.

Emily looks out toward the southeast, in the direction that Charlotte is traveling.

Dark clouds are building again over there and she imagines Charlotte looking at them from her seat in the cart and hoping that she'll reach the school before the weather breaks. Or perhaps she's dreading what awaits her at her destination.

Emily hugs the sugar loaf to her chest. Five months until she sees her sister again.

The longest they have ever been apart.

It will be hard, but she won't let the thread binding them together break. She *won't*.

As the cold from the stone step makes itself felt at last, she shivers and, jumping up, she goes indoors.

Later Tabby calls her back into the kitchen in time to see the loaves come out of the oven. They've risen and have satisfyingly crusty tops, and they smell wonderful. Emily watches anxiously as Tabby picks one up and taps its bottom. It gives off a hollow sound and Tabby says, "Ay, that'll do, I reckon."

And Emily grins at her.

 ⁊⁊

Making bread has helped her to get through the day, but when bedtime comes and she has to take her candle upstairs and go into the bedroom by herself, she is suddenly overcome again.

Sinking onto the bed, she surveys the silent room as if seeing it for the first time.

The blue-and-white jug with its mended handle and chipped rim standing in its matching bowl on the washstand reminds her of the squabble that caused these injuries — she and Charlotte, when they were small, disputing who should have the hot water first. Beside the washstand is the rush-seated chair where they both hang their clothes at night, despite repeated injunctions from Aunt that they should fold them up and put them away. On the floor just in front of the chair is the dark burn mark on the oilcloth where Charlotte once dropped the candle.

It strikes Emily with the force of a blow that she has never had to sleep in this room alone. First there were the four of them, Maria and Charlotte at the head of the bed and she and Elizabeth curled up together at the foot. When the others went off to school all those years ago, she still had Sarah, their nursemaid, to keep her company.

And then, afterward and ever since, there has always been Charlotte.

Emily suddenly becomes aware that her teeth are chattering. Undressing quickly, she puts on her nightgown, but she can't bring herself to get into bed yet. Instead she wraps herself up in a blanket and sits by the window, looking out. It's a wild night — the wind blowing down from the moor is moaning around the house. The candle flame wavers in the draft. She strains her eyes, trying to see the faintest glimmer of a star, but the sky is utterly black.

Right now her sister will be lying with a stranger in a strange bed in an unfamiliar house far away. Emily wonders what kind of reception she had and whether she's all right. With all her heart she hopes so.

She puts her lips to the icy glass of the window and whispers, "Good night, Charlotte."

"Bless thee, lass, whatever is tha doing there?" Tabby's voice makes her jump. "Get into bed now, afore tha gets chilled to the marrow."

Emily is touched. These days, since Charlotte has been trusted to behave responsibly, they see themselves into bed. She runs across the bare floorboards and clambers under the covers.

Tabby closes the wooden shutters. "It's fair wuthering out there tonight." She comes over to the bed and tucks Emily in. Patting her head, she says, "See tha gets a good night's sleep."

And then she blows out the candle and goes downstairs and Emily is left in the dark. At once she gets up and opens the shutters again. There might be nothing to see, but still, she needs to know that the sky is there, that she's not shut in.

Dashing back, she dives into the chilly bed. Within seconds she's sitting up again.

It feels all wrong to be lying here alone with a gaping empty space where Charlotte ought to be. She turns over and tries facing in the opposite direction, but that doesn't help. She can't get comfortable on her right side and she can't see the window.

She rolls over again. The sheets haven't warmed up yet; the air in the bedroom is polar. She tries to summon up thoughts of Parry, but he's not much comfort — in all his terrible ordeals, he's never without his faithful companion Ross.

If Anne had asked to come in with her, she'd have said yes like a shot, but Anne doesn't seem to have thought of it and Emily is too proud to ask her. Anyway, Aunt probably wouldn't have allowed it — she wouldn't trust Emily not to lead her pet astray.

Wrapping her arms round herself, Emily curls up into a tight ball.

"Oh, Charlotte," she breathes into the pillow. "What am I going to do without you?"

8

Emily sits transfixed as Beethoven's *Appassionata* Sonata thunders about her ears, Mr. Sunderland, their piano teacher, involving his whole body in the performance, the music pouring from him with a passionate intensity.

The music is so beautiful and it seems to speak directly to something deep inside her, something unutterably painful. She can hardly bear it.

Losing Charlotte is part of it, but not all — since Charlotte left, the dream she's had so often over the years, the one about Maria and Elizabeth, keeps haunting her and it's horrible waking up and finding herself alone. And since Charlotte went away Papa has seemed more frail and depressed than ever. She often lies awake in the early hours, her anxieties about his health multiplying uncontrollably without Charlotte there to reassure her.

Mr. Sunderland comes to the end of the piece — Branwell applauds wildly and Anne joins in more decorously. Emily is too overcome to move. The teacher turns to them, smiling, but when his eyes fall on Emily, he frowns. "Miss Emily, has something about my playing displeased you?"

Hot with embarrassment, Emily exclaims, "Oh no, not at all. It was wonderful."

Puzzled, he stares at her and she's driven to blurt, "I was just wishing that we had a piano at home so I could practice whenever I wanted. I do so want to play the music that you play — not that I'd ever be as good as you, of course, but —"

Mr. Sunderland holds up his hand to stop her. "As to that, I think it would be a very good idea. You have all reached a stage — yes, even you, Master Branwell — where it is clear that you have some musical talent. But you won't make satisfactory progress unless you practice much more than you can at present. I will speak to your father about it." He looks out of the window. "The rain has cleared. You should stay dry on your way home — but don't dawdle. There are more showers on their way, I'm sure."

Emily pulls on her cloak anyhow, too agitated to fasten it properly. Why on earth did she say that? Papa can't afford a piano. It will be awful if Mr. Sunderland does speak to him — he'll be distressed at not being able to provide something he'll decide is important and it'll be another burden on him.

On the way home she tells the others what's bothering her.

"I wouldn't worry about it," says Branwell airily, kicking a stone ahead of him up the road. He and Emily are speaking to each other again and getting on fairly well — as long as they stay off the subject of Glass Town. "You heard what Mr. Sunderland said. We are talented. We deserve a piano."

"But it's sure to be too expensive."

"Aunt will buy it for us. Especially if she thinks I might become a famous pianist." He grasps the lapels of his jacket, preening.

"I thought you were going to be a famous artist. Or a famous poet," says Emily drily.

Branwell is unabashed. "Well, I might be either of those — I like to keep my options open."

"A piano would be useful for preparing to be a governess," Anne puts in.

Emily stares at them. She certainly doesn't want to perform in public, and as for being a governess — she grimaces.

But if Branwell's right . . . if Aunt will pay for a piano . . . if she could learn to play as well as she longs to . . .

A wild and desperate hope sends her running up the hill, leaving the others far behind.

⚭

Branwell *is* right, as he often is in matters concerning Aunt. By the time Mr. Sunderland comes to speak to Papa, Branwell has talked so much and so confidently about his musical prowess that Aunt is convinced a piano of their own is an urgent necessity. Mr. Sunderland's advice is sought about where to look for a suitable instrument, and one exciting and unbelievable day their very own piano arrives and is installed in Papa's study. As soon as the wagoner and his lad have departed, they all crowd in to see it, even Tabby.

Emily catches her breath at the sight of the instrument. Whereas Mr. Sunderland's piano has a wooden front hiding the workings, theirs has a beautiful screen of maroon silk gathered into a rose; it's small, but with its two brass candle holders and stool just about big enough for two, it's perfect. She can't wait till Charlotte sees it.

"Go on, then, my boy. Let's hear it," Papa urges. Branwell takes his seat and plays some Scarlatti from memory in a flamboyant way, waving his hands and tossing his head so that his long hair flies about, but with many wrong notes, Emily notices.

"Splendid, nephew," says Aunt, patting Branwell on the back. "And I'm well satisfied with the piano — it has a beautiful tone. I'll bring down the music your mother and I used to play and you can all share it, but next time you go to Keighley you may each buy a new piece."

Emily is so overwhelmed with gratitude that she surprises Aunt and herself by planting a kiss on the old lady's dry cheek.

❧

The new arrival changes things, more for Emily and Anne as it turns out, as, after an initial burst of enthusiasm, Branwell goes back to playing the church organ, which he prefers.

"It's so much grander," he tells them.

Emily's not surprised. It's typical of Branwell to want to make a great noise and to show off what he can do with such a complicated instrument. But in this case, it's all to the good — it means more time at the piano for her and Anne.

Branwell does join in when they play a piece he's found called *The Battle of Prague*, which Papa, with his fondness for all things military, enjoys listening to. He often requests a performance in the evening.

Emily plays the piano and Branwell, as narrator, shouts out the various stages of the battle between the Prussians and the Imperialists such as *"Call for the cavalry!"* and *"The attack!"* while banging a saucepan lid with a wooden spoon to represent the drums.

Tabby always comes in to hear this one, nodding her head and tapping her foot in time to the music, but Aunt says it gives her a headache and the merest hint that it might be played sends her scurrying upstairs. No one's sorry. Without her restraining presence it's so much more enjoyable and they can be as exuberant as they like.

Gradually, over the weeks that follow, Emily and Anne make headway with their small but precious stock of music. Squashed together on the stool, they have fun playing duets. Emily is also happy to accompany her sister's singing, despite the fact Anne has a marked preference for solemn hymns. Though her voice isn't very strong, it's sweet, and often of an evening Papa will ask her to sing for him, liking the old ballads and folk songs best.

Emily's delighted to see Papa's worn face lighting up with pleasure as he nods his head in time to the music. If she comes safely home, Charlotte will be pleased to see Papa at ease like this, even if it's only for a little while, and it will be lovely to have her join them in all these musical activities.

But what Emily treasures most are the times when she can get the piano to herself.

Not content to play any old how just to amuse herself, as Branwell does, she tackles each new piece methodically, working away at it until she's mastered it, until she can play it without thinking.

When she reaches that point, she finds the music tremendously consoling — she can let out all her pent-up feelings, forgetting her anxieties about what may happen to Charlotte and Papa. Sometimes she gets so carried away she loses herself entirely.

Those are the best times.

Mr. Sunderland comes to the house now and gives them individual lessons. One day as he's leaving, Papa stops him in the hall and Emily hears Papa thanking the teacher for his part in their progress.

"Branwell — he's coming on, isn't he?" There's a note of pride in Papa's voice.

"Mmm." Mr. Sunderland sounds less than enthusiastic. "The boy has talent, but he should practice more diligently. He would do well to take a leaf out of Miss Emily's book."

"Emily?" Papa sounds surprised.

"Yes. She has the makings of a true musician. Good day to you, Mr. Brontë."

Long after the door has closed on Mr. Sunderland, Emily sits transfixed on the piano stool, cheeks glowing at his unexpected words.

She can hardly believe it, but it seems that she has stumbled into something that she can do well, and apparently better even than Branwell.

She hugs the knowledge to herself like a delicious secret.

9

Winter begins to loosen its grip and the days begin to lengthen. But Emily still misses Charlotte and constantly worries about how her sister is getting on. Is she keeping warm? Is she getting enough to eat? Above all, is she well?

Emily doesn't want to mention Charlotte to Papa in case he starts worrying too. There's no point in speaking to Aunt — she was so keen for Charlotte to go to school. In the end, she confides her fears in Tabby.

"Nay, don't fret thiself. I reckon Miss Charlotte'll be doing fine. Those friends of thi papa, the Atkinsons, they live nearby and Miss Charlotte's been a-visiting there, I believe. They'll be keeping an eye on her and be letting him know soon enough if owt's amiss."

Emily's not convinced. Charlotte would never tell the Atkinsons how she's feeling. She'd just keep it all to herself.

❧

Glass Town is never discussed now, but one day when Emily, Anne, and Branwell are sitting round the parlor table, supposedly working on stories for their miniature books, Branwell announces that he's going to write a complete history of the Young Men — the characters originating from the twelve wooden soldiers Papa gave him when he was nine, which have been at the center of many of their stories over the years.

"I'm taking it from the very beginning, complete with statistics, maps, and battle plans. And I'm doing it on my own," he adds with a challenging glare at Emily.

This is a blow. Ever since Charlotte left, she's been trying without much enthusiasm to write a Glass Town story, revisiting the imaginary world they all shared before everything changed. But her ideas don't flow as they used to and every time she tries to write she finds she scarcely produces anything. What used to be a comfort and gave her such pleasure is a struggle now. Without Charlotte and Branwell, Glass Town doesn't feel as real as it did, and she's been clinging to the hope that Branwell might change his mind and agree to work together again.

His declaration is the last straw. She grinds her teeth, then suddenly scrunches up the page she's been toiling over and throws it into the fire. If she has to make it up on her own, she doesn't want to do it anymore.

Taking another sheet of paper, she starts doodling on it, sketching horses' heads. It's completely wasteful — since paper's so expensive, they normally treasure every scrap of it that they can scrounge — and she's aware of Anne watching her, her blue eyes wide with surprise.

She doesn't care. What's the point of saving paper, if there's nothing to write?

This black mood she's sinking into has become familiar — Tabby calls it an attack of "the mopes" and it's been happening a lot lately.

Tabby says it's her age — that she's growing up.

"Don't you remember? Miss Charlotte was just the same," Tabby remarked one evening as she saw Emily into bed.

Perhaps Tabby's right. Emily can't get the idea out of her mind — she's horrified by the implications.

She's grown at least three inches this last year. Branwell says she's turning into a giraffe, but it's not funny. Her skirts are way off the ground and sometimes she doesn't know what to do with her arms and legs. From what she's seen her sister coping with, womanhood is a horrible, messy business. The very thought of it repels her . . .

Emily pulls a face and gouges the nib of her quill into the paper.

"Careful," says Anne. "You'll make a hole in the tablecloth."

"Children! Come and see what I've found." At the sound of Papa's voice calling them, the nasty retort Emily was about to make dies on her lips. And then there's an unexpected sound outside the parlor door — a short, sharp bark.

"Papa!" Emily leaps up and flings open the door. And yes, it *is* a dog, one of a good size with a brindle coat, sniffing about in their hall with great curiosity.

As Emily and the others surge out, the dog rushes up to them, baring his teeth in a grin and wagging his tail. Emily looks at Papa hopefully. "Is he ours?"

Papa, smiling broadly, winks at them. Branwell cheers and immediately stands on his head, one of his favorite tricks, causing the dog to go mad — he dances round them, letting out a volley of barks.

"What is going on?" Aunt is standing on the landing, looking down at them, her face screwed up as if she's sucking lemons.

She presses her hand to her forehead. "What is that dog doing here, Patrick?"

Her tone is sharp enough to quell them all, even the dog, who puts his tail between his legs and whines. Emily drops to her knees to comfort him and he licks her face.

Papa looks slightly abashed. "Well, now, as it happens, this fellow's a stray. He turned up the other day at the Braithwaites' farm. The thing is — they don't want him. When I was over there this afternoon, Joseph said they've already the two dogs and that's enough."

"And you're not thinking of keeping it, surely? The house is overrun with creatures as it is, what with those injured birds the children keep bringing home and that wretched cat ruining the furniture with his claws. We certainly don't want any more." Aunt's disapproval is clear in every rigid line of her body.

Emily stops breathing. She looks up at Papa, willing him with every fiber of her being not to give in.

Papa hesitates a long moment and then he says, "I am. We can give you a good home, can't we, boy?" and he pats the dog's head.

Emily breathes again. She gives a piercing whistle and the dog pricks up its ears.

Aunt erupts. "*Emily!* How many times do I have to tell you — a lady never whistles." With a sniff and a twitch of her shawl, she turns away from them all, throwing over her shoulder as she stalks back upstairs, "I hope, at least, that that animal's going to live in the peat house."

They wait until they hear the door to her room shutting and then they look at one another and grin.

Anne appeals to Papa. "He won't have to live outside, will he?"

Papa ruffles her hair. "No, but he must sleep in the back kitchen and you'd best keep him out of your aunt's way."

"What about Tiger?" Emily says immediately. "He won't like sharing his sleeping quarters with a dog."

"Well, how about moving Tiger to the kitchen? He'll like it by the range, won't he?"

"What kind of dog is he?" Branwell wants to know.

Papa puts his head on one side, considering. "Well, he puts me in mind of the Irish terrier we had when I was a boy, and if there's anything of that in him, he'll make a fine watchdog. What with him and my pistol we'll all be safe in our beds."

"What are we going to call him?" Emily is anxious. Names matter — just as much for animals as for people — so it's important to choose the right one.

Papa smiles at her. "Well, now, as to that, I've had an idea." He beckons them to follow him.

ᕦᕤ

"I'm choosing Bosun," announces Branwell. "Like Lord Byron's dog."

To Tabby's bemusement, after shutting Tiger in the back kitchen, Papa has instructed each of them to stand in a different corner of the kitchen. He's holding the dog in the middle and when he gives the signal, they are to call with their name of choice.

Emily narrows her eyes. Typical Branwell. He fancies himself Byron. But Bosun is a good name. She wishes she'd thought of it first.

"I'm having Charlie," says Anne peaceably. "What about you, Emily?"

"I'm still thinking." Emily is studying the dog, noticing the lively glint in his brown eyes, the set of his long jaws. He looks as if once he's got a hold on something, he won't let go easily.

Papa says, "Ready?" And he lets go of the dog.

They all shout at once.

"Bosun!"

"Charlie!"

"Grasper!"

The dog, confused, looks from one to another. He makes a move toward Branwell and Emily's heart skips a beat, but she goes on calling, keeping her voice low but insistent. "Grasper, here boy!"

The dog turns his head and meets her eye. He hesitates a moment and then with a sudden joyful bound he is licking her hand.

"Grasper it is, then," says Papa, smiling at her. "I'll have to see about getting him a collar."

Looking up, Emily sees Tabby watching her from across the kitchen. Tabby gives her a little nod, as if she's not displeased with what's happened. Anne, bless her, seems happy for her too. Only Branwell looks upset.

She doesn't blame him.

She wonders if he understands what she does — that from now on, whatever they may all pretend, the dog belongs to her.

10

Early the next morning Emily's woken by an unfamiliar noise. Bleary-eyed and puzzled, she listens. Of course! It's Grasper, shut up downstairs and whining and scratching at the door.

Throwing on her clothes, she goes quietly downstairs. The sky is just becoming light and no one else seems to be stirring, not even Tabby — the house is freezing. She's glad to get into the kitchen where the fire, left banked up all night, is glowing. She stops to say hello to Tiger, who's keeping a wary eye on the door to the back kitchen.

When she opens the door, careful not to let the tin bath that's hanging on it clatter, Grasper jumps up at her and barks a greeting.

"Shush, there's a good boy," she murmurs, mindful of Tabby sleeping in her narrow room overhead.

She lets Grasper out at the back and stands watching him, her arms folded tight to stop herself shivering. After racing round a couple of times, he begins a serious investigation of the yard, sniffing at everything and cocking his leg against the privy, to Emily's delight. "Clever boy," she says quietly to herself.

"What's he doing?"

Emily jumps at the sound of Anne's voice and frowns. She'd wanted to enjoy this moment by herself.

Reluctantly she makes space for Anne beside her in the doorway.

"I heard him bark," Anne whispers.

"Did he wake Aunt?"

Anne shakes her head. "I don't think anyone else heard him. Or if they did, they're not getting up."

Emily relaxes. Better Anne than Branwell — he'd never be able to keep quiet.

A wild idea springs into her head. "Why don't we take him up on the moor? I think he'd love it."

Anne's eyes widen. "You mean now? By ourselves?"

"Why not? There'll be no one about at this hour, and anyway, he'll protect us."

"But it's freezing."

"The sun's coming up. And we can put warm things on — oh, but you don't want to alert Aunt. I know, you can have my thick shawl. We'll be all right as long as we keep moving."

"Won't we get into frightful trouble?"

Emily shakes her head decisively. "We'll be back in time for prayers — they won't even know we've been out. Come on, it'll be fun."

ᐤᕁᐤ

For all her bravado, once they're outside Emily feels rather anxious about the responsibility of bringing Grasper with them, though she'll never admit it to Anne.

She daren't let him loose. What if he runs off and they can't catch him? Papa has made the dog a temporary collar from a strip of canvas, promising to get him a fine brass one as soon as he goes to Keighley. Emily has threaded a longish rope through the canvas to use as a lead, but Grasper keeps pulling on it, wanting to rush ahead.

She calls his name and she's tremendously pleased when, after a few goes, he finally comes back to her. She makes a fuss of him and gives him a morsel of the cheese she's secreted in her pocket. When they set off again, she keeps the rope short and he stops pulling and seems content to walk beside her.

Whoever had him before must have taught him to do this, which is a relief to know. She wonders if his old owners are missing him. Well, if they are it's their own fault — they should have taken better care of him.

Soon they come to the edge of the common; ahead of them lies the broad sweep of the moors. They stop and Emily gazes at the landscape before them, as if she's never seen it until now.

In a sense she hasn't, not at daybreak anyway. In this early light everything looks different, fresh and new. She breathes in deeply, expanding her lungs and feeling the cold air course through her, invigorating every part of her.

Smoke is already rising from the chimneys of scattered farms and a crowing cockerel is answered by another farther down the valley. The grass is stiff with frost and icicles glisten in the becks, but the sun is warm on her back.

Emily breaks into a grin of happiness. She's always enjoyed their walks, though not so much since Charlotte went away, because it's been strange without her sister.

But this is different.

Tabby usually sticks to well-trodden, familiar paths, warning them away from the "muck," the marshy places. She also likes to keep her eye on them, so she doesn't like them to wander far. But today, out here alone for the very first time, and unsupervised, they can do exactly as they like, go wherever they please.

She has never felt so free.

She glances sideways at Anne. Her sister seems to have overcome her doubts and is looking about her.

Gesturing at a rocky outcrop, Emily says, "Do you remember Tabby's story? About the elves living there and shooting arrows to harm the cows?"

"Oh yes. And we used to put bilberries on a leaf for them, didn't we? We were sure they would take them." Anne sounds a little wistful, as if she would still like to think the little people existed.

Emily smiles down at her. Anne is such a baby sometimes.

But Charlotte would never have agreed to this early morning adventure. Perhaps Anne isn't nearly as timid or law-abiding as they all suppose. And it's peaceful to be with her like this. Charlotte and Branwell are always full of ideas and arguments, but so far this morning Anne has let her alone to think her own thoughts. It's part of the wonderful sense of space she's had from the moment they set foot on the moor.

She looks at her little sister speculatively. It might not be so bad to have Anne for a companion. Just for now, until Charlotte comes back.

The dog stops to sniff at a clump of moor grass and Emily calls him. "Come on, Grasper. If you're not careful, the elves will get you."

And as they press on up the path, she begins to whistle a loud, cheery tune.

♋

They are late for prayers and Aunt is very cross with Emily.

"What on earth possessed you to take your little sister out into the cold? You know how susceptible to asthma she is. Do you want to make her ill?"

Emily, who hadn't given a thought to Anne's asthma, is stricken with guilt. How could she have forgotten? The nights she's heard Anne wheezing across the hall, fighting to get her breath; the severe attacks that bring Dr. Andrew with his leech jar; Anne's patient endurance when the leeches fasten themselves onto her bare arms and suck until they're fat with her blood.

Emily studies Anne. She doesn't look ill this morning — her cheeks are pink and her eyes are bright.

Putting his finger under Anne's chin, Papa tilts her face up so he can see it properly. He smiles. "I don't think she's come to any harm."

Emily breathes again.

Aunt sets off on another tack, scolding her for leading Anne into danger by going off without a chaperone, especially out onto the moors, "where anything might happen."

Papa shakes his head. "They put me in mind of myself as a lad. I delighted in going off alone to ramble in the Mountains of Mourne. It's in their blood, the love of nature" — he nods at Emily and Anne — "so there's no denying it. I know."

"But you were a *boy*," Aunt protests. "It's different for girls."

Papa shrugs. "With the dog, they're safe enough."

Emily and Anne look at each other with secret delight. However much Aunt may huff and puff about it, they take this as Papa giving them permission to go out on their own if they want.

"And if you happen to find yourselves over Ponden Hall way," adds Papa, "Mr. Heaton was saying only the other day that you're welcome to borrow books from his library at any time."

"His library! Have you seen it, Papa?" asks Emily.

"That I have not, but seeing as he's so proud of it, it *might* be worth seeing." There's a twinkle in Papa's eye as he says this. Several times he's told them of libraries he's been invited to admire on his parish visits, which turn out to consist of a few dog-eared volumes on a windowsill.

Emily's not sure about this invitation. Mr. Heaton, a mill owner and a trustee of the church, is a wealthy man, so he can easily afford books. If his collection really amounts to a library, it could be wonderful to be able to borrow books from it. But what if his taste runs to volumes about manufacturing or field sports? Besides, to visit the library would mean encountering the Heaton family. She knows them from church, of course, but she wouldn't want to have to *speak* to them.

On the whole, she's inclined not to accept Mr. Heaton's offer.

つ&く

As spring advances and the weather improves, Emily and Anne take every opportunity to slip away together with Grasper, either very early in the morning, taking care to be back in time for prayers, or after tea when Aunt is safely out of the way in her room and the mild evenings lure them farther afield.

Emily is enormously grateful to Grasper for this unexpected change in her life.

For a while now she's been finding some aspects of their daily routine stultifying — always the same chores to be done, meals to be eaten at the appointed time, and the deadly hours of sewing. She likes to blame Aunt for the rigid schedule, though, to be fair, she knows that Papa, for all his sense of fun and adventure, prefers a quiet and regular life, and since his illness this has been even more true. If Emily and Branwell start one of their arguments, at once Aunt emerges from her room to shush them.

Even when they are left to their own devices, which happens a lot, especially in the mornings or the evenings when Papa has parish work to attend to, Branwell and Charlotte (before she went away) have always been in charge, deciding what they would do.

Grasper's arrival has given her the freedom to roam the moors, and out here, she realizes, she feels more able to be herself. Without Aunt forever badgering her to be ladylike or Tabby warning her to mind herself, she can stride up rocky knolls, leap across becks, and whistle to her heart's content.

She loves Grasper for giving her this and, as she gets to know him better, she begins to love him for himself as well. He's always so good-humored and has such a zest for life. And he seems to relish being out of doors as much as she does. Now that she's confident about letting him off the lead, she enjoys watching him chase after birds or snuffing about eagerly in the heather, and when she calls him he always comes running back with his tail wagging and a great grin on his face, as if he's really pleased to see her.

It warms her heart to know that she is loved so simply and completely.

On their expeditions, Emily also gets to know Anne, learning things about her sister that she never knew.

For instance, she discovers that Anne is very observant. Whereas Charlotte admires distant vistas and sweeping views, Anne notices what is close at hand and might be overlooked. It's Anne who spots the first primroses growing in the shelter of an overhanging bank. It's Anne who suddenly stoops and stands up again, triumphantly waving a pheasant's long tail feather. And it's Anne who one evening comes to an abrupt halt and lays a restraining hand on Emily's arm.

Without a word she creeps off into the heather, removing her shawl as she goes. She crouches down and Emily can't see what she's doing, but very soon she returns carrying something carefully in both hands.

"Oh," Emily breathes. "A kestrel."

Wrapped up in Anne's shawl, it stares at them with unblinking eyes.

Emily admires its gleaming beak — a perfect cruel curve.

"Its wing is broken, I think," whispers Anne.

"Let's take it home and see if it will recover."

ᏯᏯ

Aunt makes a fuss, of course, but they are determined. Though Aunt gives in, she insists they keep the bird outside, and so that it won't upset the other birds they put it in the peat house.

Every time they go in, Emily is disturbed by the way the hawk looks at her — as if it can see into her soul and is not terribly impressed by what it finds there. She feels for the bird. It must be hateful to be imprisoned in the dark.

She studies its wild, yellow-rimmed eyes — in their gleaming depths she can see the hawk's longing to be free. She can't stop thinking about it. Does it understand that by bringing it home and shutting it up, they are trying to save its life? Or does it simply feel trapped? Just as she sometimes longs to get away from Aunt's scrutiny and the confinement of the house, is the hawk desperate to escape and once again have the whole wide sky to roam in?

They feed it scraps of meat begged from Tabby and then one morning when they open the door, it flies up at them. Startled, they step back and the hawk skims over their heads, circles, and then sails off toward the open moor.

They watch until it disappears and then look at each other with rueful grins.

Emily's sorry to see the hawk go, but she's glad it isn't shut in anymore.

∽

As spring turns into summer, their moorland walks become more adventurous and far-flung.

Aunt is still disapproving, but Papa, who knows the area intimately, is keen to hear where they've been and what they've seen. Since his illness he hasn't traveled far and he obviously misses his long walks.

For Emily it becomes part of the pleasure of their expeditions to try and conjure up for Papa the mood of the moors on any given day and the way the colors vary according to the changing light and the effects of the wind.

Papa drinks it all in and wants to know every detail, but Emily can sometimes detect a wistful note in his voice that gives her pause. Does he think he won't be able to see these things for himself one day?

She's glad that Charlotte's coming home soon, not just because she's dying to see her sister, but it will be a relief to share her worries about Papa.

11

At last, toward the end of June, the day arrives when Charlotte is due home. She's only got a month's holiday, not nearly long enough, but Emily is determined to make the most of every second of it. All morning she listens out for the carriage and keeps looking out of the window, hoping to see it coming up the lane.

The minute her older sister steps through the door, Emily sweeps her off her feet in a great bear hug.

Laughing, her victim protests, "Put me down, Emily, you silly."

Emily twirls her round before setting her down.

Charlotte looks at her in wonder. "How you've grown. You're nearly as tall as Papa."

"She's a veritable maypole now," says Branwell.

Emily cuffs him round the head, but only gently. She knows this is a sore point — Branwell has thick soles put on his boots and brushes his hair to make it stand up, but nothing can disguise the fact that he's shorter than most boys of his age.

Charlotte has hugs and kisses all round, including from Tabby, who, after embracing her, holds her at arm's length and says, "Tha's lost all thi color, Miss Charlotte. Are they feeding thee properly at yon place?"

Charlotte laughs and waves her arm dismissively, but Tabby

is clearly not satisfied. "We'll have to get some roses back into thi cheeks, lass," she mutters, retreating to the kitchen.

Emily studies Charlotte more closely. She does look pale. Emily's heart judders. Charlotte's not ill, is she? This isn't what she dreads beginning again?

"Charlotte, are you well?"

Her sister looks surprised. "Yes, of course."

Emily's not convinced, but before she can say more, Grasper arrives, wagging his tail joyfully and desperate to greet the newcomer.

Emily swallows her fear and makes Grasper sit and be introduced properly — she wants Charlotte to admire him. But to her disappointment Charlotte regards him warily and only gives him the briefest of pats. Can't she see how splendid he is?

But Charlotte has already turned away. She whirls into the parlor and stands there, as if taking it all in, her hand caressing the back of a chair.

"Nothing's changed," says Emily, following her in, with Branwell and Anne close on her heels. "It's just the same as when you left."

"I know," says Charlotte. "And you can't imagine how pleased I am to see it again — this dear room, our dear old furniture."

Branwell and Emily exchange amused glances and Branwell taps the side of his head. "Methinks her sojourn in foreign parts has mazed her mind. She is much changed and not for the better."

"No, I'm not," says Charlotte, and Emily detects an anxious note in her voice. "I'm just the same old me too."

☙

But she isn't.

Emily notices straight away that Charlotte has a different way of talking — she says words carefully, as if she's conscious of how she's speaking, and some words sound quite different from the way they did before.

There's something else too. After Charlotte's displayed with shy pride the three prizes that she's won and the silver medal for being top of the whole school, she's eager to tell them all about her experiences.

Roe Head, she says, is a roomy and comfortable house set in attractive gardens — she fetches a pencil sketch she's done and they all admire it. The surrounding area is pleasant and they have plenty of walks — Miss Wooler couldn't be kinder — the lessons are stimulating — the standard of the extras, especially French and drawing, is exceptionally high — and so on and so on.

Emily listens with folded arms: The more Charlotte says, the more suspicious she becomes. She examines her sister with narrowed eyes. What's happened to Charlotte? She doesn't usually gush.

Either she's changed or she's not telling the truth.

"Do you paint in oils?" Branwell wants to know. Since Mr. Bradley's return to the area, their brother's been going to his studio for lessons. He comes back smelling of linseed oil and turpentine and talking self-importantly about "impasto" and "scumbling."

"Oh no," says Charlotte. "Pencil and watercolor, that's all."

Branwell looks pleased and Emily wonders if he was worried that Charlotte might outdo him. Abruptly she asks, "What about music lessons? Are they any good?"

82

"Oh, I forgot to tell you. Miss Wooler has advised me to give up the piano. I have to stoop so much to see the notes and she thinks it will permanently damage my posture."

"No!" Emily is shocked and full of sympathy. "But, Charlotte, wait until you see our new piano. You won't want to stop then."

Charlotte shrugs, as though she doesn't mind giving up playing and even having their own piano is of little interest.

Emily gapes at her. She can't understand it at all. If something prevented her from playing the piano, she'd be devastated.

Branwell says, "Why don't you wear spectacles, Charlotte? She should, shouldn't she, Papa?"

Papa nods. "Yes, indeed, my dear, I really think it would be a good idea to consult Mr. Robertson while you're home."

"I'd rather not, Papa," says Charlotte primly.

Branwell snorts. "That's stupid. Why go about the world groping your way like a mole when you could see?"

Charlotte's eyes flash and then she says, with emphasis on each word, "I. Don't. Want. To. Wear. Spectacles." She sets her mouth in a firm line.

Anne says quickly, "Is there much time given to religious devotion at the school?"

"Oh yes." Charlotte sounds amused. "We go to church every Sunday, of course, but two of Miss Wooler's sisters are married to clergymen and we see a lot of them — in fact, they're practically on the staff. I don't think you'd get on very well with them, Papa — they're very keen on hellfire and damnation for everyone apart from the chosen few."

"Among whom they number themselves, I suppose?" says Papa, with a twinkle in his eye.

"I think so!" Charlotte laughs.

Emily's not interested in these clergymen. She wants to know something far more pressing. "What are the other girls like?"

"Oh, they're . . ." Charlotte hesitates. "Well, like girls of our age are, you know."

Emily stares at her and then glances at Anne, who looks as mystified as she feels. They don't know any other girls of their age.

Charlotte tries again. "They're lively . . . high-spirited."

Emily is suspicious. There's something Charlotte's not saying. She resolves to get the truth out of her when they're on their own.

"Have you made friends?" Aunt asks and Charlotte's face clears.

"Oh yes, I have made two good, good friends." And she waxes lyrical about these new bosom friends, Ellen and Mary.

Emily listens, frowning. She doesn't like the sound of this at all . . . unless exaggeration is a new habit Charlotte has picked up at school.

"Mary and I have the fiercest disputes, going at it hammer and tongs and neither giving way. I find it very" — Charlotte breaks off and looks round at everyone, as if she's suddenly become self-conscious — "exciting," she adds in a quiet voice, blushing.

"Does she like literature?" asks Branwell abruptly and Emily can tell that he's as disturbed as she is by this talk of new friends.

Charlotte laughs. "No, not at all. You should hear her comments about poetry. As it has no practical benefits, she can't see the point of it."

"Hmm." Branwell nods, as if an unspoken question has been answered to his satisfaction.

But Emily isn't reassured. She's thoroughly unsettled by Charlotte's apparent enthusiasm for this place that isn't home and these people who are strangers.

And is she really well?

She'll have to wait until bedtime to find out. But how delightful it will be to have Charlotte sharing her bed again. She can't wait to talk to her properly.

12

As soon as they are tucked up in bed together, Emily wriggles as close to Charlotte as she can get. "Oh, Charles, it's so good to have you back. I've missed you so much."

Charlotte smiles at her. "I've missed you too, mine bonnie," she says, using one of Tabby's expressions.

"Have you? Have you really?"

"Of course."

"And are you really quite well?"

"*Yes!* I told you. Honestly, there's nothing to worry about."

Charlotte seems to be telling the truth. Emily allows herself to relax.

Her sister continues, "But Papa . . ." She turns an anxious face to Emily. "He doesn't seem to have recovered as much as I would have expected in the time I've been away."

Emily doesn't know what to say. She'd like to pour out all her fears about Papa, but it doesn't seem fair to burden Charlotte the minute she's returned. She settles for saying, "At least he hasn't got any worse," and then she deliberately changes the subject.

"But tell me about Roe Head. Is it really as pleasant as you say?"

"Oh yes. It's nothing like Cowan Bridge. We didn't need to worry at all."

Emily scans Charlotte's face. Again, she doesn't seem to be hiding the truth.

"So who do you share a bed with?"

"Ellen."

Emily's not pleased to hear this, not after all the glowing things Charlotte has said about this new friend.

"What's she really like?"

"I told you. She's a gentle girl, very generous and —"

Emily snorts and Charlotte looks nonplussed. "What's the matter?"

"You make her sound so perfect. As if she's not a human being at all."

"You're right. And she isn't perfect, of course. I don't think" — Charlotte hesitates but then goes on — "I don't think Ellen has much imagination. Do you know, I can't bear to hear her read aloud." Charlotte laughs guiltily.

Emily feels a secret stab of satisfaction. Her sister's not completely besotted with this Ellen, then.

"But," and now Charlotte is completely serious, "she has been so kind to me, Emily. You wouldn't believe it."

Something in her voice causes Emily to wonder — she remembers what Charlotte said earlier. "And the other girls? Are they as nice?"

Charlotte doesn't answer.

After a while Emily puts her hand on her sister's arm. "Charles?"

Charlotte sighs. "They don't mean anything. And it's probably my fault for being too sensitive."

Emily, envisaging horrors, whispers, "What do they do?"

"They don't really do anything . . . but I hear them talking about me and laughing."

"Laughing?"

Reluctantly Charlotte says, "When I arrived, they thought it was terribly funny that I knew so little that Miss Wooler was going to put me in the bottom of the junior class —"

"But that's ridiculous. Papa has taught us such a lot of things."

Charlotte says drily, "It turns out they aren't the right sorts of things."

"Right for what?"

"For being a governess. Things like grammar. Geography."

"But you've won those prizes . . . and that medal."

"Yes, well . . ."

Emily sees all at once how terribly hard Charlotte must have worked to fight her way from the bottom of the school to the top. No wonder she looks tired.

"So then don't the girls admire you for achieving so much?"

Charlotte shrugs. "I don't think they care much about study. Of course, most of them have wealthy fathers so they're not going to have to earn their living and they don't seem to understand why I work so hard. They find me amusing."

"Oh, Charlotte, they don't."

"They do, I'm afraid. They laugh at the way I speak and the fact that I can't see properly so I can't catch a ball and they imitate the way I hold the book close to my nose and, oh, lots of things . . ."

To Emily, the humiliations Charlotte speaks of so calmly sound terrible. It's obvious what she must do. "Never mind. You're home now. And once you tell Papa the truth about it —"

"Papa mustn't know." Charlotte glares at Emily. "You're not to say anything."

"But the girls —"

Charlotte shakes her head. "It doesn't matter about the other girls."

"But —"

"Emily! Listen to me." She looks Emily in the eye. "What do you think it would do to Papa if I said I wanted to give up? He's counting on my being able to be a governess, to support myself if I should need to. I can't let him down. And anyway" — she takes Emily's hand and squeezes it — "there are lots of things about the school that are excellent and I like it, truly I do. So, you see, it's no good going on about it. I'm going back and that's that."

Emily is silenced. Just for a moment there, her heart had lifted with a marvelous hope — Charlotte would stay at home; she'd have her back for good; everything would be back to normal. But now . . . she sighs. She doesn't believe that Charlotte can really like the school, but she has a point about Papa. They must do all they can to avoid adding to his worries and risking his getting ill again.

She nudges Charlotte. "You could wear spectacles."

It's ridiculous of her sister not to. At least she'd be able to play the piano, which would be some compensation for the bullying she has to endure.

"No!"

"Why not?"

"Because I am ugly enough as it is."

"Don't be silly. You're not ugly."

"I am. Mary said so."

Emily winces. "I thought she was your friend."

"She is. And she's not afraid to speak her mind. That's one of the things I like about her. And she doesn't laugh at me and nor does Ellen. They're not like the others."

Emily can see it now — the relief of having these two friends when Charlotte is forced to live among such a spiteful set of girls.

She almost warms to them . . . almost, but not quite.

❧

". . . and at Roe Head the cooks don't boil the vegetables for hours like Tabby does."

Emily grits her teeth. It is probably nicer to have vegetables that haven't turned to a gluey mush, but she wishes Charlotte would stop going on about that blessed school. She's only been home a week, but already she's getting on Emily's nerves.

She thought Charlotte's holiday was going to be so wonderful. But her sister is forever beginning sentences with "Ellen says" and "Mary wouldn't agree with that," as if her friends, like ghostly presences, have come home with her and taken up residence in the house. And she can't stop talking about Miss Wooler, the headmistress.

If Charlotte is to be believed, this lady, who dresses in white robes and wears her hair in a plaited coronet — Branwell rolls his eyes at Emily when they hear this — is the most cultivated woman in the whole of Yorkshire.

"Miss Wooler's not just passionate about the subjects she teaches," Charlotte now declares admiringly. "She makes a point of getting to know every one of her pupils. She —"

She breaks off as Papa looks in on them, saying, as he always does, "Don't stay up too late, now."

They listen to his footsteps going up the stairs, stopping on the first landing as he winds the clock, and then continuing up to his bedroom.

Outside the light is fading from the sky, so it probably *is* time they were going to bed.

But Charlotte says, "Why don't we do the walking ritual?"

"What are you talking about?" Branwell asks.

"What we do at school before we go to bed." Charlotte explains that every evening, for the period before bedtime, Miss Wooler has the girls stroll in pairs up and down the schoolroom, conversing as they go, and she takes part in this, walking with a different pupil each time and asking them about themselves.

"What!" Emily yelps. "That's intolerable. What right has she got to pry like that? Don't you dread your turn?"

"No, not at all." Charlotte looks surprised. "I don't know how she does it, but Miss Wooler has a way of drawing you out. She seems genuinely interested in what you have to say."

Emily can't think of anything worse. She wouldn't want someone like the headmistress, a stranger, to know anything about her. But Charlotte, shy Charlotte, seems to enjoy revealing herself to Miss Wooler. What has she been saying? Emily certainly hopes she hasn't been blabbing about their family.

"So, shall we try it?" Charlotte looks expectantly at them.

Emily snorts derisively. "Why would we want to do that?"

"It's fun. You'll see." She seizes Branwell by the arm and urges him to get up. "You two pair up and follow us," she orders Emily and Anne, setting off with Branwell at a stately pace.

Anne obediently offers her hand to Emily. Grudgingly, Emily links arms with her little sister and they start walking. The parlor is small, so they're forced to go round and round the table.

Scowling, Emily directs a silent curse at Charlotte's back. This is ridiculous. At least Papa and Aunt and Tabby are all safely in bed and can't witness their making fools of themselves. She pulls a face at Anne, who giggles.

Charlotte frowns over her shoulder at them. "You've got to talk to each other."

She turns back to Branwell and they continue hotly debating an article in *Blackwood's Magazine*.

Emily sighs. Branwell was right — school has made Charlotte crazed, as Tabby would say. But since it feels stupid to walk round the table in silence, they might as well have a go. She starts talking to Anne about the Byron poem they were reading earlier, asking her sister what she most admired about it.

After a while she forgets the oddity of what they're doing and finds herself enjoying it — it's restful in the twilight and when Anne asks her what *she* thought about the poem, she discovers that the rhythm of walking seems to help her thoughts to flow.

Perhaps it's not such a stupid idea after all. But she'll never admit that to Charlotte.

13

". . . and Kirklees Park is beautiful. You can't imagine how delightful it is to roam about in the shade of the forest. And there are deer, you know."

Emily scowls. Why does Charlotte keep talking? Why doesn't she look at where she is and see how grand the moors are? Surely she can't think that a park is anything like as impressive. Perhaps, without spectacles, she's too blind to see the splendor in front of her.

Emily only feels a little bit guilty for having this mean thought.

Here they are — it's the last day of Charlotte's holiday, the sun is shining, and they're on their way to a place she and Anne have named The Meeting of the Waters, their favorite spot, and all Charlotte keeps going on about is the scenery around Roe Head. To hear her you'd think it was the next best thing to paradise.

When they come to the wide stream Emily splashes across without a thought, followed by Anne, and they laugh as Grasper frisks beside them. But then Emily realizes that Charlotte isn't with them. She looks back. Their sister is still on the bank, staring nervously at the tumbling water.

"Come on, Charlotte," she calls. "It's quite safe."

But Charlotte won't come. Sighing, Emily begins to gather some stepping-stones for her, placing them carefully in the water. Anne helps, and then, hopping across to show how easy it is, she leads Charlotte back with her.

Watching Charlotte teeter from one stone to the next, with a look on her face as if she's enduring the most terrible ordeal, Emily has to resist the temptation to push her in. For heaven's sake, it's not as if it's very deep. The worst that could happen is wet boots.

Finally they reach a point where they can overlook their destination.

". . . and Miss Wooler admires the paintings of Gainsborough, but she says —"

"Look," says Emily, gesturing dramatically and cutting Charlotte off in midflow. "Isn't it splendid?"

In front of them the ground falls away abruptly into a deep cleft and off to the left a flow of spring water is tumbling down the hillside, frothing and sparkling in the sunshine.

But rather than admiring the falls, Charlotte is peering down past her feet. "Have we got to go down there?" she says, with a quaver in her voice. "Isn't it rather steep?"

Emily grits her teeth. Charlotte isn't very brave, but she wasn't so niminy-piminy before she went to school. Putting on a patience she doesn't feel, she says, "It is a little, but we'll help you. You won't come to any harm."

She goes first, showing Charlotte where to put her feet and offering her hand at the steepest descents. Charlotte squeaks a little here and there and at one point she slips, but Emily catches her. Finally they reach the bottom.

"Here we are," Emily announces.

"Thank goodness." Charlotte puts her hand on her chest as if to steady her breathing. "We haven't got to climb back up that way, have we?"

"No!" Emily can't keep the exasperation out of her voice. They've only just arrived and Charlotte's already worrying about leaving. "There's another path we can take to get home. But Charlotte, do look."

She indicates the scene before them. Here in the bottom of the gully, the spring meets a beck at a point where it's crossed by an ancient stone bridge. The waters flow on downhill, forming brown pools edged with bright ferns and tall pink spires of foxgloves. The hillside rises all round them, cutting them off from the world so that they can enjoy the beauties of this spot in perfect seclusion, hidden from view.

Charlotte peers about vaguely.

"See those flat stones," says Emily, pointing at some slabs overhung by a clump of birch trees. "They make ideal seats. We can sit in the shade and trail our hands in the water. It will be lovely and cool."

"Or we could paddle," suggests Anne, looking excited at the prospect.

But Charlotte just says, "Mm, yes," in a halfhearted way. So they all stand around — like tailors' dummies, thinks Emily irritably — until finally she can't bear it any longer.

"Oh, do come and sit down, Charlotte," she says, and she and Anne settle themselves on a wide slab. After a moment Charlotte does join them, choosing her spot carefully and sitting down gingerly. But she can't be persuaded to put even a finger into the water.

Looking at Charlotte's stiff posture and the rather grim

expression on her face, Emily scowls. Her sister's only agreed to come to humor them. She doesn't really want to be there at all.

Suddenly scooping up a stone, Emily hurls it into the water. She only just misses Charlotte's head. Charlotte looks round in confusion and Anne exclaims, "Emily!" But she doesn't care. She had so looked forward to sharing this secret place with Charlotte, but the pleasure of the day has been spoiled and it's all Charlotte's fault.

Having dived in after the stone, Grasper searches about fruitlessly for a while and then pants back to them, dripping water everywhere and making Charlotte shrink away from him with a little squeal.

Abruptly, Emily stands up. She has had enough. "Shall we go back?"

Charlotte jumps up with alacrity, looking relieved, and they set off in the direction of home.

❧

Emily stumps along behind the others.

Charlotte must have seen how important The Meeting of the Waters was to her and Anne; she could at least have pretended. But no, all she's interested in is her new life at school. And when Emily finally broached the subject of Papa, all Charlotte could say was, "We must do our best not to worry him." And she'd followed that up with, "You'll make sure you behave, won't you, Emily?"

As if she was still a child. As if she doesn't try all the time to avoid doing anything that might upset Papa. She's even given up arguing with Aunt in case the old lady complains to Papa.

Emily kicks a stone. She's been dying to have Charlotte back, to have a really good talk with her about everything, and it hasn't happened. All because Charlotte has changed. She doesn't seem to care about the family anymore. And she certainly doesn't care about Emily.

By now the village is in sight and Emily smiles wryly as an idea dawns on her.

She calls out to the others. "Why don't we go home through Parker's field for a change?"

Anne gives her a speculative look, but Charlotte says, "Yes, all right, if you like."

They're well into the middle of the field and Charlotte is still babbling. ". . . and next term we're to begin botanical illustration and —"

She sees the cows and falters.

As if singling her out, as if they *know* she's afraid of them, the lumbering beasts crowd round her, snuffing curiously and slobbering at her with their rubbery tongues. She freezes, uttering mews of terror.

Emily feels a stab of satisfaction. It serves Charlotte right.

She waits a good few minutes before she relents and shoos the cows away. Even then Charlotte seems unable to move until Emily takes her arm and makes her come.

Over her head, Emily grins wickedly at Anne. Anne shakes her head reproachfully, but Emily can see she's repressing a smile. Good. She's glad about it too.

14

The next day, immediately after Charlotte has left to go back to school for her last term, Emily goes to the piano and plunges into one of Mendelssohn's *Songs Without Words*. She only manages a page before breaking off and staring, unseeing, at the keys.

She shouldn't have been so mean to Charlotte about the cows. It was a childish, petty act of revenge, the sort of thing they used to do to each other when they were younger. She's too old for that sort of trick now. And it was pointless anyway, since it did nothing to achieve what she wants.

Emily sighs. What she wants is to have Charlotte back again as she used to be before she went away. But now her sister has gone to that school for another five months. When she comes home she's bound to be even more different. Oh, if only everything could be as it was before Papa became ill.

Touching one or two keys lightly without pressing them down, she sighs again, and Grasper, who's been lying with his head on her foot, raises it and gives her a quizzical look. She smiles at him ruefully.

All along, without even admitting it to herself, she's been hoping that being at school would make Charlotte miss the old way they used to write. That she'd come home wanting to go back to it and they'd all join in together and everything would be all right again.

But Charlotte hadn't shown any interest in writing, not even with Branwell. She'd listened to him reading from his history of the Young Men and made enthusiastic comments, but she hadn't shown any desire to discuss new developments or write anything herself. It was as if her efforts at school had exhausted her and she just wanted to relax during the holiday.

Emily had wanted to ask Charlotte about it, but somehow she never did. And now she doesn't know what to do.

For some time now when she's seen Branwell scribbling away she's felt a pang of envy. She misses that total absorption, that experience of being carried away into an imaginary world that's so much brighter and more exciting than her dull daily life.

And she's been rereading *Rob Roy*, her favorite Walter Scott novel. It's been delightful to meet Diana Vernon, that bold and witty heroine, again and read about Frank's journey to the Highlands, where he meets the daring outlaw, Rob Roy, who fights for justice for the oppressed. Reading the story has stirred Emily up, made her full of yearning, just like when she hears Mr. Sunderland playing the piano. She wants to do this *herself*. She wants to create larger-than-life characters and send them off on thrilling adventures.

She also wants that indefinable pleasure of writing — how it begins with an indistinct feeling, something vague but pressing that builds up inside you until it emerges into a sentence, something crisp and definite that didn't exist before. It must be how God felt — "Let there be . . ." and there it is.

And oh, she wants the fun of collaboration, that excitement

where you have an idea and the other person sees a way to develop it and that gives you *more* ideas — like a tree ever-branching outward and the whole thing growing much faster and more enjoyably than if you did it on your own.

Just thinking about it makes her want to do it again, and as soon as possible!

Maybe she can . . .

Maybe writing by herself is not the only option.

Sitting up straight, she turns back to the beginning of the music and starts playing again with passionate energy.

ᘓᘑ

The next time she and Anne go out, they decide to walk to The Meeting of the Waters again. It's such a beautiful day — in the sunshine the moor is like a bronze cloth spread out for their pleasure — and Emily wonders if her sister feels as she does — that she wants to make up for their previous visit, which was so disappointing. And it's the perfect place to ask Anne the question that's been fizzing inside her.

She waits until they've settled themselves on one of the flat stone slabs. They've brought books with them, but before Anne can open hers, Emily says abruptly, "You know our Glass Town play? How do you feel about it?"

Anne looks puzzled. "What do you mean?"

"Well . . ." Emily hesitates, not quite sure how to put it. "You've been going on with it, haven't you? But are you enjoying it?"

Anne pauses and then says, "I liked it better when we all talked about it and made things up together. Do you suppose when Charlotte comes home for good, we'll do that again?"

"I don't know." Emily lifts her chin. "But do you know something? I'm tired of being ignored and told that our ideas are childish."

"Is that why you haven't been writing?"

Emily nods.

After a moment, Anne says, "Perhaps if we asked the others again when they're in a better mood, they'll let us join in properly."

Emily looks away, watching the water splashing down the hillside and spilling over the rocks, at Grasper paddling in the shallows. Taking a deep breath, she says, "I don't want to be part of what the others are doing anymore. I'd like to make up a new play, one that's just ours, you and me." She turns back to Anne. "What do you think?"

Anne's eyes, violet blue in the sunshine, are wide with surprise and Emily holds her breath as she waits for her answer.

Her sister was so young when Maria and Elizabeth died. As far as Anne's concerned, Charlotte has always been their leader. If she says no, Emily doesn't know what she'll do. Could she break away and work by herself? Could she bear to see the other three playing together and not be part of it, however unsatisfactory it's become?

Grasper trots up to where they're sitting and shakes himself, scattering water drops all over them. Anne laughs and pats his head. Then, still laughing, she lifts her face to Emily and says, "Yes."

"You want to do it?"

"Yes!"

Emily lets out a great sigh of happiness. "Good. That's what we'll do, then."

In their walks, their new shared world takes shape.

They agree that, as in all their plays, it should take the form of an island. After scouring *A Grammar of General Geography*, they call the new land Gondal and set it in the North Pacific. But Emily doesn't want the old imaginary landscapes of their plays: deserts and palm trees and fantastical cities with their palaces of lapis lazuli, streets paved with precious stones, and paradisal gardens — the sort of thing that Charlotte loves. After reading Walter Scott, her mind is full of mountains and moorlands, waterfalls tumbling into deep ravines, forests and rocky shores.

She suggests this landscape to Anne for Gondal. "It's just like here," she says, waving her arm at the scene before them. "And it's *real*."

Anne nods enthusiastically. "It's better if it's real."

Emily grins with delight. She doesn't want magical transformations either, or genii appearing and bringing people back to life. It's wonderful that Anne feels the same.

They decide that just as they used to do when they were all working on the Glass Town saga, they'll divide Gondal into separate regions, with each of them taking responsibility for developing their own main characters. They'll develop the new saga in the old way, talking about everything together and acting out various scenes and events on their walks, then writing it down at home, each working on their own bits, when they get the chance in the mornings and evenings when Papa and Aunt leave them to their own devices.

Because she loves the secrecy of it, Emily proposes that they still use the same minute print and make miniature books. "And we won't let Branwell read them, will we? Or Charlotte."

Anne looks worried. "Won't we? That seems unkind."

Emily tosses her head. "Well, they've been unkind to us, so it serves them right."

To prevent Anne arguing about it, she rushes on to outline some ideas she's had about some of her new heroes and heroines.

"I've thought of a chief man called Julius Brenzaida. At the start of it all he's a student and he's in love with Princess Rosina. She loves him, but she's not sitting around waiting for him to notice her."

She doesn't want her Rosina to be like Charlotte's heroines, who are horribly languid and never *do* anything. She wants her to be like Diana Vernon, spirited and self-willed and as Scott describes her: *Accustomed to mind nobody's opinion but her own.*

"She encourages Julius to rebel against the college authorities and they imprison him in a dungeon under the Palace of Instruction, where he undergoes horrible tortures. But the worst part of his suffering is being separated from his beloved Rosina. What do you think?"

She waits anxiously while Anne considers her suggestion. Her sister nods. "Yes, I think that sounds intriguing."

Emily feels like cheering. After having her contributions mocked and belittled by the others, it's so encouraging to receive a positive reaction. And it's so liberating to be in charge of it all. Because really she is — she's been taking the lead and Anne seems content to follow her. The novelty of having someone look up to her adds to the delight of the whole venture.

But when Emily suggests that Julius takes on himself all the responsibility for his imprisonment, Anne shakes her head. "I don't think he would feel that. It doesn't ring true."

Emily frowns. "Of course it does. It's his actions that have caused him to suffer."

"I think, however much he loves her, he would blame Rosina for urging him to rebel."

"No, that's nonsense. What do you know about love? You're just a child."

Anne raises her head and gives Emily a look.

After a moment Emily says, "Sorry. That sounded like Charlotte, didn't it?"

Anne nods.

Gazing at her, Emily sees suddenly what it might be like to be Anne, to be the youngest and therefore always somehow disregarded. "You must get tired of everyone treating you like the baby of the family."

Anne looks thoughtful and then she says, "It's quite nice to be spoiled. But sometimes I think the rest of you don't realize that I have my own ideas and am quite capable of forming my own judgment of things. Such as how Julius would feel." She gives Emily a challenging look.

Emily goes to protest, then stops and considers. Finally she throws up her hands. "You're right. He never stops loving Rosina, but he'll blame her and he'll tell her so. And she deserves it."

Emily whistles to Grasper and, as they walk on, she slips her arm through Anne's.

❧

One afternoon, walking in a direction they've never taken before, they come across a remote farmhouse.

Emily has always considered the parsonage a sturdy house, constructed with the harsh winters of the Yorkshire moors in mind, but she can see that, with its narrow, deep-set windows and stout cornerstones, this house, Top Withens, was built to withstand even more extreme weather.

It needed to be, up here.

She notices that the firs and thorns at one end of the house are slanted, their growth distorted by the force of the wind that's blowing fiercely on this autumn day.

What must it be like to live up here in the dark months of winter, cut off by deep snow? Hearing the onslaught of the gales blasting against the windows, day after day?

She tries to imagine it, peering at the house for clues. What if the inhabitants were like her Gondal people, with passions as powerful as the wind, full of bitter jealousies and resentments? How would they fare, closeted up together for months at a time, scarcely seeing another living soul? Such a situation could easily breed violence, perhaps even murder.

Excited by the possibilities, she falls into a reverie. Suddenly Anne nudges her. A face is peering at them from one of the windows. Seizing Anne's arm, Emily turns tail and flees, but when they are a safe distance away she can't resist glancing back, fixing the image of that isolated house and its situation in her mind.

15

One blustery afternoon in November Emily and Anne's rambles bring them to the hillside above Ponden Hall.

As they gaze down at the old grey stone house, Anne says, "Remember what Papa said about Mr. Heaton's library? Shall we go down and see if we can visit it today?"

Emily hesitates. Papa has recently seen the Heatons' library and he reported that it was very fine. "I don't know. I don't want to have to see the family."

Anne looks wistfully at the hall. "But just think — all those books. Can't we just have a look? We won't have to stay long."

Emily is in an agony of indecision. The lure of the books is dreadfully tempting. Like the others, she has read and reread Papa's small but precious stock of books until she knows them virtually by heart, and he can rarely afford a new volume. He has a subscription with the Keighley circulating library and will get books for them from time to time, but there's only a limited selection. The thought of having a whole library to browse in for herself . . .

"All right, but we must try not to get trapped in a conversation."

In the lane they stop and peer round a pillar at the house.

Emily's just screwing up her courage to go and knock at the door when it opens and a boy hails them.

"Pa says you're to come in, if you please."

Tying Grasper to a boot scraper, they follow the boy into the house. As they pass through the doorway, the date carved on a plaque above it catches Emily's eye — 1801.

It's a date that sticks in her memory, for it means a lot to Papa — the year of the union of Ireland with Great Britain.

Inside, Emily finds herself in a spacious room. She recognizes Mr. Heaton, with his ruddy face and thinning hair, from church. Clad in knee breeches and gaiters, he's sitting by a huge fireplace in which a tremendous fire of coal and wood as well as peat is blazing away. Opposite him, with some knitting in her lap, is his wife, a round, comfortable-looking woman. The boy joins his little brothers at the table; there are open books in front of them, but they're far more interested in their visitors.

Having five pairs of eyes gazing at her is too much for Emily. Her instinct is to turn and run, but Mr. Heaton has risen and is greeting them. "Miss Emily, isn't it? And Miss Anne? How do you do, young ladies? I hope I see you well."

"We are very well, thank you, Mr. Heaton." Anne blushes furiously. "Aren't we, Emily?"

"Yes," says Emily stiffly. This is a mistake. They should never have come in.

She offers monosyllabic replies to Mr. Heaton's inquiries about Papa's health and that of the rest of the family. He addresses them all to her, but she refuses to look him in the face. She hates it when strangers peer at you as if they've a right to know what you're thinking and feeling. Her eyes dart round the room.

It's nothing like their parlor at home, but nor is it the luxurious room Emily would expect of a wealthy man like Mr. Heaton — a room with crimson and gold furnishings and crystal chandeliers such as Charlotte described in the palaces of Glass Town.

It's more like a farmhouse. A great oak cabinet fills one end, the shelves above laden with silver jugs, enormous pewter dishes, and gleaming tankards. Overhead, legs of beef and ham dangle from hooks in the dark wooden ceiling and a rack of drying oatcakes hangs at one end of the room. Instead of a picture above the fireplace, there are some fearsome old guns.

Emily can't believe that somewhere in this house there can be any library at all, let alone a "fine" one.

By now, an awkward silence has fallen. Anne nudges her and she forces herself to say, "Mr. Heaton, Papa said your library is very impressive."

"Ah yes, indeed." Mr. Heaton smiles expansively. "I would say it's the largest hereabouts. We have a Shakespeare First Folio, you know. You'd like to see it, no doubt?"

"Oh yes, please."

The oldest boy is out of his seat in a flash. "Let me show them, Pa."

His father laughs. "Aha, I see one of you has made a conquest. Which of the young ladies has won your heart, William, my boy?"

Flushing scarlet, the lad studies his boots.

Emily is puzzled. What does Mr. Heaton mean? But when his father says, "Go on, then, son, show the young ladies the way," and the boy raises his eyes to hers, she sees a look in them that she's only ever seen in Grasper's eyes — one of dumb devotion.

She cringes inwardly as they follow him upstairs. Silly boy, what does he think he's doing looking at her like that? He can't be more than twelve.

The sight of the library drives all other thoughts from her head.

Mr. Heaton wasn't exaggerating — there are more books here than Emily has ever dreamed of. She dives at the shelves, scanning them wildly. History, biography, travel . . . and here are the poets: some she's heard of — Burns and Moore — and others unfamiliar to her. She's tempted to seize volume after volume from the shelves and fill her arms with this treasure.

Taking a deep breath, she makes herself calm down. She looks again more carefully and eventually selects just one book — Byron's *Don Juan*.

Soon she's so deeply immersed in it she's hardly aware of the boy creeping out and leaving them to it, or of Anne turning pages occasionally.

⌘

"Well, now, Miss Emily." Mr. Heaton's abrupt entry into the room makes her jump. "I don't want to spoil your entertainment, but Mrs. Heaton was wondering whether it wasn't time for you to be getting your sister back to the parsonage. I'll take you in the gig, if you like."

Emily doesn't want to leave this wonderful room. It's like being inside a cocoon — she feels completely relaxed and safe. But glancing out of the window, she sees that dusk is falling. They had better go. But they certainly don't need a lift.

Unfortunately Anne is already saying, "Thank you, Mr. Heaton. That's kind of you."

Emily gives her a look. Now they'll have to talk to him all the way home.

Mr. Heaton says, "Before we go, is there a book you'd each like to take with you? And when you bring your sister back to return it, Miss Emily, you're welcome to choose another."

Emily and Anne exchange delighted glances and rapidly make their choices.

"What is it to be, then?" asks Mr. Heaton, looking at the books in Anne's hand.

"I can't decide between Bishop Horsley's *Sermons* and Gilbert White's *The Natural History and Antiquities of Selborne*."

Mr. Heaton looks at her with an expression of surprise mingled with amusement.

"What serious books for a girl of your age! But by all means, take them both. I expect your papa would like to read the Horsley. And possibly the White. You're fond of nature, are you, Miss Anne?"

"Oh yes."

"And you, Miss Emily?" He looks at the title and frowns. "Moore's *Life of Lord Byron*? Hmm, now then, that's not a very suitable choice for a young lady, is it? I'm not sure your father would approve. I think you should pick something else, don't you?"

Emily clasps the book to her chest and gives him a dark look. Mr. Heaton is just like Aunt — she's always harrying Papa for letting them read whatever they want instead of something tedious and improving, like Mrs. Edgeworth's *Moral Tales for Young People*. "Papa will be quite happy for us to read this. He's very fond of Byron's poetry himself, and we have read a great deal of it. And Papa has said he'll get Moore's *Life* for us as soon as he can."

Mr. Heaton looks discomfited. "Ah well, in that case . . . I tell you what, bring it with you and I'll just check with your father that he's happy about this."

Emily scowls. Does he think she's lying? She's tempted to say something rude, but she bites it back. It would be a mistake to offend him and spoil her chance of visiting the library again.

⟨∞⟩

Later, with Anne and Branwell, she laughs about the expression on Mr. Heaton's face when Papa expressed his gratitude for the loan of the book. "We've all been wanting to read this since it came out," he told Mr. Heaton cheerfully, and that good man looked "as if he'd choked on a prune stone," as Branwell put it.

After they've described the library, Branwell is eager to see it for himself. "And he says we can borrow books whenever we like?"

"Yes. And he says we won't be bothered. Though I'm not so sure." Anne giggles. "The eldest boy is smitten with Emily."

"He is *not*." Emily glares at Anne.

Branwell makes retching noises. "If he is, he must be blind."

Emily throws a cushion at him.

⟨∞⟩

At bedtime, when she goes in to say good night to Anne, she tells her off. "Don't say that kind of thing in front of Branwell — he won't stop teasing me now. And anyway, it's not true."

"Sorry." Anne is contrite. "But I do think that boy admires you. And it's no wonder — you're so pretty."

Emily stares at her sister. Has she gone mad? "Pretty!" She screws up her face in disgust.

"You are," Anne insists.

"Good night." Emily wants to put a stop to this absurd conversation.

But, alone in her bedroom, brushing her hair, she studies her face in the looking glass: wide-spaced blue-grey eyes, a long straight nose like Papa's, a determined set to her mouth. Does this amount to prettiness?

As she gazes at herself, a realization strikes her like an electric shock.

This is what she looks like.

It's like meeting a stranger. For the very first time in her life, she's seeing *herself*. This is how other people see her — as a being, separate from all other beings on earth, with her own unique recognizable identity.

This is who she is.

She nods to herself in the mirror: a greeting to the only Emily Jane Brontë in the world.

16

"Ponden Hall, tha says?" Tabby pauses in her rolling of pastry and looks at Emily inquiringly. "I can't say as I've ever been inside myself. But folk say it's a grand place."

"The library is amazing," says Emily. "You can see that the family's wealthy. But, do you know? They live in one room downstairs like any cottager."

"He's all reet, is Mr. Heaton." Tabby resumes her rolling. "Not one to get above himself. And good-hearted too, though it hasn't always served him well."

Sensing a story, Emily draws up her chair to the table.

"If tha's going to set there a while, tha might as well make thiself useful. Chop those carrots, why don't tha?"

Emily picks up a knife. "Go on, Tabby. What happened to Mr. Heaton?" She's not the slightest bit interested in the man himself, but she can't resist Tabby's tales.

"Well, his sister, Eliza, got herself into trouble with a fellow from Leeds, John Bakes he were called. Near broke her father's heart, it did. Old Mr. Heaton got them married here at Haworth and paid to have the bairn made legitimate, like. But Bakes were no good. While Eliza worked herself to death in his grocer's shop, he drank all the profits. Eliza got consumption in the end and her father fetched her and the little lad, Arthur, back to the hall, but it were too late." Tabby shakes her head sadly. "Pass us pie funnel, lass."

Emily passes over the small ceramic dome that Tabby uses to hold up the piecrust. "What happened to Arthur?"

"Well, now, that's a sad thing too. Bakes insisted on taking his son back and the boy led a terrible life, by all accounts — working all hours and beaten and abused. But then Bakes died. By this time old Mr. Heaton had passed on too and our Mr. Heaton were living in the hall with his wife and young family. He felt sorry for Arthur and took him in, but it didn't go well."

While she's been talking, Tabby has cut out some pastry leaves to go on the top of the pie, and she pauses to concentrate as she marks the veins with her knife. Emily's impatient to hear the rest of the story, but she knows it's no good trying to rush Tabby. Only when the pie's safely in the oven and Tabby has wiped her floury hands on her apron does she settle in her chair and resume her tale.

"Arthur were a sullen lad, by all accounts. Least that's what Hannah the housekeeper told me. She said she couldn't abide his look sometimes — if he were crossed, his black eyes glittered as if the devil hisself lurked in them."

Emily is enthralled. The image of those eyes conjures for her the whole boy — a dark, gypsy-looking lad with tousled black hair. She doesn't ever remember seeing him.

"Did he never come to church with the Heatons?"

Tabby shakes her head. "He wouldn't. According to Hannah, the lad said his father claimed to be God-fearing even as he were thrashing him and that had turned the lad against religion. As far as Hannah were concerned, Arthur were a godless heathen and she could find no good in him. She didn't trust him with little maister William — you'll have met him, I warrant? The Heatons' eldest lad?"

"Yes." Emily answers abruptly — she doesn't want to think about that boy and the way he looked at her.

"Well, at the time I'm speaking of he were nobbut five year old and Hannah would find bruises on him that couldn't be explained. Mrs. Heaton weren't happy about the situation, but Mr. Heaton would keep making allowances for Arthur. Things went on uneasily for a time, but matters came to a head when they discovered the lad up to tricks even Mr. Heaton found unforgivable."

Tabby stops, and to urge her to keep going, Emily leans forward in her chair. But Tabby has paused to check the progress of her pie in the oven; satisfied, she resettles herself and carries on.

"Mr. Heaton were holding a meeting of church trustees in his library when little William bursts in. He were red in the face and laughing and he began to curse and blaspheme his head off. His father were shocked and embarrassed and no doubt the worthy gentlemen were horrified by these antics.

"Mr. Heaton caught up his son and carried him from the room and 'twere then he discovered that the bairn were drunk, would you believe? Very soon the little lad were as sick as a dog but after a spell in bed, anon he recovered and no harm done.

"It turns out Arthur had put him up to it. Mr. Heaton were all for giving the lad a good talking-to, but Mrs. Heaton wouldn't rest until her husband agreed to send him away. The maister were in the middle of sorting out an apprenticeship for the lad with a cabinetmaker back in Leeds, when it seems Arthur took matters into his own hands. One night he disappeared and he's not been seen round these parts since."

"Does no one know what became of him?"

Tabby shakes her head. "Hannah says there's not been a word these last six year. There's rumors that he went to be a soldier or ran away to sea, but they're just tales, I reckon," Tabby says, getting to her feet. "More like he's come to a bad end somewhere. Now, Miss Emily, if tha's finished those carrots, will you skift out of here and let me alone, for I've a pile of ironing to get done."

∾

That afternoon, when Emily and Anne are discussing the Gondal saga, Emily says, "I've been wondering about a new character. What do you think of the idea that, when Julius is fighting to take the kingdom of Almedore, he comes across a boy, a dark orphan, half-wild and neglected, and he decides to adopt him as his own son."

"Hmm, interesting." Anne nods her head. "Have you thought of a name for him?"

"I'm not sure. What do you think about Alfonso? And now that Julius is Emperor of Angora, he'll be Alfonso Angora. And when he grows up, he's going to turn against Julius and make him regret his kindness."

"Why would he do that? It seems very ungrateful."

Emily pauses to watch a kestrel hovering, holding itself remarkably still, despite the breeze. The next moment it plummets, falling out of the sky like a stone and disappearing into the heather.

She turns to Anne. "I don't know yet. We'll have to think about it, won't we?"

After tea, the three of them continue with *The Life of Lord Byron*, which they'd begun the evening before. After they've each taken a turn to read aloud, they pause to talk about it.

"Byron sounds just like you, Branwell," Emily comments.

"Indeed, 'a mind too inquisitive to be imprisoned within limits,'" Branwell quotes, puffing out his chest.

"I was thinking more of his idleness and his temper." Emily's tone is wry.

Branwell scowls at her.

Anne giggles. "Yes, fancy him tearing his smock when he was small, just because he was cross with his nurse."

"Better than tearing someone else's clothes. Don't you remember? You tore Charlotte's apron when she wouldn't let you have *The Arabian Nights*."

"I was only little," says Branwell.

"You were seven. Much older than Byron and quite old enough to know better."

Branwell smirks, not in the least repentant.

"I feel sorry for him," says Anne.

"For *Branwell*?"

"No, for Byron. When he was young, at any rate. The doctors were cruel, torturing his poor clubfoot like that. And his mother sounds like a dreadful woman — doting one moment and then raging at him the next. No wonder he grew up to be wicked."

"Is that what you think? That he was wicked?"

"Well, yes. Don't you?"

"I don't know." Emily hesitates. "He seems quite vulnerable

to me. You know, how he threw himself into sports like fencing and boxing, as if to prove to everyone that his maimed foot didn't matter."

"Yes! He's a boxer, just like me!" Branwell swaggers about the room, throwing punches. "And I'm going to be a famous poet too!"

Emily pointedly ignores him. She's still thinking about Byron. It wasn't his fault if he was attracted to women who happened to be married, was it? He was obviously a passionate person. Look how he fell in love with Mary Chaworth when he was only fifteen. And how hurt he must have been when he overheard her say, "Do you think I could care anything for that lame boy?"

No wonder he ran away.

She gives Branwell a sideways glance. Does he have his eye on someone? Maybe one of the girls he sees at church? And then she looks at her brother's freckled face and inky fingers and laughs to herself.

Branwell as a pining lover? Preposterous!

Byron must have been quite different. She can see now how much of himself he put into his poetry, how his heroes — Conrad, Manfred, Cain, those dark, defiant men with their inner loneliness and sorrow, who have committed dreadful deeds and yet feel no remorse — are all, to some extent, self-portraits.

If only she could be like them. Not that she wants to commit dreadful deeds, of course, but how fine it would be to do as you pleased and express your deepest feelings freely and fearlessly, and not have to be hemmed in by petty restrictions.

Emily sighs. And then brightens. Her own life might be quite ordinary, but she can live out her dreams through her Gondal people. They can be whatever she chooses — courageous outlaws and rebels, passionate lovers ... just like Byron's characters.

She can't wait now to get back to Ponden Hall and see what other inspiring books are to be found there. But in three weeks' time Charlotte will be back home for good, and she's bound to want to visit the library. It will be much better to go to the hall with her. If anyone tries to speak to them, Charlotte can deal with them — after all, at school she's had plenty of practice in making conversation.

17

"I suppose you've learned everything they can teach you," says Emily as she walks round the parlor table with Charlotte on her first evening home from school.

In Charlotte's honor Tabby has been allowed to lay a good fire and, with the shutters closed tight against the cold December night, the parlor is warm and cozy.

Charlotte blushes. "Don't be silly. I don't expect Aunt can afford any more fees."

Emily wonders what her sister is really thinking — whether she's really happy to have come home. But she's not going to ask her.

When she knew Charlotte was coming home for good, she made a decision — she's not going to fret about her sister anymore. If Charlotte wants to restore their old intimacy it's up to her to make the first move. And if Charlotte wants to go back to writing about Glass Town with all of them joining in together, then she's going to be disappointed. Emily's very happy working with Anne and she wants to keep Gondal to themselves.

But she can't help wondering what difference the past five months will have made to her older sister. And what will it be like to have her living with them again?

"So . . ." Charlotte grips her book tightly, looking self-conscious. "You first, Emily. What is rhubarb?"

Emily raises an eyebrow. "Come on, Charlotte, you know I know what rhubarb is."

Charlotte purses her lips. "Go on, answer the question."

Emily sighs. "All right. Rhubarb is a plant with pink stems that are delicious when cooked with sugar, especially in pies. Oh, and if you eat too much, it makes you run to the privy a lot."

Anne giggles and twin spots of color appear in Charlotte's cheeks.

Emily almost feels sorry for her. This was a bad idea of Papa's — that once the Christmas holiday was over and they took up their lessons again, Charlotte should teach her and Anne. It's all very well him saying it's good practice for Charlotte for when she has to be a governess and it's better for them because he's so often called away on parish business. It isn't — it's boring.

Papa's lessons are much more fun. Emily would much rather study what she's interested in instead of following the dreary textbooks, and Papa's always so easily diverted into telling stories.

"Emily, please."

Hearing the pleading in Charlotte's voice, she relents. In a monotone she rapidly recites, "'Rhubarb is the root of a tree growing in Turkey, in Asia, and Arabia Felix; used for medicinal purposes.'"

"Correct. Now, Anne —"

"But honestly, Charles, what is the point?" Emily is serious now. "Why do we have to learn the answer word for word, like parrots? Why can't we just say it in our own words?"

"Because . . ." Charlotte casts about for an answer. "Erm . . ."

"Because you need to know whether your pupils have learned it properly?" Anne offers.

"Yes, that's it." Charlotte shoots her a grateful look.

"But it's so mindless. And anyway, why does anybody have to learn all this stuff? What's it *for*?"

Charlotte stares at her for a long minute. "I don't know," she admits finally.

"You see." Emily's triumphant. "It's pointless. Come on, Charles, haven't we done enough for today?" She puts on a beseeching look, and after a moment's hesitation Charlotte shuts the book.

"All right. What shall we do instead?"

"We've got writing to do, haven't we?" Emily turns to Anne, who nods.

"Oh?" Charlotte sounds surprised. "Something for Glass Town?"

"No," says Emily flatly.

Charlotte's face falls.

Emily is unrepentant. Too often in the past Charlotte's done this to her — shutting her out from what she and Branwell were doing.

Now the tables are turned, and Charlotte will have to get used to it.

৩৲৩

As soon as Charlotte hears about the library at Ponden Hall, as Emily predicted, she's eager to go and see it. But even with

Charlotte's protection, once it comes to it Emily's daunted at the thought of having to face the Heaton family again. She almost doesn't go, but then at the last minute, when Anne and Charlotte are putting their cloaks on, she rushes to join them — the thought of all those books is too tempting. And, as luck would have it, the servant is happy to show them to the library and they don't have to talk to anyone at all.

Charlotte's enthusiastic about the library and as winter gives way to spring they begin to visit it regularly. But, though Charlotte reads as much as ever, Emily notices that she doesn't seem to do nearly as much writing as she used to, spending a great deal of her time drawing instead.

To Emily's amusement Charlotte persuades Anne to model for her, covering her head and shoulders in a tablecloth cunningly arranged to look like fine drapery. Anne's quite pleased with the end result, though, as Branwell isn't slow to point out, the artist has made Anne's neck look about twice as long as it really is.

But then Charlotte asks Emily to sit for her. Emily thinks she's joking at first, but when she realizes Charlotte's serious, she says firmly, "No. And it's no good asking me again, because I won't." The very idea! How can Charlotte possibly think she'd want to dress up like an idiot and sit still all that time?

Charlotte's forced to return to copying portraits of society beauties, lovingly reproducing every tiny detail of their curls, their elaborate headdresses, and their jewelry. She gives these fine ladies the names of her Glass Town heroines, but seems less interested in writing about them.

Emily wonders about this. She's determined not to ask, but eventually curiosity gets the better of her and she says to Charlotte, "You seem keen on drawing at the moment."

"Yes. I enjoyed it so much at school that I want to keep on with it."

"Do you like it more than writing?"

"No!" Charlotte turns to look at her. "Why do you say that?"

"Well, you don't seem to be doing as much at the moment."

Charlotte gazes at Emily. She seems to be making up her mind about something. Then she says, "You're not to say anything to anyone."

"I won't." Emily is mystified. Whatever's coming?

Charlotte bends her head closer and says quietly, "I want to try and be an artist."

"An artist?"

"Yes. I want to earn my living painting miniature portraits."

Emily's mouth drops open.

"Don't look so surprised." Charlotte looks hurt. "I suppose you think I'm not good enough."

"No . . . I mean . . . I . . ." Emily flounders and then gathers herself. "I thought you were going to be a governess."

Charlotte pulls a face. "I don't think I'm suited to it. Look how hopeless I am with you and Anne. And, do you know something? I've realized I don't like children. When I visited the Atkinsons, the children there were dreadful — completely spoiled and uncontrollable. I'd hate to have to teach them."

"I see." Emily looks at her sister doubtfully. They've all taken it for granted that Branwell might become a professional artist, but it's never entered her head that Charlotte might want to be one too.

Charlotte seizes her arm. "I know it sounds mad, but I've thought about it and it's what I really want to do. Being at school has made me realize that there's a whole world out there of cultured people who spend their lives immersed in painting and poetry and music and . . . I want to be part of it."

Emily's stomach clenches. This is what she feared — Charlotte wanting to move away from the family. And don't most artists live in London? If Charlotte lives far away in the capital, they'll never see her.

But it may not happen. Charlotte's talented, of course, but could she really earn her living as a painter?

Abruptly she asks, "Are there many women artists?" She means *any*.

"Of course." Charlotte laughs as if she's being stupid and Emily flinches. "Miss Wooler has a fine collection of prints by women."

Oh, Miss Wooler. If she's behind this, no wonder Charlotte's so keen. Clearly her sister has lost none of her admiration for that wretched woman with her white dresses and daft notions.

"Shouldn't you speak to Papa about it?" With any luck he won't like the idea and that'll put a stop to it.

"I will, but not yet. I want to practice as much as I can and then —" Charlotte stops and looks round to make sure they're still on their own. Then she comes close and says quietly, "I want to enter some drawings for the Art Society's summer exhibition. If they're accepted, then I'll speak to Papa. But mind, till then, you mustn't tell anyone. And I don't want anyone else to know about my plans until after the exhibition."

"Not even Branwell?"

"Especially not Branwell."

෬ശ

Emily can't stop thinking about their conversation.

Fancy Charlotte confiding in her — her, and not Branwell!

But perhaps it's not so surprising. She can't imagine what Branwell's reaction will be when he finds out — anything from scorn of Charlotte's abilities to alarm at no longer being the only artist in the making in the family. Whatever it is, he won't hold back.

But anyway, Branwell isn't important.

What matters is that Charlotte chose her.

It's what she's been waiting for. It's just like the old days when the two of them used to make up plays in bed that they didn't tell the others about.

But as for Charlotte's plan — she doesn't like that at all. Why can't Charlotte be content to stay at home, to go on as they always have? Why must she want to be something in the world?

A horrible thought strikes her. What if Anne has ambitions she doesn't know about? What if she wants to go away too?

As soon as there's a chance, she asks Anne, making it sound casual. "Have you ever thought there's something you'd like to do?"

Straight away Anne says, "I'd like to travel and see more of the world. I'd love to see the sea, wouldn't you?"

Emily shrugs. "I've never thought about it. What I really mean is, have you an idea of what you would like to be? You know, if anything were possible?"

Anne frowns, thinking. And then she says, "I would like to be a better person."

Emily snorts. "Don't be silly. You're the goodest person I know. I don't see how you can be improved upon."

Amused, Anne shakes her head. "That's not true and you know it." Then she says quietly, "I often fall short of what I ought to be."

Emily doesn't say anything. When Anne talks like this, she never knows what to say. She's sure they don't have the same ideas about religion. For her sister, it's all about duty and leading a virtuous life — Aunt's influence rather than Papa's. But she'd never want to hurt Anne's feelings by arguing with her.

"And I would like to do some good in the world if I could." Anne sighs.

Emily groans inwardly. Here are both her sisters hankering after "the world." She can't understand it at all. What does the world have to offer in comparison to staying at home and being able to "live," as it were, in Gondal? How can her sisters want the dull real world when their imaginary worlds are so much more exciting?

⁕

Later, helping Tabby clear away after tea, she suddenly asks her, "Did you ever have ambitions when you were younger, Tabby?"

"Ambitions?" Tabby pauses in her wiping of the table. "I can't say as I did. I had a hope of marrying, which I did, and then, when I were left on my own, like, I hoped I'd find a place where I could see out my days comfortably and be of some use. Which I have." She smiles broadly at Emily, but Emily can't smile back. Tabby's answer hasn't really helped.

Tabby looks at her closely, serious now. "What's put this into thi head, lass?"

"Oh, nothing." She'd love to tell Tabby about Charlotte's plan and talk it through with her. But, of course, she can't betray Charlotte's confidence.

"Is there maybe something tha's hankering after?"

"No!" Emily seizes the broom and begins briskly sweeping up the crumbs on the floor. "Nothing at all."

Which, of course, isn't true. What she's "hankering after" is to stay exactly where she is, doing exactly what she does, and for everyone else to do the same.

18

One day toward the end of May Charlotte announces that
Papa's said she can invite her friend Ellen to stay.

This is astonishing news. Apart from people seeing Papa on
church business, they rarely have visitors. There are the curates,
of course, who supposedly come to discuss spiritual matters
but who seem more interested in Tabby's pastries, and the
Sunday school teachers, who are invited to tea once a year, but
no one has ever *stayed* with them before.

Emily gets straight to the point. "Why do you want this
Ellen to come here?"

Taken aback, Charlotte doesn't answer immediately.

"You see," Emily crows. "There isn't a reason for her to visit."

Charlotte shakes her head. "Of course there is. Apart from
anything else, it's the proper thing to do after she was kind
enough to invite me to her house."

"Oh, proper." Emily shrugs her shoulders dismissively.

"Anyway" — Charlotte's tone is assertive — "I *want* to see
her. She's my friend."

Emily is completely baffled. She stares at her sister, and
can't think of a single thing to say.

෨෬

Later, she grumbles to Anne. "This is going to disrupt our routine completely *and* create more work for Tabby, which isn't fair."

"I suppose it will be nice for Charlotte," says Anne mildly.

"Probably. Very nice, but not for the rest of us. Especially me. Do you know, Charlotte's decided that Ellen's going to sleep with her and I've got to make do with the pallet bed?"

Anne clucks her tongue sympathetically.

Her sister's response is consoling. But she doesn't tell Anne the thing that's bothering her most — that she doesn't want this Ellen, this *friend* of Charlotte's, here, in their house. She doesn't want to have to face up to how close her sister is to this stranger.

The last straw comes when Charlotte declares that they shouldn't do any writing while Ellen is staying with them.

Emily exclaims, "Well, of course we wouldn't, not in her presence. But there's nothing to stop me and Anne going off and doing whatever we want, while you talk to her."

"You can't do that."

"Why ever not?" Emily is outraged.

"It would be rude. We should do all we can to entertain her."

"So we've got to talk to her every minute of the day?"

"Don't be silly. We can do other things. But I don't want to write because Ellen would want to read it and . . . you don't know her, of course . . . but I think she'd be shocked if she saw what I wrote."

Emily frowns. "Why ever would she be shocked?"

"Ellen's very religious." Charlotte pauses. "I think, maybe partly because of Papa being a clergyman, she believes I'm better than I am."

Emily laughs. "And you don't want her to find out the awful truth."

A red tinge creeps into Charlotte's face. "No, I don't," she admits. "Sometimes, you know, I shock *myself* by the things I write."

"*What?*"

"It's true," Charlotte sighs. "Instead of dwelling on the Duke of Zamorna and his adulterous affairs, I ought to be writing about nobler subjects, people who are wholly good."

"But there aren't such people." Emily is surprised that Charlotte can't see this. "Basically, everyone acts from self-interest, don't they?"

Charlotte's eyes widen. "Emily! You don't believe that, do you? What about people who do altruistic acts? Like the Good Samaritan? And our Lord who sacrificed Himself for our sake?"

"I don't know about our Lord, but I reckon most people do good deeds because it makes them feel good. And in the Bible people are told to do good so they can go to heaven. So they're getting something out of it, aren't they?"

"That's a dreadful thing to say."

Emily shrugs. "Anyway, I'm sure there are a lot of people who behave like your Zamorna, or would if they got a chance. You're only telling the truth. And that's what we're always being told to do, isn't it?"

Charlotte looks doubtful. "Ye-es. In real life. But perhaps writing is different. In any case, I'd rather not risk it with Ellen. And you won't say things like you just said about religion in her hearing, will you?"

This Ellen is sounding worse by the minute. But Charlotte needn't worry about what she might say. She'll do what she always does when visitors come — she won't say a word.

∽

A few days later, when Emily and Anne are supposedly learning some riveting geographic facts, Emily can't help noticing that Charlotte's looking round the parlor and frowning. Finally her sister bursts out, "Don't you think the furniture in here looks awfully shabby? I wonder if we could cover up the sofa with something."

Emily exchanges a look with Anne and then says, "Why on earth would you want to do that? The horsehair cloth's a bit worn, but it's perfectly serviceable."

"Well, Ellen's family is well-to-do and The Rydings is such a well-appointed house. In the drawing room they have comfortable upholstered armchairs and little tables and whatnots."

Emily snorts with exasperation. "What on earth is the point of such folderols? We have enough chairs to sit on and a table to sit at. Why would you want anything else? It only means more things to dust."

Charlotte doesn't look convinced. "Ellen will think it odd that we don't have curtains."

"You could tell her why," Anne says quietly.

"You don't think it makes Papa seem eccentric?"

"It seems perfectly reasonable to be afraid of fire," Emily exclaims. "Especially if you've seen the suffering and horrible deaths that result from it, as Papa has."

"I suppose so." Charlotte lapses into thought and then sighs.

"Now what?"

"I was just thinking, I hope Papa doesn't use his spittoon while she's here. It's not a very genteel habit. And if he tells any of his stories, I hope they're suitable."

Emily snaps her book shut. "If you're so ashamed of us, why not write and tell Ellen not to come?" If only Charlotte would!

"Of course she must come. And I'm not ashamed." But Charlotte's face is reddening.

"I think you are. And I think it's despicable."

Charlotte's head shoots up and her eyes flash.

But before she can say anything, Anne intervenes. "I think you're worrying too much, Charlotte. After all, she's coming to see you, not to inspect the house or judge us. And if she's as nice as you say she is, she'll accept us as we are."

Charlotte gazes at her for a moment and then says, "You're probably right." She chews at her finger and then says to Emily, "But you'll behave, won't you?"

Emily gives her an innocent look. "What do you mean?"

Charlotte purses her lips. "You know exactly what I mean."

※

"You're not familiar with Penzance? Ah, it's well worth a visit. The climate is so balmy that we had palm trees in the garden and camellias flowering in February."

Branwell and Emily roll their eyes at each other.

In honor of Ellen's arrival, they are using the silver milk jug and sugar basin and, as well as bread and butter, there's a pink ham and Tabby has made cheesecakes. Papa has joined them for tea, passing dainties to Ellen with grave courtesy, but it's Aunt, wearing her best cap, which is even bigger and more ridiculous looking than her everyday ones, who holds the floor.

She's taking the opportunity of a fresh audience to trot out the reminiscences of her younger days the rest of them have heard far too many times before. ". . . and for dancing we wore such lovely gowns. One I remember — the underdress was cream silk and over it was gauze woven with pink and blue silk threads . . ."

Emily glances at Ellen. She's listening with a polite smile on her face and no indication of the boredom she must be feeling. Or perhaps she isn't. When she admired Aunt's ghastly teapot with its cheery message, *To me to live is Christ, to die is Gain,* she sounded perfectly sincere.

At least she doesn't stare, as if she's trying to work you out or find fault with you. But why does Charlotte like her so much? She seems to be . . . well, nice, but not in the least bit interesting.

In fact, and Emily grins to herself at the thought, she's rather like a milk pudding — sweet and bland.

❧

Tea over, Aunt fumbles in the folds of her black silk dress and produces a small silver box. Out of the corner of her eye, Emily sees Charlotte stiffen. They both know what's coming.

Opening the box, Aunt offers it to Ellen, who shrinks back in alarm. Aunt laughs girlishly. "Only teasing, my dear."

She takes a pinch of snuff and with a deft turn of her wrist carries it to her nose. There's a pause in which Emily steels herself and then Aunt gives a mighty sneeze. She completes the ritual by blowing her nose on a multicolored handkerchief. A look of shock and disgust flashes across Ellen's face, even though it's quickly masked.

Emily knows how she feels. The skin above Aunt's mouth is permanently brown and her handkerchiefs are the color of a peat bog. It's a puzzle that Aunt, who's so particular and has such a lot to say about cleanliness and godliness, indulges in such a revolting habit. But wouldn't it be good if Ellen is so put off by it that she cuts her visit short?

Emily checks to see how Charlotte's bearing up. She can't help feeling a little sorry for her. Her sister is gazing at Aunt in an agony of embarrassment. Aunt hasn't realized the effect of the sneeze: The curls peeking from her cap have slipped and, now askew, are clearly revealed to be false.

Emily can't help smirking and Branwell stifles a snigger, but Ellen remains perfectly straight-faced.

She's been well trained in polite behavior, then. But perhaps it simply means that she doesn't have a sense of humor.

19

While Ellen's staying with them, since they're not allowed to write, in the evenings they fall back on their other favorite occupation and take turns reading aloud. Emily's not surprised when Charlotte insists on choosing the reading matter, sticking to safe poets like Milton and Wordsworth or picking out the more serious articles from *Blackwood's Magazine*.

Heaven forbid that pious Ellen should be exposed to anything shocking, such as the evil Byron!

By the third evening, Emily, lying on the rug with Grasper, observes, from Ellen's fidgeting and stifled yawns, that she isn't relishing the entertainment.

Charlotte's obviously noticed too, as several times with a worried frown she glances over at Ellen drooping on the sofa. Eventually she breaks off from her reading. "That's enough of that, don't you think?"

Ellen sits up at once, a look of relief on her face.

A slightly uncomfortable silence falls, which is eventually broken by Ellen.

"Do you always spend your evenings alone like this?"

Charlotte says, "After nine o'clock, yes. But before he goes to bed Papa sometimes sits with us, if he's free. Aunt too, occasionally, in the summer, but in the winter she prefers the comfort of her own room."

Ellen looks slightly embarrassed. "I meant, do you never have visitors? Or pay social calls?"

Charlotte smiles a tight little smile. "We are not so fortunate as you, Ellen, in having a wide circle of friends and relatives living close by. In truth, we know hardly anyone in Haworth."

"What stuff and nonsense!" Branwell bursts out. He turns to Ellen. "I know a whole set of fine fellows from round and about, but my sisters are too stuck-up to mix with the hoi polloi."

Anne exclaims in protest and Charlotte reddens with annoyance. "That's not fair, Branwell, you know it isn't. It's easy for you because you're a boy. We girls are constrained by social etiquette, the need for introductions and so forth, and since Aunt never leaves the house except to go to church and Papa is too busy for social calls, we receive no invitations."

"What a pity." Ellen clearly finds their situation horrifying.

"I don't think so," says Emily abruptly. "We're quite happy without *visitors*." To her satisfaction, Ellen blushes.

Charlotte frowns at Emily and says, "But even if we wanted them, I don't think it would make any difference if Aunt were the most sociable creature in the world. We are not rich enough to be of interest to the good gentlefolk round here. And I believe they think we are odd creatures because we read so much."

"I see." Ellen looks uncomfortable, as if she wishes she had never broached the subject.

Another silence falls.

Anne says shyly, "Shall we do something else? What would you like to do, Ellen?"

Ellen brightens.

"Why don't we play some games?"

"Games?" echoes Charlotte, sounding as if Ellen has suggested that they swallow a dose of rat poison.

Emily has no interest in games either, at least not the sort of games she thinks Ellen means.

She can still remember the one time when she was small and was invited along with her sisters to tea at one of the grand houses. There were other children there and games were organized, supposedly to amuse them all, but they were so ridiculous she and her sisters didn't want to join in. They didn't have any idea what to do anyway, so they just stood there feeling stupid while the other children stared at them.

Of course, their own games are different — she loves their imaginary plays and the word games Papa has shown them, riddles, conundrums, anagrams, and the like.

She was delighted when she discovered, all by herself, that two of her favorite words were linked — that HEART could be turned into EARTH.

She doubts that Ellen would enjoy such puzzles, but this might be the chance she's been waiting for — to show Charlotte that her friend is rather a simpleton. "That sounds like a good idea," she says cheerily, ignoring Charlotte's frown. "What shall we play?"

Ellen gathers them round the table and they watch, bemused, as she rolls a short length of wool into a small ball.

"The idea is, we all try to blow it off the table and the person it falls by has to pay a forfeit. It's very funny!"

Emily can't believe it. This is supposed to be amusing? Ellen really is a complete ninny.

She glances at Charlotte and is pained by her sister's expression — Charlotte looks puzzled, but so eager to understand and anxious to please.

Can't Charlotte see she's worth twenty Ellens?

After Branwell's paid the first forfeit and imitated a donkey with his usual dash, braying loudly and throwing himself onto the floor and kicking up his legs in a wild fashion, Emily's determined to make their guest lose — she blows ferociously and the little ball flies into Ellen's lap.

Bright-eyed, Ellen cries, "What forfeit must I pay, Emily?"

"Put yourself through the keyhole."

"Emily!" Charlotte warns.

Ellen's face has fallen. "Oh. I see." She clearly doesn't. "Is it a joke?"

"No." Emily regards her steadily. "It's simple." She stands up and, taking a piece of paper from the side table, she tears off a strip. On it she writes YOURSELF, holds it up to show everybody, then rolls it up and pushes it through the keyhole.

"Oh, it's a trick." Ellen laughs uncertainly and Charlotte says quickly, "Very funny, Emily. We'll do something else now, shall we?"

"Why not?" says Emily. And before anyone else has a chance to speak she adds, "How about Conundrums?"

"What's that?" asks Ellen, and now there's a definite note of anxiety in her voice.

Branwell says reassuringly, "It's not difficult. I'll go first and you'll soon see how it works. Right, Emily, where did Charles the First's executioner dine and what did he eat?"

Emily ponders a moment. "Oh, I know. He took a chop at the King's Head."

"Correct."

"It's rather clever." Ellen looks worried.

"Isn't it?" says Emily. "My turn now. Ellen, why are bankrupts more to be pitied than idiots?" She smiles inwardly. Surely this will be beyond their visitor.

"Oh!" Ellen exclaims as if she's bitten her tongue. She turns red, says, "Excuse me," and rushes out of the room.

In the silence, Emily says, "What was all that about?"

Charlotte looks grim. "I'm not sure, but it could be something to do with the fact that our friend Mary's father is bankrupt. Honestly, Emily, you are the limit." And she sweeps out.

Branwell gives Emily an ironic look. "Well done."

"How was I to know about Mary's father? And it's only a game."

"I think Ellen must be very sensitive," says Anne. "Perhaps you'd better apologize."

"I suppose so." Emily pulls a face. All this fuss about nothing.

"Anyway, what's the answer?" Branwell wants to know.

"What?"

"Why are bankrupts more to be pitied?"

Emily smirks. "Because bankrupts are broken while idiots are only cracked."

"Hah, good one, Em."

∽

Ellen seems embarrassed by Emily's muttered apology. "No, it was my fault. I misheard you — I thought you said why are bankrupts *like* idiots. I'm such a noodle."

Charlotte is less forgiving — when Ellen's out of earshot, she rounds on Emily.

"What on earth were you thinking of? It's a mercy Ellen's so good-natured, or you might have damaged our friendship. Behave properly and be nice to her, or if that's too much to ask, at least be polite!"

Before Emily can say anything in her own defense, Charlotte stomps off.

Emily sighs. Instead of loosening Charlotte's attachment to Ellen, all she's managed to do is make Charlotte angry with her and protective of her friend.

Well done, Emily, indeed.

ତଠ

The fortnight Ellen is with them seems to last forever.

Emily is deprived of playing the piano alone, and she doesn't get a single chance to talk to Anne about Gondal. As the days pass, she desperately misses the experience of being immersed in their imaginary world. She manages to hide her feelings and "be nice" to Ellen, though she sometimes wonders why she's bothering, since Charlotte continues to be cool toward her.

It doesn't help that everyone else seems to be enjoying Ellen's company, and by the time her holiday is drawing to an end she seems to have almost become one of the family; even Tabby, who is normally hard to impress, is won over, Emily notes gloomily.

In particular, Ellen seems to have charmed Aunt, who, embarrassingly, frequently praises Ellen's "beautiful manners" in her hearing. To their astonishment, Aunt suggests that as a treat for their visitor on her last day the young people should go on an excursion, which she will pay for.

After much debate they settle on Bolton Abbey as their destination. At first Emily's happy to go along with the scheme — the place is somewhere she wouldn't mind seeing. But then Ellen suggests that, instead of coming to Haworth to collect her, her brothers could meet them at Bolton Abbey and they could all spend some time together before she was taken home.

"We could have breakfast at the Devonshire Arms!" Ellen beams at everyone.

"What a brilliant idea." Branwell grins enthusiastically.

Emily shoots a desperate look at Charlotte, but after a moment Charlotte says, in rather subdued tones, "That will be very pleasant, I'm sure."

Later Emily catches her alone. "Why did you agree to Ellen's idea?"

"What else could I do? It will be fearfully expensive, I know, but —"

"Never mind the expense. It wasn't too bad when it was just Ellen, but now we've got to meet her family. And eat in a public place!"

Charlotte blinks at this last complaint, but says crisply, "Her brothers are very nice. I'm sure you'll like them when you meet them."

Emily stares wildly at Charlotte. Why doesn't she understand? Other people, people who aren't family, expect you to behave in a certain way. If you don't, they give you that look — mostly disapproving, occasionally amused, but *always* judging you, criticizing you. She just wants to not be noticed.

Desperately she flings out, "Well, I won't see them, because I'm not going now."

Charlotte narrows her eyes. "Ellen will think it so peculiar if you don't come. It will spoil her last day."

"But —"

"No buts. You're coming."

20

Aware of Charlotte's eyes on her, Emily passes the journey to Bolton Abbey in silence, but inwardly she's seething.

It's bad enough having to be part of this charade, but Branwell could have let her have a go at driving. For someone who thinks he's such an expert, he's behaving absurdly. With the velvet collar of his coat turned up and his shirt wristbands protruding from his sleeves, he's flourishing the whip in an extravagant fashion and crying "Gee up!" and "Halloo!" in a loud voice. It's completely unnecessary since, whatever he does, the horses plod steadily on at their own pace.

The only good thing about the day is that they're going to Bolton Abbey.

She loves Turner's painting of the place — a favorite of Papa's that he has hanging over his desk. She has spent hours gazing at it, admiring the delicacy of the ruined priory set against the majestic crags of Barden Fell, the whole scene bathed in a silvery light. She wants to see what it's really like, especially as it might be a landscape she and Anne could borrow for Gondal.

But first there's the ordeal of breakfast.

At the door of the Devonshire Arms Branwell makes a great show of stopping the carriage, shouting "Whoa," and heaving on the reins, though the horses have already come to a standstill of their own accord.

The two ostlers lounging outside the stables make no effort to stir themselves, but mutter something to each other and laugh. Only when Branwell shouts "Hey!" does one finally saunter up and say, "Yes, sir?" in sneering tones.

At that moment a light carriage dashes into the inn yard, drawn by a pair of gleaming chestnut horses. Ellen waves and calls out before scrambling down to greet her brothers.

As the other ostler darts forward to attend to the newcomer, Branwell goes red and Charlotte tightens her lips.

Emily can't understand their embarrassment. So they're poorer than Ellen's family. What of it? What does it matter what these stablemen or anyone else thinks of them?

Once they're inside the inn and settled at a table, Emily, shielded by the menu, gives Ellen's brothers a covert glance. They're older than she expected. One has a moustache and the other hasn't, but she doesn't know which is which.

Having satisfied her curiosity, she keeps her gaze down. The last thing she wants is for one of them to catch her eye, to start that probing inquisition.

But here is the waiter to take their order and it's her turn and she must speak, so casting her eyes wildly at the menu, she sees at last, gratefully, the one familiar dish.

"I'll have porridge."

She's aware of a slight stir on the other side of the table.

"Porridge, Miss Emily? That's a little spartan, isn't it? Can you not be tempted to something more exciting? I believe their deviled kidneys are particularly fine." The voice is amused and, glancing up, she sees one of Ellen's brothers, the one without the moustache, watching her.

Is it Henry, the older of the two, or George? She doesn't care.

She punches out, "Porridge," and closes her mouth. Whatever they say to her, she won't speak again.

Luckily, as their breakfasts arrive and they all tuck in, the conversation flows on merrily without her. She only half-listens — she's wishing Grasper were here to sample the porridge, which comes with sugar *and* cream.

She notices that if there's a lull in the talk, Branwell's eager to fill it, though an edge has crept into his lively humor.

She thinks she knows why.

Compared to Ellen's brothers, he seems like a boy, and maybe he feels it too. But it would be better if he stayed quiet rather than showing off by spouting poetry and quoting bits of Greek and Latin. As his voice gets shriller, it tends to crack more, and she sees the brothers exchanging amused glances.

At last, they're all finished. There's an awkward moment when Henry insists on paying for everything. Emily can see that for all her anxiety about the cost, Charlotte doesn't like this at all.

Emily doesn't see why Charlotte should be so bothered — after all, this was Ellen's idea. For herself she's relieved to escape from the table, from that stuffy room, and to head along the lane toward their goal. But as they reach the path leading down to the priory, she comes to an abrupt halt.

The grassy slope in front of them is dotted with people. Strolling in pairs and small groups, laughing and talking, they seem only interested in their own chatter; hardly anyone is taking notice of the ancient monument. Foolishly, she'd imagined them having the place to themselves, of seeing the priory in all its haunting solitary beauty, just as in Turner's picture.

Instinctively she moves closer to Anne.

Her sister glances up at her. "Horribly crowded, isn't it?"

Emily nods, soothed a little. At least one person here today shares her feelings.

She goes with the others to stare at the ruins and stands there patiently while Henry gives a long-winded account of the history of the place; they walk along the riverbank and she puts on an appropriate expression whenever anyone points out some fresh beauty — an ancient oak tree or the tumbling waters of the Strid. But all the time she's longing for the moment when they can start for home.

She stares into the shadowy depths of the water. If only, right now, she could be a fish, hiding in the cool silence at the bottom of the river.

ᢙᢌ

They reach a ford where Henry and George stop to help "the ladies" across.

Ignoring George's proffered hand, Emily strides through the shallows, careless of the splashes dampening her skirts. She stops on the other side to wait for Anne, but it's Ellen who joins her first, assisted by Branwell, who clearly doesn't want to be outdone in a display of gallantry.

Ellen immediately links her arm through Emily's and suggests they walk on. She smiles up at Emily and says confidingly, "I was hoping for a chance to speak to you before I go. There's something I particularly wanted to talk to you about."

"Oh?" At once Emily is on her guard. What could Ellen possibly have to say to her?

"It's Charlotte."

"Charlotte?" Emily can't imagine what might be coming.

"I wanted to know your opinion of Charlotte's plan."

A cold feeling begins to creep up Emily's spine. "Her plan?"

"Yes, her hope of becoming an artist."

Emily stops walking. After a moment's struggle, she manages to say, "You know about that?"

"Oh yes," says Ellen blithely, apparently unaware of the effect of her disclosure. "And the thing is, I'm no judge of such matters — a complete dunce when it comes to art" — she laughs — "but you are clearly gifted, so —"

"What makes you say that?"

Ellen recoils a little at Emily's sharp tone. "Um . . . well . . ." She hesitates and then admits in a rush, "Charlotte showed me some of your drawings. I hope you don't mind. The one of Grasper is lovely."

Emily is speechless.

Ellen plunges on, "I think Charlotte is very talented, of course, but I just wondered what her chances of success are. It would be so distressing for her, if it doesn't work out. You're the obvious person to ask . . . knowing about art and caring so much for Charlotte . . ." She trails off.

Emily tries to pull herself together. This is not Ellen's fault. "I'm flattered you think I know something about the subject . . . and I appreciate your concern for my sister . . ." She knows she sounds stilted, but it's the best she can do. "The truth is, Ellen, I don't know. All we can do, I suppose, is hope for the best."

Ellen will never guess, of course, that the best as far as she's concerned is that Charlotte doesn't succeed.

Ellen nods. "Yes, that's what we must do." At that moment George comes up to join them and Emily drops behind.

She walks on in a daze. She hardly knows which is worse — Charlotte showing Ellen *her* private drawings or revealing to their visitor what was supposed to be a secret shared only by them. How could Charlotte have treated Ellen, a stranger, as if she was one of the family? What was she thinking of?

She's hardly aware of Henry announcing that it's time they were heading home, of the Nusseys departing amid general farewells that she takes no part in.

As they get underway themselves, Charlotte relaxes back into her seat. "Well, I think that went well, despite everything, don't you?"

Branwell and Anne agree eagerly, but Emily doesn't say anything, not then nor for the whole of the long journey home. As soon as they get back, she goes to the piano and hammers out a Bach fugue. It helps, but only a little.

❧

It's bedtime before she and Charlotte are alone. They undress in silence, but, once Charlotte is in her nightgown, she comes over and touches Emily's arm. "What's the matter? Did someone say something to upset you?"

Emily concentrates on doing up her buttons. "You could say that."

Charlotte frowns. "Who was it?"

Emily faces her. "It was you."

"Me? What do you mean?" Her sister's eyes are wide with astonishment.

"You told Ellen about wanting to be an artist."

Charlotte is clearly perplexed. "Yes?"

Emily shrugs. "Well, then."

"I don't understand. That's what's upset you?"

"I'm not upset. I'm angry."

"But why?"

If Charlotte doesn't even know what she's done, then that makes it worse. "You said I wasn't to tell anyone. I thought it was a secret."

"It is, at home."

Emily gives Charlotte a long hard stare. Charlotte opens her mouth to speak, then shuts it again.

"I'm not allowed even to tell Branwell, but Ellen can know."

Charlotte shrugs, then, turning away, she unfastens her braids. "I'll tell the others eventually. I just don't want to do it yet." She starts brushing out the kinks in her hair with long smooth strokes.

Emily is left standing there. She wants to fight about this, but Charlotte won't. Frustrated, she bounces onto the bed, causing the springs to squeak in protest.

"And you showed Ellen my drawings. Without asking me."

The brush stops. Charlotte looks sideways at Emily. "I didn't think you'd mind."

"Well, I do."

"I'm sorry."

Is she? Is she really sorry? Emily doubts it. She climbs under the covers, her own hair unbrushed, and turns away from Charlotte. She thought Charlotte sharing her secret with her meant that they were close again, that they understood each other, that things were back to normal. Now she sees it meant nothing, nothing at all.

Charlotte slides into bed and the mattress rustles as she turns over to take up their accustomed sleeping position. Emily can feel her sister's breath on her neck, the pressure of her body against her back.

She endures it for a moment or two and then she slips out of bed and into the pallet bed, still in place from Ellen's visit.

"What are you doing?" asks Charlotte sleepily.

"It's too hot to be together," says Emily. "I prefer to be on my own now."

21

One July morning, not long after Ellen's visit, Papa asks Emily to take a note to John Brown. It's only a step to the barn across the lane, where she can hear the sexton at work, but Emily's glad of a chance for some fresh air as it's such a hot day. And luckily Mr. Brown is so absorbed in engraving a new headstone that he doesn't engage her in conversation.

On her way back, she lingers at the parsonage gate, hoping for the slightest breeze from the moor, but the air is thick and still. She's trying to think about Gondal, to be ready for talking about it with Anne, but Charlotte's treachery keeps rising up and blotting out other thoughts. She can't forgive her sister and she can't stop feeling aggrieved about what's happened.

That morning at breakfast, at last Charlotte shyly told the family of her hope of having her work chosen for the Art Society's summer exhibition. After some initial surprise, Papa was encouraging, and said that he and Branwell would take the drawings to Leeds for Charlotte.

Thinking about it now, Emily tells herself that she doesn't care if Charlotte becomes an artist and goes away — it won't make any difference to her at all.

Lifting her head, she sees a sheepdog coming down the lane toward her. It has distinctive markings — an almost completely white face with a black patch over one eye — but she doesn't recognize it.

As it approaches and she gets a better look at it, all thoughts of Charlotte fly out of her head. Poor thing! Its tongue's hanging out and it's panting rapidly, its thin sides heaving. It must be dying of thirst.

Running into the back kitchen, Emily fills Grasper's bowl with water and carries it out. The dog's biting at a stone near the gate, trying to eat it. Perhaps it's starving too.

"Don't eat that! I'll get you some food in a minute. Here you are." She puts down the bowl of water. The dog looks at her. It has a cowed, anxious expression and as it approaches the bowl cautiously, she sees that it's trembling.

"Poor boy. Have you been ill-treated?" She puts out her hand to pat it, to reassure it, and the dog lunges forward and sinks its jaws into her arm. Emily exclaims and tries to pull her arm away, but the dog hangs on. She has to beat at its head to make it let go.

"Sorry, sorry." Emily feels terrible for hitting it. Clutching her throbbing arm, she backs away. She's still hoping that the dog will drink, but it seems paralyzed and just stands there with its mouth open. And then she sees something that sends a chill up her spine — foam dripping from the dog's lower jaw and pooling in the dust.

Inching backward, Emily feels for the gate and, slipping inside, she shuts it tight. Peering over it, she's relieved to see the dog lolloping back up the lane. At least it's heading for the open moor and not toward the town.

But the dog is not her main concern.

Rolling up her sleeve, she examines her arm. There are deep

puncture marks and the dog's fangs have lacerated the skin — blood is oozing from between the jagged edges of the wound.

Stupid, stupid Emily. How often has Papa warned her about touching strange dogs? And that story he told about the farmer who was bitten by a rabid dog . . .

She shivers.

As she's looking at her torn arm, her vision begins to blur. Immediately she claps her hand back over the injury. This is no time to faint. Think . . . think! What did Papa say the farmer should have done?

Taking a steadying breath or two, she runs back into the house. There's no one in the kitchen, but there on the stove are two irons Tabby has left to heat up.

Snatching up a cloth, she seizes one of the irons and claps it on her injury. There's a sizzling sound and a smell like charcoal as the hot metal bites into her flesh. The pain is terrible — she has to grit her teeth to stop herself from crying out. But it must be done; she must cauterize the wound to stop any infection from spreading.

When she can't bear it any longer, she carefully replaces the iron exactly where it was and rolls down her sleeve. Then she lets out her breath. All she can think of is reaching the bedroom without being seen, but as she moves toward the door, she staggers and has to sit down.

As luck would have it, at that moment Tabby comes into the kitchen, grumbling to herself. "That Mr. Greenwood certainly likes his coffee. Here I am with all that ironing to do and I've to make another pot. It's not as if —" She breaks off at the sight of Emily. "Ee, lass, whatever is the matter? Tha looks as if tha's seen a boggart."

"It's the heat, I think. I forgot to take my bonnet and it's sweltering out there." Surreptitiously Emily moves her arm to conceal her bloodstained cuff under the table.

Tabby gives her a sharp look. "Tha's not usually done in by it." She sniffs the air suspiciously. "What's tha been up to?"

"Nothing. I'll be all right in a minute. Could you get me a drink?"

Shaking her head, Tabby fetches a glass of lemonade and Emily gulps it down, glad of its cold sweetness on her tongue.

Her arm feels as if it's on fire and she's terrified of what that means, of what she might have brought upon herself so unthinkingly. She longs to tell Tabby what's happened, to have Tabby comfort her and look after her as she's always done in the past whenever Emily was upset or hurt.

But this time it's different. She has done this to herself and until she knows what the consequences are to be, she can't tell Tabby. She can't tell *anyone*.

Gripping the edge of the table, she makes herself stand up, but she can't help swaying and Tabby regards her with concern. "Tha's not at all reet, my lamb. Mebbe tha should have a lie-down?"

Emily forces herself to say lightly, "No, I'm all right. I'll just have a wash — that'll cool me down."

∽◯∾

The minute Emily reaches the bedroom she rummages in the chest of drawers for something to bind her arm.

She finds a worn muslin pillowcase and manages to tear a strip from it with her teeth. She should probably put something on the wound, some ointment maybe, but she doesn't know what, so she just wraps the bandage round it and ties it as best she can — a fiddly thing to do one-handed. She's not made a good job of it, but all she can do is hope for the best.

She hides the ruined cuff at the back of her drawer — she can put it on the fire later — and then scrubs at her sleeve where some of the blood has seeped into it. Luckily it doesn't show much on the dull brown material. Then she finds the deepest cuffs she possesses and puts them on.

She's just about presentable when Charlotte appears in the doorway, looking worried.

"Tabby said you might have a touch of sunstroke."

She can hear the sympathy in her sister's voice and it almost undoes her.

She could admit the truth to Charlotte, couldn't she? It would be such a relief to have someone to share this with . . .

But she only hesitates for a moment. No, she can't tell Charlotte. After what happened with Ellen she no longer trusts her sister. What if she tells Charlotte and she blabs it to the rest of the family? No, this is all her own fault and she must deal with it by herself.

She steels herself and replies coolly, "I'm all right. I'm coming down now." Then she makes herself walk steadily past Charlotte and down the stairs, doing her best to appear normal.

Branwell and Anne look up as she enters the parlor, but she avoids their eyes and, picking up a book, sits down on the sofa and pretends to read. Grasper jumps up beside her and she strokes him unthinkingly. Her arm is horribly painful and she'd like to cradle it, but she doesn't want to draw attention to herself. Almost worse than the pain are the frantic questions whirling round in her head.

How soon will she know if the worst has happened? What are the telltale signs? And if it's true, how long till . . . ?

She balks at the idea. She can't face it, not yet.

෬෪

She doesn't feel like eating, but there's no avoiding dinner. She manages a mouthful or two of potato, a sliver of cold beef, and then she puts down her knife and fork, defeated. Aunt, who seems to know all about the events of the morning, gives her a sharp look. "No walk for you this afternoon, young lady. You'd better stay indoors."

With Papa out of the way — he went off with Mr. Greenwood before dinner — nothing could suit Emily better. As soon as the others have left the house and Aunt has retreated to her room, she slips into the study.

Papa's medical book isn't on the shelf in its usual place, but then she sees it on his desk, open at "sunstroke." That means someone has already spoken to Papa. Good. That will help her to conceal the truth.

She flicks back the pages until she finds what she's looking for:

HYDROPHOBIA. (Rabies)
Caught from a rabid animal, hydrophobia is an infection that destroys the brain. It is untreatable.

Emily stops reading. She closes her eyes a moment, as if somehow this will make the sentence disappear. She breathes deeply once or twice and then opens her eyes.

The sentence is still there.

She forces herself to read on. She learns that from being infected it can take several weeks for the first symptom — *headache* — to appear. After that she can expect *acute pain* followed by *terror and hallucinations.* Her heart fluttering, Emily skips to the stark words at the end of the paragraph: *delirium, coma . . . death.*

She sinks onto Papa's chair. Minutes pass as she sits there, feeling numb, unable to move or think.

Only when the grandfather clock chimes the hour does she rouse herself. The others will be back soon and they mustn't find her here. Because she knows now for certain that however tempted she is to confide in someone, she mustn't. If the rest of the family find out about this, they will be utterly alarmed. She couldn't bear it. To be the object of so much attention would be suffocating, but worse than that would be to know that she, by one stupid action, has caused all that distress.

Why, the shock of it might kill Papa! Emily's heart lurches in her chest.

She clenches her fists. No, the others simply mustn't find out. She mustn't betray by a word or a look what has happened.

She has done what she can to save herself. Now all she can do is wait.

22

Emily manages to get through the next few days only by summoning every ounce of her willpower. The pain in her arm, now swollen and bright red, is intense, but she forces herself to bear it. There's no point in calling upon God — He won't do anything. She must cope with this herself. It's just a sensation and it will pass — she won't let it overcome her.

What she finds harder to cope with is her fear.

She tells herself, "Nothing's going to happen; you're not going to die."

For a while it works, and she feels calmer, but then dread at the prospect of what she might have to suffer comes surging back and infects everything.

If she tries to distract herself by reading or playing the piano, she can only manage it for a few minutes at a time. She begins to write, but then worry looms and she finds herself thinking about her own situation rather than the goings-on in Gondal.

Even walking with Anne doesn't help — the first day after she was bitten and they're out together she tries to talk in their usual way, but it's so hard to pretend that nothing's wrong. The trouble is, though, she's desperate to go out — being out alone on her beloved moors will surely bring her some relief, even if it's only temporary. She wrestles with the problem for a while and in the end she decides there's nothing for it.

The next morning she finds Anne in the study dusting the piano and without any preamble says, "You know, I'd rather you didn't come with me on walks anymore. I want to go alone."

Anne looks so hurt that Emily feels sorry at once. But she can't take back what she's said — she'll just have to stand by it. She braces herself for Anne's reaction.

"Is it because of what I said about Julius?"

"Julius?" She can't think what Anne's talking about. Then she remembers.

The last time they'd discussed Gondal, Anne argued with her because she'd decided Julius was to have an affair and father an illegitimate child. Anne said it was sinful to write such things. Emily disagreed hotly and said she was sick of Anne being such a goody-goody, that she was going to stick to her idea and Anne could go to the devil.

The dog bite has driven all this out of Emily's head. Thinking of it now, she feels ashamed of herself. She wants to say sorry, but she mustn't soften, not now.

"No, it's nothing to do with Julius. It's just how I feel at the moment. I'm sure Charlotte will go with you." And she rushes out before Anne can say anything else.

∽✺∽

That afternoon Emily sets out with Grasper and discovers that she was right — striding rapidly across the moors with her sleeves rolled up and her hair uncovered, giving herself up to the rhythm of her footsteps and her breath, letting go of her thoughts and feelings and allowing the wind to carry her along and the rain of the summer storm to wash over her, she can, for a while at least, forget what has happened to her and what might be to come.

She stays out longer and later than usual, returning with wet hair and damp clothes.

"Bless the lass," Tabby cries when she sees her. "Tha's soaked to the bone."

"I like to feel the rain on my skin," Emily explains. "It makes me feel alive."

"Tha'll catch thi death of cold, more like," says Tabby drily.

Emily grimaces to herself. If only Tabby knew.

She must keep out of Tabby's way — of all of them, she's the one most likely to notice her distress. But she can't hide herself away from everyone.

During the evening Anne keeps giving her worried glances, but at least she doesn't pester her. It's harder to evade Charlotte, who at bedtime doesn't hold back.

"What's the matter?"

"Nothing."

"It can't be nothing — you're hardly eating anything. If you go on like this, you'll fade away. And last night I woke up and you were just lying there and you obviously hadn't been to sleep. What's going on?"

"Nothing, I tell you."

Emily curses herself for not managing to hide it better and she redoubles her efforts to appear normal, making herself join in merrily and chatter as usual. But Charlotte won't let it go. The next day she tries again when they're making Charlotte's bed.

"I asked Tabby about you, and she said, maybe it was your age, you know, that you're outgrowing your strength, but I don't think it's that."

"Why are you discussing me with Tabby?"

"Because you won't tell me what's wrong."

"There's nothing to tell." Emily concentrates on tucking in the sheet so she doesn't have to look at Charlotte.

"I think there is. You're just not yourself. Are you ill?"

"No!"

"Well, is something on your mind? Because that's what it looks like to me."

"The only thing on my mind is that I wish you'd leave me alone!"

Emily's annoyance with Charlotte is nothing compared to her annoyance with herself. It's cowardly and weak to be so fearful — she should be strong. She resolves that from now on she's going to be as proud and fearless as her heroine Rosina, Princess of Alcona. She will outface anything that fate threatens her with and she will not allow herself to think of dying.

☙

But on the Sunday morning five days after the dog bit her, Emily wakes up with a headache.

This is it. It's beginning.

Terror seizes her with a stomach-churning jolt. Without warning she is thrown back into that familiar state that she has been running away from all these years — the state she was in after Elizabeth died.

The terror of abandonment.

But then she was suffering from *being* abandoned. Now it is she who is faced with letting go, with abandoning everything that she loves — her family and Tabby and the moors where she feels most at home — and being exiled and outcast, separated from them for all eternity.

Her throat closes up — she can't eat a spoonful of breakfast, she can barely speak.

Morning service passes in a blur as she stands, kneels, mumbles responses at the appropriate moments like an automaton. She tries to listen to Papa's sermon, but she can't take it in and as she sits there in a tumult of anxiety, her eye falls on the plaque on the wall.

The words carved on it are as familiar to her as her own heartbeat, but still she reads them through:

Here lie the remains of Maria Brontë, Wife of the Rev. P. Brontë . . .

Also the remains of Maria Brontë . . . who died in the twelfth year of her age

And of Elizabeth Brontë, her sister . . .

Oh, Elizabeth! Her best beloved sister has walked this path before her. Doesn't this mean that she's not really alone?

If Elizabeth were here now, she could tell her all about it, and impossible as it would be, Elizabeth would find a way to comfort her.

But . . .

By now, she supposes, all that is left of Elizabeth and of Maria and Mama are their bones. She is quite, quite alone.

She shivers as the truth that she has been desperately trying to avoid crashes in on her — the truth of what will happen to her. Soon, all too soon, she will be joining Mama and her sisters in that dark vault under the cold slabs of the church floor.

Her own bones ache at the thought of it.

Ever since the dog bit her, she has not once been visited by her familiar nightmare, with all the pain of finding her sisters and losing them all over again.

What does it mean? That all along, deep down, she's known that she's about to die? That she has no need to dream of her sisters, because she will soon be with them?

That's what Papa professes to believe and preaches to his flock in the words that Emily knows so well — *God so loved the world, that He gave His only begotten Son, that whosoever believeth in Him should not perish, but have everlasting life.*

It's a wonderful, comforting idea . . . that one day, perhaps not so very far off, she will again meet Mama and Maria and dear, dear Elizabeth and rejoice to see them.

If only she could believe it.

When Mama died, she remembers asking, over and over again, "Where is she?"

And they said, "In heaven."

But when she wanted to know where heaven was, no one could give her a satisfactory answer. And she could never understand why, if Mama was safe in her "eternal home," as Papa said, he was grey and silent for so long after she'd gone.

"In the name of the Father, Son, and Holy Ghost . . ." Papa intones, signaling that the service is about to end.

Emily struggles to raise herself from the pew. She is utterly wrung out.

Fixing her eyes on Elizabeth's name on the plaque, she prays, "Please, let me not die. Let me not die, not yet."

23

By the time they reach home, the pain in Emily's arm is so severe she can't think about anything else. In the hall she catches Aunt's arm. "May I be excused from dinner? I'm feeling a little unwell." It's an effort to get the words out, almost impossible to sound as if she's just feeling under the weather.

She waits, unsteady on her feet, willing Aunt to just say "Yes" and let her go upstairs. But, of course, with Aunt, it can't be so simple.

Aunt has to scrutinize her thoroughly before pronouncing, "You are very pale." She lays a cool hand on Emily's forehead. "And you're rather hot. Do you feel feverish at all?"

Emily is saved from answering by Papa's arrival. Aunt says, "Patrick, I'm rather worried about Emily. She's been looking peaked for a few days now and I think she might have a fever. Do you think we should send for Dr. Andrew?"

Emily rouses herself and in desperation cries out, "No!"

Her father looks alarmed. "Emily, my dear, what ails you?"

"It's nothing, Papa, really. There's no need to send for the doctor." If only they'd all stop looking at her. This is the very kind of fuss she was hoping to avoid. And now Papa is worried. Why don't they just let her go?

"Very well. Go and have a rest on your bed and then we'll see how you are."

Emily flees upstairs.

In the bedroom she pulls back her sleeve. Gritting her teeth, she rips off the bloodstained muslin sticking to the wound. It doesn't look good — blisters have formed on the surface and it's oozing yellow pus.

Suddenly, as she's staring at the injury, Emily's stomach heaves and she just manages to make it to the basin before she vomits. Shaken, sweating, she sinks onto the bed. She reaches for the towel to wipe her face and at that very moment Charlotte bursts in.

"Emily! You look terrible."

"What do you want?" Emily snaps. She must get rid of her as quickly as possible.

"Papa sent me up to see if you needed anything."

"I don't." Surreptitiously Emily tries to cover her arm with the towel, but Charlotte is peering at her.

"What's the matter with your arm?"

"Nothing."

Charlotte reaches forward and tweaks the towel off. Her mouth drops open. "My God, Emily! What have you done?"

"I haven't done anything." Emily yanks down her sleeve to hide the evidence, but Charlotte is already on her way out of the room, calling, "Papa! Aunt! Come quickly."

∞

Throughout the commotion and interrogations that follow, Emily manages to keep hold of the one important thing — they mustn't find out about the dog.

To every question she gives the same answers. No, she "doesn't know how it happened," her arm "just went like this." To her utter dismay Papa declares that in the morning they must send for Dr. Andrew.

She gives Charlotte a baleful look. This is all her fault.

At long last they stop talking about it, Aunt binds Emily's arm with a fresh dressing, and she is put to bed in Charlotte's bed.

Emily doesn't object — it's the only place where she can be free from all their anxious, puzzled eyes. And by now she's actually feeling very ill — sweating and shivering by turns. Her joints seem to be on fire and every now and then she's overtaken by nausea and has to vomit into the bucket that Tabby has put by the bed. All she can do is lie there, expecting the hallucinations to start any minute and dreading that Dr. Andrew will be able to tell what's wrong with her.

After dinner Tabby comes to sit with her. Her presence is comforting and luckily she doesn't ask any questions, but in any case Emily feels too wretched to talk — she doesn't want to eat anything and even sipping water brings on the nausea again. She dozes on and off, aware at some point of Tabby creeping out and, later, of Charlotte coming to get her nightgown and hairbrush.

Vaguely Emily wonders where her sister is going to sleep, but she doesn't want to risk any conversation so she keeps her eyes closed and very soon she's asleep herself.

೧೭

The following morning, after Dr. Andrew has examined her, he takes Papa and Aunt out onto the landing. In a hushed voice he pronounces his diagnosis: ery . . . something. Emily doesn't hear the word properly. At least he's not saying hydrophobia, so her secret is still safe.

"How serious is it?" Papa wants to know.

"It can be very serious. We should know one way or another within the week."

Which means, Emily supposes drowsily, that you can die from this disease too, whatever it is. Everyone will still be fearful . . . Dimly she's aware that she should be bothered about this, but really, she feels too strange, too ill to care.

"Now then, young lady . . ." Dr. Andrew's abrupt return to the room with Aunt startles Emily awake. Adopting the falsely jovial tone he always uses with them, the doctor commences his treatment. And Emily sees, with a lurch of her stomach, that it's her turn for the leeches.

Anne has endured this more than once. If her little sister can bear it, surely she can.

She's surprised when the doctor asks her to clench her right fist — it's her left arm that's injured. Having raised the vein, Dr. Andrew pierces it with his lancet — Emily flinches, but makes herself watch — and when the blood wells out, he places a glistening leech on the cut. He then turns his attention to her injured arm, putting three of the black creatures in the most sensitive part of the wound, where they fasten on greedily. Emily braces herself, but after an initial stinging sensation, she can't feel them at all.

She lies still, staring at the ceiling, not thinking of anything at all, just letting herself float. Odd how she's never noticed those fine cracks before, as if a spider were clinging to the plaster right above her head.

After a while she becomes quite light-headed. Black spots appear before her eyes and her tongue feels too big in her mouth. She tries to say, "I think I'm going to faint," but the words won't come out. She's just starting to panic when Dr. Andrew pronounces himself satisfied and pulls off the bloated leeches.

Dimly Emily hears him telling Aunt to ply her with cooling drinks. "Lemonade is best, and you can mix in half a teaspoon of Dover's powder — that should increase the sweating, which will help her to throw off the infection. Keep the wound uncovered, but bathe it with laudanum three times a day. And when our patient feels like eating again, a light diet of sago and the like is best." His voice fades away as he leaves the room with Aunt and Emily is left in peace at last.

She drifts in and out of sleep, a troubled sleep in which figures loom at her threateningly from the shadows and voices whisper words that she strains to hear. Often she comes to with a start, bathed in sweat, with her teeth chattering and her heart thumping with terror. At times she's aware of a dim figure being in the room, of someone persuading her to sip cool drinks or wiping her face with a damp flannel, but when she tries to open her eyes, her eyelids feel like heavy weights and she gives up and sinks back into sleep again.

⚬⚬⚬

Emily opens her eyes. Blinking, she sees that she's in her bedroom. How strange — Tabby is here, sitting over by the window. And stranger still — Tabby's hands are resting in her lap. Tabby never just sits — her hands are always busy with some work or other.

But then Emily realizes that the room is quite dim and she sees that the shutters are closed. How odd. Because it's definitely daytime — she can see cracks of light at the edges of the wooden panels.

She tries to speak, but all that comes out is a croak. She clears her throat and tries again, murmuring, "Why don't you open the shutters, Tabby? Then we'd both be able to see."

Tabby is across the room in an instant. "Bless thee, my lamb. Tha's properly awake at last." Emily feels Tabby's rough hand on her forehead and a beaming smile spreads across Tabby's face. "Cool as a moorland spring. Tha'll be all reet now, for sure."

All right? Then Emily remembers. The doctor was here — she has been ill. Her eye falls on her left arm and she sees a wound — healing now, but still an ugly red weal . . .

With a start of alarm she remembers everything. She tries to sit up, but she can't — she has to sink back onto her pillow.

"Bless thee," says Tabby. "Tha's as weak as a fledgling fallen from the nest. Don't tha be trying to sit up yet awhile, not till tha's got thi strength back."

"How long have I been in bed?"

"A week."

"A week?" Emily can't believe it. But what was it Dr. Andrew said? If she's got whatever it was he said and she's all right after a week, then it means she's going to recover.

"And tha's to stay there a mite longer, my lass, at least until doctor's been to see you. If tha fancies a bite to eat, I'll go and get thee summat light to try — tha needs to build thiself up."

Tabby bustles from the room.

Emily almost wishes that she could go on being asleep for a while longer. Because now she can't stop thinking. She feels better, but does it mean anything? Was Dr. Andrew right about her illness? Is she safe now?

⟡

After another two days in bed Emily still feels weak, but she's impatient to get up now — she's had enough of being confined to the bedroom and is desperate for some fresh air. Dr. Andrew comes and declares that all danger is past and the patient can now resume her normal life, though she mustn't overdo things to begin with.

Everyone, apart from Emily, cheers up. That, at least, is one relief — she no longer has to worry about the effect of her illness on Papa. She is glad to be back among them all again and especially glad to see Grasper, who licks her face furiously, wagging his tail as if he'll never stop.

But the shadow of her fear still hangs over her.

As soon as she gets the chance she consults *Modern Domestic Medicine* again. By now she's found what she's supposed to have had: erysipelas. Reading about it, she can see how similar it is to rabies, at least at first. Perhaps Dr. Andrew was right after all. A small glimmer of hope flares up inside her.

But then she turns to the page about hydrophobia and, reading it properly, sees what she missed the first time she read it — the incubation period can be months, sometimes as long as a year.

Emily closes the book. She still can't be sure. Perhaps she did have erysipelas, but that doesn't mean she won't get rabies. She will have to go on with her silence about the dog bite and wait to see if any other symptoms develop. It will be ages until she knows that she's truly safe.

Gradually Emily resumes the pattern of her normal life. Now that her arm is healed and she feels better, it becomes harder to remember that she still needs to be watchful. When she's absorbed in playing the piano or reading a book, she can forget her fears entirely.

Since it's easier now to pretend that everything is all right, when she feels strong enough, with some embarrassment, she asks Anne to walk with her again. She's eager to go to Ponden Hall again for some new books — while she's been convalescing, she's read and reread the last ones she borrowed. More than anything, though, she's longing to plunge back into Gondal again. But how will Anne feel about it, after Emily went off by herself?

Anne, bless her, gladly agrees to resume their outings again, which gives Emily pause for thought. Why can't she be more like Anne and forgive Charlotte? But it's no good — she hasn't Anne's sweet nature. Anyway, what Charlotte did was different — she didn't need to confide in Ellen, whereas Emily simply had to be alone.

Anyway, recent events have only confirmed Emily's feelings about her sisters — Anne has been so sensitive and kind to her, whereas Charlotte has been unhelpful, persisting in questioning her and then letting the cat out of the bag.

ფ

It's a relief to be back with Anne again and soon they are immersed in developing more adventures for the people of Gondal.

Emily creates a new character, a young man who, warned by a specter that he is destined to die early, keeps the knowledge to himself. He will die, she decides, but writing about him is strangely cathartic — when she's finished she really does feel a sense of relief, as if something has been resolved. When she reads this to Anne, her sister is enthusiastic, declaring that the episode is very moving.

No one mentions the erysipelas now, though one night when Charlotte catches her examining her scar — Emily's back in the pallet bed now — she says, "*Why* didn't you tell us?"

It's a question everyone's been asking and Emily replies as she always does. "I've told you before — I didn't want to worry you."

Charlotte looks anguished. "But to have suffered that alone! You could have told *me*."

Emily shrugs. "I wanted to keep it to myself. *I* can keep secrets."

Charlotte flushes, showing that the bolt has hit home. And then she says, "Have you any idea how you caught erysipelas? Papa said you can get it from pigs. But you hadn't been near any pigs, had you?"

Emily puts on a deliberately vague expression. "Do you know, I really can't remember."

24

Not long after Emily's up and about, the news comes that Charlotte's drawings have been accepted for the summer exhibition, which is due to take place in three weeks' time. Everyone except Emily professes to be delighted about it, though Emily's not sure that Branwell is as pleased as he pretends.

The day of the trip to the exhibition turns out to be one of those fine August days when the sky is an unbelievable blue. Instead of spending the day shut in a stuffy building, among crowds of strangers, Emily would much rather stay behind with Aunt and Tabby and take the opportunity for a long walk, but she reluctantly agrees to go. Despite her estrangement from Charlotte, she can't quite bring herself to spoil her sister's pleasure. Once she would have had no hesitation in taking revenge, but now it seems mean and petty.

Anne is keen to go, though she expresses her enthusiasm more quietly than Papa and Branwell. As for Charlotte — she's almost too elated to speak, especially when she finds that her drawings are hanging in the same room as a painting by Turner.

Emily is pleased to see another example of Turner's work — this one is of Venice and she has never seen such light in a painting, such a piercing blue — but she can't understand her sister's excitement. Charlotte's drawings have been hung in a dim corner, too high up to be properly seen. And they are the only people taking any notice of them.

"Well done, my dear." Papa squeezes Charlotte's shoulder. "A fine achievement."

Charlotte glows pink with pleasure.

Papa suggests that they move on to look at some of the other exhibits. He's particularly interested in seeing William Robinson's portraits. Emily's not very impressed by these — the people look so wooden and lifeless — and she's soon bored, especially as Branwell insists on lecturing them about the various techniques the painter has employed.

As they stroll on, Emily's head starts to ache — the heat, surely, she hastens to tell herself, rather than a symptom to be dreaded — but then Anne tugs at her arm. "Look!"

Emily looks. And the hairs rise on the back of her neck.

She's never seen anything like it: a huge sculptured head, over six feet tall. She can't stop gazing at that face. There's such proud scorn in the eyes, in those lips curled in a sneer, and yet the expression is one of deepest despair.

It's beautiful . . . and chilling.

"Who is it?" she whispers to Branwell, who is standing beside her, equally transfixed.

"It's Satan. By Joseph Leyland." Branwell turns to Papa. "Do you know anything about him, Papa?"

"Leyland? Ah, he's a local fellow, like Robinson." Papa studies the sculpture. "A fine piece of work, to be sure. It puts me in mind of *Paradise Lost*. Do you remember? When Satan addresses the sun. We must look it up when we get home."

When the others move on, Emily can't tear herself away — she stands there, absorbing every detail of the face. She keeps coming back to the eyes, drawn by their inhuman power; it's as if Satan is gazing deep into her soul and knows everything there is to know about her.

༉

On the way home, Branwell and Charlotte are debating the merits of the various paintings they have seen when Papa, who has been sunk in thought, suddenly says, "Branwell, I have it in mind to ask William Robinson if he will tutor you. What do you say to that?"

Branwell stops dead in the road. All the color drains from his face and then his cheeks flush pink. "Papa!" is all he can manage to say, but his eyes are bright with excitement.

Emily looks sideways at Charlotte. Her sister is biting her lip, but otherwise she's giving no sign of what she must be feeling.

"I'll need to speak to your aunt first, of course," says Papa.

Emily knows what that means. It will presumably cost a great deal to engage the services of such a famous man as Mr. Robinson. It can't be done unless Aunt will help.

༉

In the event, Aunt is in full support of the idea, especially after Papa tells her more about Mr. Robinson. When she hears that he's been a celebrated artist in London, she urges Papa to approach him.

In no time at all Papa has arranged an appointment and taken Branwell to meet the painter at his studio in Leeds. When they return with the news that Mr. Robinson has agreed to take Branwell on as a pupil, Aunt's normally dour face lights up.

"Oh, Branwell! Very likely, Mr. Robinson will introduce

you to the highest echelons of society and, with your talent, you will be such a success." She regards her nephew fondly.

Charlotte, Emily can see, is doing her best to look pleased for him, but obviously she minds very much. Despite everything, Emily feels aggrieved on her sister's behalf — it's not right that Branwell has all the attention and the opportunities while Charlotte's overlooked. As soon as they're alone, she says to Charlotte, "You should be having lessons with Mr. Robinson too. It's not fair. Tell Papa about your idea."

Charlotte shakes her head. "I might speak to Papa, but not until the exhibition ends."

"Why wait?"

"Because I want to know if anyone has bought my drawings. It'll be a sign, you know . . ." She trails off.

Emily does know. It will be horrible for her sister if her drawings don't sell.

ର୍ଚ୍ଚ

In the weeks that follow, Emily finds Branwell insufferable. She can't begin to imagine what Charlotte must be feeling. Their brother is now certain that he's destined for success. He won't stop talking about his projected future: the life he's going to lead in London's artistic circles and the money he's going to make.

Emily is dubious. She can't believe that it's all going to be as easy as Branwell expects. She also wishes, for Charlotte's sake, that Aunt and Papa weren't so caught up in his dreams of glory. Apart from anything else, they seem prepared to spend any amount of money on him. His lessons cost two guineas a session, and then when Branwell complains that his bedroom is too small for him to paint in, they decide that the upper store-room is to be converted into a room especially for him.

This involves a lot of dust and disruption as Fred Harper blocks up the outside door and knocks through a new doorway to the landing. After consultations with Mr. Robinson, Papa orders an easel and all the paraphernalia the budding artist might need and Branwell takes possession of his new "studio."

For a few days all is peaceful. But then Branwell emerges complaining that copying isn't satisfactory and he needs to practice "properly" — in other words, he wants his sisters to sit for him.

Emily instantly refuses.

"Come on, Em," says Branwell, putting on his most winning expression. "This is important for my career."

"I don't want to have my likeness taken," says Emily truthfully. She adds mischievously, "Though I doubt I'd be recognized if you painted me."

Branwell frowns.

"I'll do it," Anne offers quickly.

"Bless you, little one," says Branwell, recovering his sunniness. "What about you, Charlotte?"

Charlotte hesitates.

Emily's not surprised. How could Charlotte possibly put up with Branwell's posturing and preening as he plays at being the "Great Artist"?

At that moment Papa looks in at the door. Branwell appeals to him at once. "Papa, I want to paint the girls and they're being obstreperous. Tell them they've got to sit for me."

"I said I would," Anne protests.

Papa looks at Branwell mildly through his spectacles. "Well, son, I don't think we can force your sisters to do anything against their will."

Branwell frowns.

"But, do you know," Papa looks round at them all, "it would gladden my heart to have a portrait of you all — you too, Branwell, if you can manage to fit yourself in. What do you say, girls?"

Of course, the appeal is irresistible — they can't disappoint Papa, and so Branwell ceremoniously leads them to his "studio" and, with much huffing and puffing, he sets to.

෨ᗅᑙ

It takes several days and he won't let them see it till it's finished. Finally he announces that it's done and they all cluster round to look at it.

Privately Emily thinks he's not done too badly as far as she and Anne are concerned, but poor Charlotte has ended up looking like a prissy schoolmarm.

She sneaks a look at Charlotte to see how she's taking it.

Charlotte's lips are pursed, but she doesn't say anything. She doesn't need to — Aunt and Papa's comments are fulsome enough even to satisfy Branwell.

Seeing him reveling in their praise, Emily can't resist. "Have you got the perspective right? You've made yourself taller than me. Or are we supposed to imagine you're standing on a box?"

Branwell turns a furious red at once. "Don't be stupid. You're sitting down. And it was the only way I could fit my head in."

Papa lays a restraining hand on his shoulder. "It's very fine, Branwell. If it's all right with you, I'd like to hang it in my study."

Branwell smirks, and when Papa has carried the picture from the room, he says to Emily, "See, Miss Ignoramus, Papa can appreciate fine art, even if you can't."

Emily doesn't deign to reply. As for Charlotte — she looks as if she would like to punch Branwell.

ᗧᑐ

To Emily's amusement, Charlotte finds her own way of getting back at their brother.

While she's been waiting to hear about the fate of her drawings, Charlotte has taken up writing again and, helped by Branwell when he can spare the time from painting, she's added a kingdom called Angria to the Glass Town confederation. Among its inhabitants is one Patrick Benjamin Wiggins.

Charlotte reads out her description of him with malicious delight, emphasizing certain details as she does so: "A *low*, slightly built man . . . a bush of *carroty* hair . . ."

Emily glances at Branwell, who's looking distinctly uneasy.

Wiggins, according to Charlotte, is extremely boastful, and in imagining his own epitaph he depicts himself in the most glowing terms: "As a musician he was greater than Bach, as a poet he surpassed Byron, as a painter, Claude Lorraine yielded to him . . ."

Anne laughs out loud and Emily smirks.

Nettled, Branwell looks round at them all. "I don't know why you're finding that so funny. With all my talents, you've no idea what I might achieve in the future. And I do know one thing."

"What's that?" asks Emily.

"I'll achieve more than any of you silly girls." And with that he affects a lofty manner and stalks out of the room.

25

A few days later, Emily at last finds the time to reread some of *Paradise Lost*. She's been thinking of it ever since they saw the statue of Satan at the art exhibition, and she looks first for the passage Papa mentioned.

Reading it now, she finds it especially poignant in a way she didn't when she was younger.

The sun reminds Satan of what he once was: Lucifer, star of the morning, brightest of all God's angels. He regrets all that he has thrown away by trying to overthrow God. But he realizes that the only way he can achieve God's pardon is by submission and this awakens his spirit of rebellion again. Bidding farewell to hope and fear, he deliberately chooses evil.

Emily shivers as she comes to the line: *Evil, be thou my good.* She puts the book down.

She feels a stirring of sympathy, even admiration, for this being who refuses to subject himself to another's authority. Why should God have all the power?

As this outrageous thought forms of its own accord, she sits up, feeling a prickle of excitement tinged with fear. She holds her breath, half-wondering if God is going to strike her dead.

But minutes pass and nothing happens.

What does that mean?

Aunt is always telling them, "God sees you. He knows your every innermost thought." Either it isn't true, or else, as Emily has suspected for some time, God has far more important things to concern Himself with than everyone's thoughts.

Or maybe — a new idea occurs to her — maybe God, if He exists, is far too mysterious and unknowable for petty humans to understand. Maybe not all the things that are said about Him in the Bible, the things that Papa believes in so unquestioningly, are true.

Thinking this gives Emily the strangest sensation . . . as if her head is expanding and her thoughts, untethered, are floating away. She feels excited and afraid, but mostly excited, enjoying this wonderful new sense of lightness, of freedom.

Lacing her fingers, she stretches her arms over her head. It strikes her that some of Satan's characteristics would suit her heroine Rosina. The princess is already powerful, but she can make her even fiercer, a woman who nurses a deep sense of grievance. Yes, that will be perfect.

Charlotte comes into the room and Emily nods at her, but she's still caught up in her thoughts.

She's so glad now that she went to the exhibition after all — seeing the statue and reading Milton's poem has really inspired her. She can't wait to tell Anne her latest idea. She'll have Rosina treat her enemies with a cold and scornful pride and . . .

She notices that Charlotte's holding a letter. It's hard to be dragged from the exciting world of Gondal, but Emily can see from her sister's face that it's not good news.

Dutifully Emily asks, "What's happened?"

"The organizers of the art exhibition want me to collect my drawings. They haven't sold."

"Oh, Charles." Emily can't help feeling sorry for her sister. There's no comfort she can offer, though; if she tries, it will only make Charlotte cry — she can see that she's struggling to hold back her tears — and that will make her feel worse.

"So you see, it's just as well I didn't tell Papa." There's an edge to Charlotte's voice, but for once Emily doesn't retaliate.

"No, you were quite right," she says meekly.

☙

Summer passes into autumn. The days shorten: They wake up to feathers of frost on the windows and their breath coming out in clouds; Aunt banks up her fire and swathes herself in two thick shawls; they have to light the candles earlier and earlier.

As the year turns Emily begins to relax — it's been so long since the dog bite, surely she would know by now if she'd contracted rabies? Charlotte seems to have got over the disappointment about her artistic ambitions; though Papa is looking frailer and his hair is grey now, he hasn't succumbed to any more illness; she and Anne are still happily immersed in Gondal. In short, everything is as it should be, and she is content.

But she has reckoned without Branwell.

Throughout the autumn he sometimes stayed at the Black Bull after sessions of the boxing club, but not long after Christmas he begins to go to the inn on other evenings as well, waiting till nine o'clock when Papa and Aunt go to bed before slipping out. He's always back before eleven, but in such an excited and talkative state that it's hard to persuade him to go to bed.

Emily can see that he's not just enjoying the company at the inn, but is also developing a taste for alcohol. She'd be inclined to let him alone for now — the main thing is to keep this from Papa — but Charlotte becomes increasingly agitated about him, and one evening, when their brother's out as usual and they are writing in the parlor, Charlotte suddenly puts down her pen and says abruptly, "What are we going to do about Branwell? We can't let him carry on like this."

"Shall we tell Papa?" Anne's eyes are wide.

"No!" Charlotte and Emily both speak at once and then Emily says, "We can't do anything. Except hope it's just another of his enthusiasms that he'll tire of eventually."

Charlotte drums her fingers on the table, thinking. Then she looks at the others. "I think we should talk to him."

Emily sighs. "It won't do any good, Charles — he won't take any notice of us."

"Well, I think it's worth a try." Charlotte gives them a martyred look. "Even if I have to do it by myself."

⚬⚬⚬

As Emily predicted, when Charlotte tackles Branwell in the hall one evening just as he's putting his coat on prior to going out, he's unreceptive. "Don't preach, Charles. It's only a bit of fun. And a fellow can't be expected to spend all his time at home with only his sisters for company."

And with that he leaves, shutting the front door quietly behind him.

Emily heard this exchange through the open parlor door and when Charlotte joins her and Anne again, her sister looks so hurt that Emily refrains from saying, "I told you so."

What they can't understand is where Branwell gets the money from — none of them are given any pocket money. They suspect that Aunt indulges him with the occasional shilling or half crown, but not often enough to support his new drinking habit.

"Perhaps Mr. Brown treats him," suggests Emily. Branwell sometimes refers to a "jolly evening" in the sexton's company.

"Maybe." Charlotte frowns. "Or maybe," she adds drily, "the visitors pay for their entertainment."

In a recent development, a boy sometimes appears at the back door with a message for Branwell, typically something like, "Mr. Sugden sends 'pologies, but he says there's a salesman from York staying over and wanting to meet Master Branwell, if it pleases him to come."

Of course, it does please Branwell mightily to be getting such a reputation at the Black Bull for his witty conversation and he never misses a chance to hold forth to an admiring audience or demonstrate his amazing memory or his ability to write with both hands at once.

That's what he tells them he's been doing when he comes home, flushed and in high spirits, and never a word about drinking, though they can smell it on his breath.

Charlotte gives up trying to talk him out of it, but Branwell's behavior makes her tight-lipped and disapproving. Emily doesn't say anything to her sister, but she finds it paradoxical that Charlotte is happy enough to imagine a life of utter dissipation for her Angrian heroes, but can't tolerate their brother's departure from the straight and narrow.

She herself doesn't find Branwell's drinking offensive, but she's anxious about Papa finding out — he'll be shocked and disappointed in Branwell and the distress might bring on another attack of pleurisy.

In an effort to prevent this happening, she does everything she can to conceal Branwell's antics: After he's come in, she checks that he's bolted the door, and later she peeps into his room to make sure he hasn't left his candle burning. Branwell, of course, has no idea that she's doing these things and he continues blithely to please himself.

෨෬

As if it wasn't bad enough to have Branwell to worry about, one morning Charlotte announces that her other school friend is coming to stay.

"I asked her sister Martha too, but she can't come this time. So it will just be Mary."

Emily frowns.

As if to forestall her objections, Charlotte declares, "Papa and Aunt are both delighted at the idea." But then a doubtful look crosses her face and she adds, "Though Mary isn't like Ellen."

"What is she like?" Emily wants to know.

"You'll see."

26

Mary bounces into the house, laughing, talking, and behaving as if she has known all of them all her life.

She's not in the least shy, not even with Papa and Aunt, and she has, Emily discovers, as her hand is seized and pumped up and down, a direct way of speaking and of looking at you, so that Emily finds herself compelled to meet Mary's gaze.

To her surprise, for once she doesn't feel threatened — the expression in Mary's eyes is quizzical and warm. It helps that their visitor seems to like Grasper — she makes a big fuss of him and when she says, "Aren't you a handsome fellow?" it sounds as if she means it.

Emily's disarmed, and her curiosity about this other friend of Charlotte's prompts her to go with the rest of them as they take Mary on a tour of the house, which ends up in the backyard.

They say hello to Tiger, who is basking in a patch of sunshine, stop by the cage to see Jasper, Snowflake, and Plato, the one-legged magpie, and then Anne opens the peat house door to introduce Mary to the latest additions to their menagerie: a pair of plump geese.

"They're called Adelaide and Victoria," says Anne. "After the queen and the princess."

Mary claps her hands. "Capital! What a joke. That puts the monarchy in their proper place — scratching for crumbs in the dirt."

"But we didn't mean any disrespect." Charlotte looks confused. "The princess is one of Emily's heroines."

"Is she now?" Mary shoots Emily a direct, disconcerting look.

Emily bows her head and takes refuge in rumpling Grasper's ears. But she suddenly feels uncomfortable about admiring Princess Victoria so much.

"You don't approve of royalty?" Branwell asks.

"No, indeed. Why should people have such power and privilege, just by virtue of being born into a certain family? We should be able to choose our rulers. All of us, men and women alike," she adds fiercely.

Branwell and Charlotte immediately start to argue with her, but though she's outnumbered, Mary doesn't give way.

Emily doesn't join in. She doesn't care for politics as the others do — they take after Papa in their passion for it, whereas she doesn't see that it would make much difference to her life who ruled. But perhaps her view of Princess Victoria has been childish. Perhaps she's only seen her as a fairy-tale princess, rather than a real person who might influence the government's actions.

Fancy — Mary has made her question herself, and she hasn't been in the house more than an hour! And what she says about privilege is worth thinking about.

She looks at their visitor.

Before she came, Emily was set on disliking her. For one thing, she doesn't care for poetry. But now, listening to Mary and watching her, her grey eyes alight, her face animated as she argues, Emily's fascinated.

To her surprise, rather than finding the prospect of this visitor tiresome, she finds herself wanting to spend time with Mary.

❧

A day or two later they are all in the parlor sitting by the fire, except for Branwell, who has gone off with a friend from the village. Mary, who is sharing the sofa with Grasper, suddenly says, "I am interested in your aunt's situation. Does your father support her?"

Anne gives a little gasp and Charlotte looks embarrassed. She glances up at the ceiling, where Aunt is in her room above them.

Emily's amused. One of the things she's discovered about Mary is that she speaks her mind. Most people hypocritically hide what they're really thinking and call it politeness, so this is refreshing. Perhaps Mary is interested in people's financial situations because of her own family's predicament. Emily wonders how they manage with their father bankrupt.

Responding in kind, she answers Mary directly. "No, he doesn't. She has her own money — inherited from her father."

"Ah, I see." Mary nods. "She's lucky, then. And do you think she's single by choice?"

Emily's surprised. The question has never occurred to her.

"We don't know." Charlotte looks as if it's a new idea to her too. "She's always talking about the balls and beaux of her youth, but whether she ever received a proposal . . ." She shrugs and then looks at her sisters. "Lucky for us that she didn't marry."

Emily grimaces. She knows she should feel grateful for all that Aunt has done for them, but sometimes she thinks they could have easily managed just with Tabby and got along far more comfortably.

Mary meanwhile is giving Charlotte a droll look. "Lucky for you, yes. And possibly lucky for herself too," she says crisply.

"How can you say that?" Charlotte protests. "By not marrying she has missed so much."

"Such as?" Mary looks amused.

"Well . . ." Charlotte stops, then she says in a rush, "A chance for a warm, close intimacy . . ." She stops again and blushes.

Emily stares at her sister, shocked. "You want to be married?"

Charlotte's cheeks turn scarlet. "Oh, I'm not speaking of myself. Besides, who would have me, plain and penniless as I am?"

"You're not plain," says Anne loyally.

"Oh, but I am. Mary said so, didn't you, almost the first time we met."

It's Mary's turn to redden. "Oh, my wretched mouth! How it will run away from me. I'm so sorry, Charlotte."

"No, you spoke the truth and it did me a lot of good. It certainly has kept me from vain fancies." Charlotte looks down and an uncomfortable pause follows.

Emily is still musing on Charlotte's revelation. Though her sister's denied it, it's obvious she *was* talking about herself. She wants intimacy with a man? Some stranger she's not even met yet? What an absurd idea . . .

But then it strikes her — maybe it's not so absurd to Charlotte. Maybe it's all of a piece with her hankering after a world beyond the family, that world she imagines as exciting and full of possibility?

Mary, clearly keen to lighten the atmosphere, says teasingly, "Why think only of who might have you? What about a man *you* would like to have?"

Charlotte rouses herself and looks arch. "Oh, there I am spoiled for choice! What men do I meet? The curates, of course!"

Emily splutters and Anne giggles. Since Mary looks mystified, Emily explains, "The curates are really boring — they invite themselves to tea and all they do is eat and argue. And they treat Tabby dreadfully, ordering her to bring them more bread or beer, as if it was their house."

Charlotte says, "Yes, Mary, you've never seen such a self-seeking, empty-headed bunch of young men."

"I'm glad to hear it. So you're safe, at least for now. But really, Charlotte" — Mary drops her lightness and speaks in earnest — "you must know that there's no guarantee that, by marrying, a woman will have a warm, close attachment."

Hear, hear! Emily's glad that Mary said that. Because after all, Charlotte could just as easily find what she wants here at home, if she didn't have such "daft" notions, as Tabby would say.

Charlotte goes to speak, but Mary has the bit between her teeth now. "What is more certain is that a wife would have to bend her will to that of her husband and subordinate her wishes to his."

"But would she not want to, if she was deeply attached to him?" Charlotte protests. "Would she not be willing to die for him?"

Emily groans and Mary snorts rudely. "Oh, Charlotte, what a romantic you are. Such nonsense."

Anne pipes up, "I think Charlotte's right." They all turn to look at her, and she shrinks back into her chair.

"Well, I don't want to die for anyone," Mary declares. "And I certainly don't want to be financially dependent."

Charlotte sighs. "You have a point. If only it were possible to be married and also have control of one's own money."

"Well, it's not. And that being the case, I shall never marry." Mary emphasizes her words with a decided nod.

Charlotte, who has been looking fondly at her friend, says quietly, "But what if you fall in love, Mary?"

"Oh, that." Mary waves her hand dismissively and, bending her head, she begins to play with Grasper's ears.

ᘉ

Emily thinks a lot about this conversation afterward.

Marriage is not something she's ever discussed with her sisters. She had no idea that Charlotte had even thought about it, let alone had visions of what it might be like. And as for Anne agreeing with Charlotte . . . astonishing!

Emily tries to think of the married women she's seen, women she's scarcely ever taken any notice of. There are the village women, of course, thin with overwork and too often grieving at the graves of their little ones. Or the well-to-do wives who sit in the best pews at church — they seem more interested in each other's clothing than in their spouses. None of them look as if they are glad to be married.

And in books, it's all about love — seeing someone and yearning for them and sometimes being lucky enough to win them. But the books always end with the wedding and never go on to describe married life. Perhaps it's because it's too dull to bother with.

As usual when she has a question, Emily seeks out Tabby, the only person she knows well who's been married, apart from Papa, and of course she can't ask him.

"What's it like to be married?" Tabby scratches her head. "Well, now, that's nigh impossible to answer, lass."

"Why?"

"Well, because . . ." Tabby's clearly struggling. She tries again. "It's like . . . tha does thi best and sometimes tha's happy enough, and sometimes tha's not." She waves her hand as if that's all she has to say on the subject. "Why's tha asking anyways?"

"Oh, it was just something we were talking about with Mary."

Tabby's face breaks into a smile. "That lass, she's a proper caution."

"Yes, she is," Emily agrees.

Mary is not like anyone she's ever met. Talking to her is like standing on a hilltop with the wind blowing through you — you feel buffeted, but also invigorated, *alive*. And Mary doesn't seem afraid to speak her mind, apparently not caring what anyone thinks of her.

Emily remembers, with glee, the conversation Mary had with Aunt that morning. Aunt was proudly telling Mary how she had made her nieces sew pincushions and needle cases for the charity basket in the belief that it did *them* more good than the recipients of their handiwork.

Mary gave her one of her looks and said, "How so?" and Aunt was left speechless, gaping like a fish.

Emily smirks. She loves the fact that Mary's outspokenness extends even to the old lady and that she's quite prepared to argue with her instead of treating her with the deference she expects.

Not that Emily agrees with everything Mary says, but she certainly approves of her view of marriage.

If Emily were to bind herself to some man, she'd have to leave home and go live with him, just as Mama had to leave Penzance when she married Papa. That would be terrible. And fancy not being able to please yourself, but to have to put your husband's wishes before your own. Why, she'd even have to give up her own name. Emily winces at the thought.

The answer is obvious. She, like Mary, will never marry.

27

On Mary's last afternoon — a fresh March day, with the breeze sending cloud shadows scudding across the moorland — Emily finds herself walking ahead with their visitor, who seems to enjoy striding out as much as she does.

For once Branwell hasn't joined them, though he's not missed any other walks during Mary's stay, and they soon leave Charlotte and Anne behind.

Much as she is beginning to like Mary, Emily feels shy about talking to her and, unusually, Mary doesn't seem to have anything to say, so they walk in silence. But it's an easy silence and Emily feels relaxed.

After a while, feeling warm, Emily unthinkingly rolls up her sleeves.

Mary says casually, "My word, that's a nasty scar on your arm."

"Yes, a dog bit me." At once Emily is aghast.

What on earth made her say that? It must be because she was feeling at ease and had let her guard down.

She doesn't very often think about the threat of rabies now — after so many months she's begun to believe that she's safe. But as long as there's the faintest chance of it flaring up, it must be kept from her family.

How could she have been so thoughtless?

She looks sideways at Mary. "I know this sounds mad, but would you mind not mentioning this to Charlotte? Or to the others?"

"They don't know?" Mary sounds surprised.

"No, that is . . . they know about my scar, but not how I got it."

Mary looks at her closely a moment and then says, "I see. Right. Well, of course, I won't say a word."

Emily chews the inside of her lip. Can she trust her?

Mary says lightly, "At least it hasn't put you off dogs. I can see how attached you are to Grasper." She nods to where Grasper is investigating a clump of cotton grass.

Emily seizes on the change of subject gratefully. "Oh yes, I am."

"And he's obviously devoted to you. I like dogs and Grasper is a splendid fellow, but if it was me, I don't think I'd cope very well with his attentiveness."

"Oh? Why's that?"

"I wouldn't want to be so *needed* . . . I'd rather be free of such dependence."

Emily hesitates, but there is something so open about Mary that she is compelled to candor herself. "If it was a human being dependent on me, I would feel the same, but with Grasper, it's different; I don't know why."

She reflects for a moment and then says, "I think it's because he's so easy to be with. You know exactly where you are with him — he can never tell lies. And he doesn't judge me — he doesn't care what I look like or whether I behave 'properly.' He doesn't ask anything of me at all, so it is easy to love him."

Suddenly embarrassed by this disclosure, she looks at Mary

to see if she is laughing at her, but Mary's face is serious and she nods as if she understands what Emily is saying.

"I can see why you value him. How refreshing not to be judged! I suspect that, like me, you suffer from the expectations your aunt has of girls. She is like my mother. They both believe that a girl should learn early to busy herself with pointless, trivial activities. It's so unfair. My brothers have a lot more freedom to please themselves. Do you find that?"

"Oh yes. Branwell doesn't have to do any household chores. And he is always favored before us girls."

"It's the same in our house. And when visitors come they always take more notice of the boys, whereas Martha and I are expected to sit there quietly." She sighs heavily. "It's a conspiracy to prepare us for a lifetime of patient passivity. Such wicked nonsense when we have the same capacity for action as men. Far too many women ruin their lives by waiting for their fortune to come to them instead of setting about making it for themselves."

Emily almost cheers. This heady talk accords exactly with what she believes. And it's just what she tries to do in her writing, giving her heroines adventures in which they can create their own destinies.

For a wild moment she's tempted to tell Mary about Gondal, but then reason asserts itself.

Though they've talked a lot, she doesn't know Mary well enough. Charlotte has said that, though Mary loves reading, she has no interest in poetry or fanciful ideas. She probably wouldn't understand the lure of creating imaginary worlds.

No, she mustn't say anything. Gondal is private, only to be shared with Anne.

Mary is still talking. "And as for those who swallow the line that they have a duty to devote themselves to others . . ." She grimaces as if she's swallowed sour milk.

"You don't agree with that?"

"Good Lord, no. I believe we women have a duty to act in our own interests. We should do all we can to improve our lives and consider our own pleasure. If we don't, we have only ourselves to blame." She looks at Emily, her eyes glowing with passion.

Mary's opinion is the exact opposite of the dreary creed that Aunt's dinned into Emily and her sisters since they were small: duty, duty always before desire.

Emily beams at Mary. She stops walking and throws out her arms, causing Grasper to bark and jump up at her excitedly. "You are right! And Aunt is wrong! Away with lace collars and cross-stitch needlecases!"

It feels wickedly exhilarating — like deliberately smashing Aunt's teapot, which she's sometimes felt like doing. She'd never be able to say these things to Anne.

Mary chimes in. "Yes, yes! Away with embroidered tray cloths and pointless samplers!"

"Oh!" Emily exclaims and drops her arms.

"What is it? Have you bitten your tongue?"

"No. It's nothing. Let's walk on."

It was Mary's innocent mentioning of samplers that did it. Without warning the box buried deep inside her has sprung open and the monsters are here. As she walks, she clasps her hands to her chest where the pain is and bends as if she's battling against a fierce wind.

"Emily?" Mary's voice is full of concern.

She can't tell her, she can't . . .

She looks at Mary, sees her warm grey eyes watching her.

Could she, for once, take the risk of exposing herself to someone who is a stranger? Mary's eyes . . . they're so like Elizabeth's. And her reaction to Emily's disclosure about the dog bite was so sensitive — she didn't pry or make tactless comments.

Emily takes a deep breath. She will do this, she wants to take this risk, but she can't look directly at Mary. If she keeps her eyes on the ground, she might be able to manage it.

"When my sister Elizabeth died," she begins carefully, as if she's telling a story. Because after all, that's what it is, a story, and she will tell it to Mary, who is listening intently. But it needs a different beginning. She starts again.

"I loved my sister Elizabeth very much, and after she died I was very . . ." She pauses and then chooses a word. It's not at all the right word, but it will do, for now. "I was very upset and a few days after the funeral, Aunt called me into her room and said, 'You can have this.'"

She looks up at Mary. "It was the sampler Elizabeth made just before she went away to school. She'd had an awful tussle with Aunt over it . . . she hated sewing and Aunt kept making her unpick the stitches and do it again. But she did finish it, finally."

Emily pauses. She lays her hand on Grasper's head a moment before going on. "When Aunt gave it to me, I stood there holding it, looking at all those wobbly stitches and thinking of Elizabeth's poor pricked fingers and the pointlessness of it all . . . and then Aunt said" — she swallows, takes a breath — "Aunt said 'I thought the text would comfort you.'"

Mary leans toward Emily. "What text was it?" Her voice is quiet for once, gentle.

Emily closes her eyes, opens them again. She quotes, "'I shall not die but live and declare the works of the Lord.'"

Mary winces.

"Yes." Emily shakes her head. "I read it, standing there in front of Aunt, and I felt sick. Elizabeth was dead and Aunt thought this stupid piece of material with its stupid, stupid message was going to help." She looks at Mary directly. "I threw it on the fire — right there and then, onto Aunt's fire — and it blazed up and was gone."

"What did your aunt say?"

"I don't know. I think she was too shocked to say anything, and by the time she could speak I'd gone. I went to the nursery and lay on the bed Elizabeth had died in and I wouldn't get up, not for ages."

Mary doesn't say anything, but her grey eyes are full of sympathy. They walk on in silence, but it's still a comfortable silence. It wasn't a mistake to tell Mary about the sampler.

After a while Mary observes, "I can't imagine what it would be like if I lost my sister. Or even one of my brothers, annoying as they are sometimes. Charlotte has sometimes spoken of Maria — I can tell she meant a lot to her."

"Oh yes, Charlotte, and Branwell, loved Maria very much. I did too, of course, but . . ." Emily hesitates. "Maria was so good. I mean, she was good at everything, but also, she never did anything wrong. Aunt was always saying, to all of us, 'Why can't you be more like Maria?'"

"That must have been tiresome."

"It was. It wasn't Maria's fault, but she was rather like a saint, so when she died it almost seemed inevitable, you know, as if she'd spent her life preparing to go to heaven. But Elizabeth was different."

"Not saintly?"

Emily smiles. "No. At least, not in that way. She was . . . ordinary. But that made it easier to love her. And . . . you know, we didn't have Mama, but Maria and Elizabeth did their best to make up for it. Maria tried to look after us all, but Elizabeth took special care of me." She frowns, trying to find the right words, to *explain*. "You know, it was as if she belonged to me and I belonged to her."

Mary nods, as if she does know what Emily's talking about. "You must miss her very much."

Emily hunches up her shoulders. Then she says, simply, "Yes."

And now she doesn't want to talk about it anymore, but it's all right because they've reached a stream, swollen with winter rain, and they'll have to negotiate their crossing carefully.

Grasper splashes across at once. Emily reckons she can jump over, but perhaps the stream's too broad for Mary. She hesitates, but then surprises herself by giving her companion a stiff bow, like a cavalier saluting his lady, and offers her hand, intending to help Mary pick her way across.

Mary smiles and makes a curtsy in return. Then, without warning, she retreats a few paces, runs up to the stream, and leaps over, landing safely on the other bank. She stretches her arm out, inviting Emily to join her.

Emily hangs back. She doesn't need any help. But then something impels her to reach out and take hold of Mary's hand as she jumps. They are only in contact for a second, but Emily experiences a shock like a charge of electricity.

As they walk on, she can still feel the impression on her skin — the strength of Mary's grip, the warmth of her palm.

☯

That night Emily lies on her pallet bed, wide awake and feeling restless. Eventually she sits up, making the straw in the mattress rustle. A foot away from her, sharing the bed, Mary and Charlotte are fast asleep.

Emily gazes at Mary. Tomorrow she's leaving them. Emily has never been sorry to see a visitor go, but she's sorry now.

Mary's strong, striking face, surrounded by a cloud of dark hair, is still for once. With its hollows and planes clearly defined in the moonlight, she resembles a statue carved from alabaster of some goddess or otherworldly creature.

Catching herself thinking this, Emily's amused. How Mary would laugh at her if she were to say such a thing to her face. Because really there's nobody more sensible and part of this world than Mary. In that she's very like Elizabeth.

As the thought forms, Emily sees with a small shock of recognition that, just as she did with Elizabeth, with Mary she feels safe.

Perhaps — her heart starts fluttering at the idea — perhaps Charlotte will invite her friend again. She's so fond of Mary that she's bound to. And then perhaps Mary will become *her* friend too.

Emily is astonished at herself — here she is, for the first time in her life, hoping to make a friend.

Settling down on the prickly mattress, she pulls the covers up to her chin and lies there in the dark, smiling to herself.

28

Some weeks after Mary's visit, a letter arrives for Charlotte.

Emily, bringing it into the parlor to give to her sister, recognizes the bold, sprawling handwriting and feels a pang of envy — of course Mary will write to Charlotte, it's only natural. But when Charlotte breaks the seal and examines the folded pages, she says, with surprise, "Mary's enclosed a note for you, Emily." She passes it over.

Emily seizes the thin sheet of paper and scans it eagerly.

. . . how I am missing the serenity of your parsonage, where it is possible to have a civilized conversation without being interrupted! My brothers are all at home just now, turning the house into a veritable bear pit with their falling out and squabbling . . .

Emily frowns as she reads. Mary probably means she's missing talking to Charlotte or Branwell — the letter is friendly, but there's nothing to suggest that Mary's thinking specifically of her. And then she comes to the last paragraph:

Have courage, my dear, and don't let the tyranny of sewing, et cetera, prevent you from following your heart's desires.

Give Grasper a hug from me. Farewell.
Your friend, Mary

Emily clasps the letter to her chest. *Your friend!* And that
clear reference to their last conversation. Mary *is* thinking of
her, and not just being polite.

"What does Mary say?" asks Charlotte.

"Oh, nothing in particular — complaining about her
brothers."

"Poor Mistress Mary! She would do better with a wondrous
brother like me," says Branwell.

Charlotte retaliates at once, and in the ensuing banter Mary's
letter to Emily is forgotten. Emily's glad. She'd rather keep it to
herself.

But now she's faced with a problem — she'll have to send a
reply. Having never written a letter to anyone, she feels daunted.

She takes a piece of paper from her writing desk and uncorks
the ink bottle. Then she chews the end of her penholder. How
does one begin? Trying to use her best handwriting, she carefully inscribes:

Dear Mary,
Thank you for your letter . . .

She stops writing and pulls a face. That is so stilted and
boring. What on earth is there to say? She glances at Mary's
letter again. Of course! Mary writes if she's talking to her, so
that's what she must do. She dips her pen into the ink again
and adds:

. . . which was a lovely surprise. You say you miss our quiet house. Well, it has seemed quieter without you, more's the pity. I too miss the lively conversations you provoked . . .

Better to keep it general and not let Mary know how much their talks meant to her. She doesn't want to embarrass Mary or herself by saying too much.

୧୦

The next time Emily and Anne are out on a walk and talking about Gondal, Emily announces, "I've decided that Julius's illegitimate child doesn't drown with her mother, but is saved, and Julius acknowledges her as his own and has her brought up in a manner suitable for his daughter."

"I still don't think you should give him a child out of wedlock, but if you insist, that sounds a better idea. What's going to happen to her?"

"I don't know yet. But I think she's going to play a big part in the story. Her name's Augusta Geraldine Almeda, and she has grey eyes and black hair."

"Oh! Like Mary."

"Yes." Emily blushes slightly. "She is rather like Mary, I suppose. She's going to be brave and passionate and she won't be beholden to any man, but strides about the world creating her own destiny."

"That could be exciting."

"Yes. I think so."

Anne looks at Emily speculatively. "You like Mary, don't you? I noticed you wrote her a letter."

Emily stiffens. "I did . . . but only because she wrote to me, you know." She's reluctant to admit to Anne how much she admires Mary. Well, she doesn't want Anne to be upset or jealous, does she? She hastens to add, "I didn't tell her anything about Gondal, you know — that's just between us."

Anne says lightly, "I wouldn't mind if you told her. I think it's nice that you've made a friend."

Emily stops in her tracks. "Really?" She suddenly gives Anne a big hug. "Oh, you are so *good*!"

Anne laughs, looking bemused. "I don't think so. You are funny sometimes, Emily."

ᕽᕽ

Emily is so caught up with her latest character, Augusta, that she misses an astonishing piece of news.

She only finds out what's going on when Anne runs into her bedroom, where she's busily writing. "Emily, you'll never guess what's happened. Papa has been to see Mr. Robinson and Branwell is to try for the Royal Academy."

"The Royal Academy?" Emily repeats, puzzled. She's still in the world of Gondal, where no such place exists.

"Yes, you know. The school of art in London."

"London?"

Anne laughs at her. "Wake up, you dozy thing, and come and congratulate our remarkable brother."

Downstairs, under the cover of Branwell's noisy jubilation, Emily sneaks a look at Charlotte. Her expression is inscrutable. But when it emerges that their brother will spend three years in the capital, Charlotte says, "Oh, Branwell, London!" and there's no mistaking the envy in her voice.

When they're by themselves in the bedroom, Charlotte doesn't mention her own feelings. All she says is, "It's obviously a marvelous opportunity for Branwell, but I'm worried about him."

Emily doesn't need to ask why. Alone in London, with no one to keep an eye on him, it's all too easy to see their brother being tempted into drinking houses and who knows what else.

"We'll just have to hope that Branwell's sensible."

From the look Charlotte gives her, she can see that her sister is no more convinced of that likelihood than she is.

"And there's another thing." Charlotte frowns. "I don't see how Papa's going to pay for Branwell's living expenses. I imagine everything costs more there, don't you?"

"Aunt will help, won't she?"

"I expect so, but even then, it will be a burden."

Emily feels a spasm of alarm. Papa's always anxious about money. Only the other day, she heard him tell Tabby to light just one candle, now that the evenings were drawing out. This extra worry could make him ill again. But what can they do about it?

She can't think of anything useful to suggest.

Charlotte sighs. "We'd better go to sleep. Good night." She turns on her side and closes her eyes.

Emily wishes there was something she could say. She feels so sorry for Charlotte. Once again her sister has to see Branwell having something that she would dearly love herself. But Charlotte won't want her to mention it, and there's no point in upsetting her.

Feeling sad, Emily lies down in her pallet bed and sends a quiet "Good night" toward the other bed.

Not long after this conversation, Charlotte comes into the parlor one morning, where Emily and Anne are writing. She's holding a letter and looking thoughtful.

"What is it?" says Emily.

"Miss Wooler has written to offer me a position at the school. Her sister is getting married."

"A position?" For a moment Emily feels genuinely mystified. And then she realizes. "Oh. I see."

Charlotte has already squared her shoulders and adopted the familiar mask that means she's burying her feelings.

Emily can't bear it. "But you don't have to accept it, do you?"

"I think I must. It's fortunate that it's come just now when Branwell is to go to the Academy. It will be a help to Papa if I am off his hands and this is a much better prospect than going as a governess to people I don't know."

Emily groans to herself. Surely Charlotte isn't going to do this and cast it in the light of a noble sacrifice for Branwell's sake?

But before she can say anything, Charlotte taps the letter, giving Emily a penetrating look that makes her feel as if an insect is crawling down her back.

"What?"

"Miss Wooler is also offering a place to one of you," Charlotte blurts out. "As a pupil, I mean . . ."

Emily freezes.

"It's not free, of course . . . I mean, she'll reduce my salary to cover it . . ." Charlotte stumbles on unhappily. "But it's a marvelous opportunity for one of you."

She's looking at Emily pleadingly.

There's a long silence in which Emily and Charlotte stare at each other.

Charlotte looks away first. "I have to tell Papa about this," she mumbles. And she whisks out of the room.

Anne puts out her hand and clasps Emily's wrist. "I could go," she offers.

Emily shakes her head. Papa and Aunt wouldn't dream of sending "little Anne" away from home. And they're right.

She puts her own hand on top of Anne's. She can feel her sister's thin bones.

"It will be me."

She means it to be reassuring, but, as she says it, her grip on Anne's hand tightens.

Like a distant echo, she hears the sound of an iron gate clanging shut.

29

"Congratulations, Emily." Papa is beaming. "To have this chance to be educated . . . and for nothing. Why, isn't it a heaven-sent stroke of good fortune?"

Emily mumbles, "Yes, Papa."

"It's so generous of Miss Wooler. What a kind woman she is, to be sure."

Emily bites back what she would like to say — that the proposed arrangement is to Miss Wooler's advantage. Another pupil won't cost much, but she'll be getting Charlotte's services at a bargain rate.

Papa puts out his hand and tilts her chin up so that she has to look him full in the face. "My dear, of all my children, you are most like me. Just as I struggled all those years ago to make something of myself, I know you'll make the most of this opportunity to better yourself. And it will be a great relief to me to know that should anything happen to me, you'll be able to provide for yourself. This is a blessing indeed."

"Yes, Papa." And with that Emily has to flee, his words ringing in her ears: a blessing that sounded more like a curse.

༄

In the bedroom, on her own, she makes herself face it.

It's a disaster — the very last thing she would want to happen.

What is to become of Gondal? How can she go on with it without Anne? How can she live without Grasper? And how can she leave Papa and Tabby and everyone?

Unbidden, Mary's words float into her head: *We have a duty to act in our own interests.*

Oh, if only she could. If only she had the courage to say, "No, I don't want to do this."

But at once she imagines Papa's face, how disappointed he would be. That is the flaw in Mary's philosophy — if you put yourself first, you can hurt other people.

She can't refuse this. Not when Papa's counting on her and expecting there to be one less mouth to feed.

Besides, somewhere inside her there's a hard nugget of pride, a voice saying, "It would be weak to run away from this."

She thinks of her Gondal heroines sailing off to distant lands, of Lord Byron going to fight in Greece. That's the kind of strength she admires. Compared to those ventures, this is nothing. She will accept this challenge.

୧୦୬

She writes to Mary to tell her the news. Without meaning to she must have sounded woebegone, because Mary writes back by return of post. Emily opens the letter eagerly, but she's not altogether comforted.

I have to admit that I didn't enjoy school as much as Charlotte seems to have done, but there is much to be gained from it, if you can put up with its drawbacks.

*There's no need to feel any anxiety about the teachers.
They are generally tolerable apart from Miss Catherine, who
is somewhat of a martinet, but even she will not trouble you
if you keep to the rules. I suspect you will find that rather
hard, dear Emily, but it can be done! If I managed, I'm sure
you can too!*

Emily doesn't like the sound of that at all. Rules! How will
she live by rules?

As she looks over her clothes with Aunt to see whether she
has what she will need; as she listens to Charlotte's advice on
what things to take and what to leave behind; as Branwell
fetches the bags from the lumber room and she begins to pack,
she manages to cope by gritting her teeth and refusing to think
about what is to come.

ベン

On the last evening Papa calls her into the study and, after speaking seriously about how she must work hard and try her utmost,
he looks at her with his mild, kind eyes and says, "It's a pity that
you'll be away for your birthday, but of course we'll all be thinking of you. You will never be far from my thoughts, my dear."

Emily's resolve almost weakens.

She wants more than anything to throw herself into his arms
and cry, "Don't send me away, Papa; don't make me leave
home." But by holding her breath and digging her fingernails
into her palms, by looking over his white head rather than at
him, she manages to stop herself doing any such thing. And she
even manages to say, "I'll do my best not to disappoint you,
Papa." Her voice is paper thin.

Papa takes off his spectacles and rubs his eyes. For a terrible moment, Emily thinks he's going to cry. If he does, that will finish her. But then he nods to himself and says, "It is a comfort to me that at least you and Charlotte are together; yes, that is a comfort indeed."

But we won't be together, she thinks. Teachers and pupils inhabit different worlds — that much she can remember from the last time she went to school. But of course she won't say that to Papa.

As soon as she can, she escapes from the study and goes upstairs to finish her packing.

Charlotte, who finished *her* packing hours before, is already in bed, sitting up with her nightcap in her hands. Without saying a word, she watches Emily fold up the last few items and then get ready for bed. But as soon as Emily climbs into her own bed, she says, "Well."

"Well, indeed," says Emily. What else is there to say?

"You know, it won't be as bad as you think it's going to be."

Emily looks at her sister. Charlotte has no idea how bad she thinks it's going to be. But all she says is, "No, probably not."

Charlotte fiddles with the strings on her nightcap. "One thing, though, Emily . . ." She stops.

"What?"

"I don't suppose you were thinking of saying anything at Roe Head about our writing?"

Emily gives her a look.

"No, of course not. Good. But, well, it might be prudent to keep some of your more unusual ideas to yourself. The people there might think you're a bit . . . well . . . odd."

"Mary didn't."

"Not everyone's like Mary. She's a bit unusual herself."

"Don't worry. I won't show you up."

Charlotte flushes. "That isn't what I meant. You know it isn't."

Emily's not so sure. But rather than go on with this, she lies down. "Let's go to sleep. Tomorrow's going to be a long day."

Charlotte hesitates, but then she settles down too. Soon she's breathing deeply. But long after Charlotte has fallen asleep, Emily lies awake, staring at the night sky.

Where will she be tomorrow night? What will she be able to see from her bedroom window?

The stars glitter back at her, cold and distant and silent.

30

The next morning Emily gets up very early, before anyone else, and takes Grasper for a walk. When they return she rests her hand on his head for a moment before shutting him in the back kitchen. After breakfast she asks Anne to feed him and when Anne looks surprised she says, "You might as well begin today."

She doesn't go near the back kitchen again.

As soon as the carriage arrives she climbs into it without a word. She can't say good-bye or even look at everyone gathered in the lane to see them off — it takes all her willpower not to betray how desperate she feels. Giving them a half wave, she faces in the direction they are going and as they set off she doesn't glance back.

She's glad that Charlotte's quiet on the journey. Emily can guess what her sister might be feeling about going back to Roe Head as a teacher, but she can't think of a single comforting thing to say. All she can do is sit there, gazing out at the passing scenery without seeing it, dread lying like a heavy stone in her stomach.

When they're nearly there, Charlotte rouses herself and begins to point out features of the area — "Look, Emily, there's Kirklees Park . . . and the Calder Valley beyond" — as if she's trying to imply: *It's beautiful here too.*

Emily looks dully out of the window. Charlotte's wasting her time. This pleasant, gentle landscape with its trees and parkland is far too tame, with too many signs of human occupation.

This isn't her world.

As they turn off the road and pass through a pair of gates, she recognizes the school from Charlotte's drawing — a grey stone building with bay windows set in an expanse of grass with trees and shrubberies.

Looking at it, she feels a kind of horror. What is she doing here? What does this house have to do with her?

They are shown into an oak-paneled parlor where Miss Wooler greets them graciously enough. The headmistress is shorter and stouter than Emily expected from Charlotte's admiring description. And rather old to be wearing a white dress.

They are introduced to the other teachers, Miss Wooler's sisters, but Emily is too anxious to take in which is which. When one of them says, "Come, Miss Brontë, I'll show you round the house," it takes Emily a moment to realize that the teacher's addressing her. With a backward glance at Charlotte, she's led away.

Her guide — is she the strict one, Miss Catherine? Or is she Miss Eliza? Whoever she is, she doesn't talk much but goes at a brisk pace, and Emily is left with a confusing impression of staircases and rambling passageways. In one of the upstairs rooms, the teacher points out a bed by the window. "That's yours. Put your clothes in those drawers and I'll be back for you shortly." And Emily is surprised to see her box there, looking out of place in these unfamiliar surroundings.

Left alone, she sinks onto the bed and stares around her. The room is decorated in a style someone must have supposed girls would like — the wallpaper is covered with tiny sprigs of rose-buds, while the curtains are patterned with stiff garlands of unnatural-looking pink roses. There are three other beds in the room and she wonders who they belong to. And then she remembers, with a lurch of her stomach, that she will very likely be sharing hers.

How can she possibly sleep with a stranger?

Fighting her rising panic, she goes to the window and looks out. The bedroom is at the side of the house overlooking a garden — more roses planted in rows in rectangular beds and straight gravel paths. But at least she can see the sky, which today is a clear blue and cloudless. If only she could float up into it and be carried away from this place . . .

She remembers with a jolt that the teacher will be return-ing at any moment and she hurries to unpack her things. This doesn't take long. Then she sits on the bed again and waits.

Every now and again there's a burst of noise from down-stairs, girls' voices, excited and shrill, and laughter. She wishes she could just stay here in this quiet bedroom, that she doesn't have to go down and face them. But finally the teacher looks in and beckons her and she's forced to follow her down the stairs.

"The schoolroom," says the teacher, opening the door with a flourish.

As they enter the room, silence falls and all heads turn in her direction.

Although she lowers her eyes immediately, she has the impression that she's come upon a troop of exotic creatures like the flamingos in an Audubon watercolor. When she lifts her gaze she sees flowers — pink, blue, lilac — floating on delicate muslins or some shiny material she doesn't recognize; bare arms and shoulders; gleaming, elaborate topknots; and finally a blur of faces in which the eyes stare hard at her, curious, assessing . . .

She looks away. Now that she's seen these girls she can tell that Charlotte's advice was pointless. In her drab green dress, with her hair hanging down, lank and loose, she doesn't even have to open her mouth for them to judge her as odd. And then she thinks of Mary. Mary can't have fitted in here very well either. But she would have been brave enough to be herself and not pay any attention to what they thought of her.

Emily squares her shoulders. She will try to be like Mary. Instead of being afraid of their judging her, she simply won't care.

The teacher breaks the silence. "Girls, this is Miss Brontë, who is coming to join you. I know you'll make her feel welcome." And with that she turns on her heel and leaves the room.

Almost immediately a girl with brown hair and eyes and creamy skin comes forward and, holding out her hand, says, "Hello. I'm Julia, Julia Caris." After a moment's hesitation, Emily shakes the hand and mumbles her name, but of course they all know it already, and from somewhere at the back of the room she hears a mocking echo: "Emilee Brontee."

"That's an unusual name." The girl is looking at her, not unkindly.

"It means 'thunder' in Greek," Emily blurts out. And realizes immediately that she's made a mistake.

There's a ripple of sniggers round the room and the same voice as before calls out, "Oooh! Thunder!" in mock fear.

Julia frowns and goes to say something, but Emily turns away and walks over to the window. There's a surprised silence and then someone laughs, and a voice calls, "Well done, Julia.

Perhaps your welcome wasn't warm enough!" There's a general tittering, and after a moment they all start talking again.

Emily stares out across the garden, her heart racing. She can hear what the other girls are saying and it's all trivial nonsense. She can't hear anyone discussing an interesting subject, anyone who talks like Mary.

She focuses on the view in front of her. There are hills, certainly, as Charlotte promised, but the landscape has been spoiled by a great industrial sprawl with chimneys belching smoke.

But she has nowhere else to look, nowhere else to go.

When a bell rings she follows the others into a dining room. She's glad to sit down — she feels exhausted, worn out with the strangeness of it all. She takes a bite from a slice of bread and butter, but, after struggling to swallow it, she puts the rest back on her plate; she manages a few sips from a cup of tea that she nurses until it's cold and is taken from her. Then she sits silent and ignored in the midst of the chatter going on around her.

She looks for Charlotte and sees her across the room at the teachers' table, listening to Miss Wooler, nodding. To Charlotte, she remembers, this house is familiar, the teachers known to her. She isn't surrounded by strangers.

She thinks of Anne and Branwell having their tea in the kitchen with Tabby. They'll find it strange without her and Charlotte. She imagines Anne, too upset to eat. And Grasper whining at the door, waiting for her to come home.

A longing to be there with them rises in her throat, so painful it threatens to choke her.

She slams the door on that vision.

She mustn't think of them. That's the only way she'll survive this.

31

After tea she follows the others back into the schoolroom, where the girls form small knots and talk on, chirruping away like a flock of birds. How can they have so much to say to one another? All this inane chatter.

Better to be silent if there's nothing worthwhile to say.

She takes up her position by the window again until a teacher looks in and says, "Off to bed now, young ladies." There's a general movement to the hall, where lit candles have been put out for them, and, having picked one up, Emily trails behind the others.

Most of the older girls head toward the same door, so she follows them, and there in the corner by the window is the bed with her nightgown on the pillow.

While waiting her turn at one of the washstands, she secretly observes the other girls. There are only six after all, though downstairs there seemed far more of them. It looks as if they're all paired up for sleeping which means — oh, blessed relief — she can sleep by herself.

She relaxes just a little bit.

One girl, Lydia, seems to be their ringleader. With her blonde hair and blue eyes she's striking to look at, but her expression is petulant and dissatisfied.

As soon as they see Lydia's nightgown, the others cluster round, uttering little coos of admiration and fingering the fine lace and ribbon trimmings. In response to an inquirer, she drawls, "It's French, of course," in a dismissive way, as if having expensive foreign clothes is nothing special.

When at last Emily is able to wash, she finds very little water left in the jug, but she does her best with it and then retreats to her corner. With her back to them all, she undresses quickly. As she dons her own nightgown, sewn by herself under Aunt's direction and made from cotton with no trimmings whatsoever, she pulls a wry face, imagining what the other girls will say about it.

She has barely slipped under the covers when the teacher who showed her round appears at the door and stands there, arms akimbo, surveying the room. The stragglers hurry into bed and the teacher paces the length of the room, checking from side to side. When she reaches Emily's corner, she frowns.

"Miss Brontë, your shoes."

Emily blinks. She has no idea what the woman is talking about.

"I don't know what you were accustomed to do at home, but while you are here, rather than just kicking your shoes off and leaving them anyhow, you will place them neatly under your chair."

Emily can't believe this. What on earth does it matter where her shoes are? With an inward sigh she gets out of bed and moves her shoes. She looks at the teacher to see if she's satisfied, but she's wrinkling up her nose in an expression of distaste.

"And that is no way to leave your clothes. Fold your undergarments and cover them with your dress."

Emily is on the verge of uttering a tart retort, but she bites her tongue and rearranges her clothes on the chair, aware that the others are watching this charade with great amusement.

At last she's allowed to get back into bed and, having extinguished their candles, the teacher leaves them.

Emily shuts her eyes, but she can't close her ears and block out the voices, which pipe up as soon as the teacher's footsteps have died away.

"Astonishing how *some people* are brought up, isn't it?" Emily recognizes the languid voice as Lydia's.

Titters greet this remark.

Lydia goes on, "If I had underwear like that, heaven forbid, I wouldn't dream of displaying it to the world, would you? And fancy wearing stays instead of a proper corset — when you're as flat as a board, you need all the help you can get!"

More titters and someone says, "Lyddy, you're so droll."

Emily grits her teeth, but she forces herself to stay silent. They're not worth her scorn.

Another voice pipes up. "I know something you don't know."

"What?"

"Harriet has a beau."

"No!"

"You hush, little sister."

"Come on, Harriet, spill the beans. Is he handsome?"

"He has very nice eyes. And he dances divinely."

"What about you, Lydia? Have you had any *special* dancing partners?"

"Oh, dancing." Lydia's drawling enunciation invests the word with world-weary boredom. "I can see that dancing with boys is exciting for you children, but I've had other fish to fry."

Squeaks of delight follow this announcement. "Oh, do tell, Lyddy."

"It's not for your tender ears, *mes enfants*," she replies loftily, which has the presumably desired effect of inciting her audience to a frenzy of protests and questions.

"Enough!" She silences them. "Never mind about me, what about our new friend, Miss *Brontee*? Has she any admirers, I wonder? Some rustic swain who's drawn to that 'Oirish' accent? Who finds that natural I've-just-come-in-from-a-hayfield look irresistible?"

Gales of laughter greet these witticisms.

Emily wishes she had the power to launch a thunderbolt at them all.

The next moment the door opens and a sharp voice says, "Young ladies, if this noise does not cease immediately, you will all receive a black mark." The door shuts, but there are no footsteps, suggesting that the teacher is hovering outside to check that her threat has had the desired effect.

Surprisingly to Emily, it does — there are one or two muffled giggles, but no one says another word, and soon the room fills with the deep regular breathing of people sleeping.

In the dark the pattern of garlands on the bedroom curtains looks like stripes.

Or bars.

Oh, Emily, what have you done?

From misplaced pride and a desire to please Papa, she has trapped herself in this alien place among these strangers.

If only Mary were here . . .

She suddenly sees what it must have meant to Charlotte to discover two kindred spirits here. No wonder she grew so close to them, even to Ellen. She would hardly have been able to help herself.

Her own behavior toward Charlotte over that business of sharing her secret with Ellen now seems petty and shameful. Why couldn't she have been as generous to Charlotte as Anne was to her about Mary? Why couldn't she have been glad that her sister had made a friend instead of holding on to a ridiculous grudge for far too long and cutting herself off from Charlotte?

Emily's heart twists with a sudden pain — to have realized this now when it's not possible to make amends. For here Charlotte is on the other side of the impenetrable barrier that divides teachers from pupils. And Emily is alone.

So. Just at this moment she has only one option — herself. Tomorrow is her birthday and she will be seventeen. Time enough to become self-reliant. And after all, it's not the first time she's been in this situation.

She runs her fingers over the raised scar on her arm.

She managed to cope with the dog bite without anyone's help. By exerting her willpower, she endured that horrible physical and mental suffering without giving herself away. She faced the prospect of death . . . and survived.

Surely this can't be as bad?

As long as they leave her alone . . .

32

"Trappist monk."

"Vestal virgin."

Having delivered these sallies, Lydia and her ally, Harriet Lister, go sniggering down the corridor.

Emily doesn't even turn her head. She is learning not to care. If those loathsome creatures choose to amuse themselves with snide remarks at her expense, what does it matter?

In the letter that she's writing to Mary, she tells her friend what's just happened.

She can't write to Anne — it hurts too much to think of home and her sister and what they would be doing if she were there right now. And she doesn't want Anne to worry about her. But Mary knows what it's like here — she's endured it herself — and it helps to share things with her, such as all the spiteful comments the other girls make about her, jeering at her clothes, her hair, her mannerisms, and in particular her silence, which seems to goad them more than anything.

I keep hoping that if I don't react they'll eventually grow tired of the game. They haven't yet. But I can bear it . . .

She tells Mary about other tiresome things, sure that Mary would have found them tiresome too.

Like the rules . . .

You were right to warn me about them, but it's no good. I simply can't remember them all: "walk, don't run"; "use this staircase, not that"; "set out your work this way." How on earth did you manage not to break them? I keep failing and so of course I am given black marks, and what with my bad spelling, I've had to wear "the black sash" no end of times. It's all so petty and ridiculous, isn't it?

And the deadly walking ritual . . .

No one will walk with me, so the teachers are forced to partner me. I think it must be as trying for them as it is for me — the conversation limps along like a man with one leg and inevitably collapses.

How different it would be if Mary were here — the talks they would have. But then everything would be different if Mary were here. Emily would have an ally who would surely agree with her about the appalling narrow-mindedness of the school's ethos.

It seems to me that the basis of the regime here is hypocrisy: Girls are being trained to pretend to be what they're not.
Witness this sample conversation between Miss Wooler and Miss Lydia Marriot, whom Miss W. has just reprimanded for being too bold:

Miss W: "Timidity and reticence are becoming in a woman. It is what men like to see."

Miss L: "But what if you're not timid?"

Miss W: "Then you must feign it."

Can you believe it? Well, I'm sure you can because you experienced all this yourself. And the result is to turn out a set of simpering, affected ninnies, without a shred of originality or an intelligent idea among them.

As for any education we are supposed to be getting . . . where is it? Certainly it's not to be gained from all this learning by rote. Didn't you hate it too? So dull and pointless. At least on account of Charlotte's teaching at home, I can keep in the middle of the class without too much trouble and not draw unwelcome attention to myself. I really can't see the point of trying to win medals, as Charlotte did. Why work yourself to death just to sit at the top of the table?

She can't resist telling Mary about the experience of having Charlotte teach her.

Charlotte has made it clear from the start that here I am a pupil and not her sister, and she goes out of her way not to show me any favoritism. She's always finding fault with me and picking me up for small mistakes. But it's a waste of time because, whatever she does, the others, quite unjustifiably, make nasty comments about Charlotte's partiality.

But Emily's not very comfortable with this. It seems disloyal to criticize her sister, especially as Mary is Charlotte's friend too. What happened to her resolve to be kinder to Charlotte? She shouldn't have mentioned it.

Even though she's only writing the letter in her head and she's never going to send it.

∽✕∽

What she can't tell Mary, even in a pretend letter, is what she finds unbearable.

She hates having every minute of her day organized for her and never having a moment to herself. Even going out doesn't provide any relief — the deadly walks where they're organized into an orderly crocodile and move at a funeral pace to supposedly picturesque spots.

These places are too soft and cushioning. She feels suffocated.

What she wants is the exhilaration of tramping over the moors, feeling the wind blow through her. She longs to be able once more to lose herself out there in those wild spaces under that wide sky.

She can't even release the pressure of her feelings by playing the piano because it's in the corner of the schoolroom and whenever she's at leisure the other girls are there too. It's intolerable to have to spend every minute of her day in their company. It's not just that they're uncongenial and don't care about anything that matters to her.

The point is she is never, ever alone.

Even when she tries to hide herself in the garden while the others are playing ball games, as soon as she settles down in some secret nook in the shrubbery, the little Cook sisters track her down and start chanting doggerel from a safe distance.

Emil-ee Bront-ee
Tall as a pine tree
Emil-ee Thunder
Made a big blunder

She longs for solitude, to be able to escape into her imagination, into the world of Gondal. She's brought an unfinished story with her and hidden it in the drawer under her clothes. Sometimes she takes it out at night and just holds it, like a talisman, a promise that one day she'll be able to go on with it again. Knowing that she can't at the moment makes it almost too painful, but she can't help herself.

ⱺⱺ

One afternoon, Emily's late going up to wash for tea — Miss Catherine kept her back to reprimand her, not for the first time, for leaving her boots where someone might trip over them instead of stowing them neatly under the bench in the cloakroom.

As she approaches the door of the bedroom, which is ajar, Lydia's voice rings out. "Alfonso Angora! He sounds like a rabbit."

They have found her Gondal story! Paralyzed, her heart pounding in her chest, she's forced to listen.

"Go on, Lyddy. Read us some more."

"I couldn't. It's such childish claptrap."

"Oh, it's not that bad." Julia Caris's voice. "It is rather melodramatic, I grant you, but I think she has something."

"I'll say she has! A bad case of brain fever is my diagnosis. I mean, why write in such tiny print that you can hardly read?

And listen to this. 'At the approach of the ghastly specter, Alfonso —' "

Galvanized at last, Emily bursts into the room and snatches the paper from Lydia's hand. "How dare you! How dare you go into my drawer and take this. It's private."

Lydia doesn't turn a hair. "If it's so private, you shouldn't wave it around at night when people can see you. We thought it was a love letter, didn't we, Harriet? But alas, nothing so interesting."

Speechless with fury, Emily can only glare at them.

Julia has the grace to look embarrassed, but the others are obviously amused.

"Come, *mes enfants*," Lydia drawls. "Let us leave Miss Brontee to commune with her muse while we lesser mortals go and eat."

They straggle out, giggling.

Emily feels hot tears pricking her eyes. She bites hard on the inside of her lip. She won't cry. Those monsters won't make her cry.

She looks at the crumpled piece of paper in her hand. They don't know anything. They're stupid, ignorant, vile beasts. But their intrusion into her private world has ruined this story for her.

Pressing her mouth into a grim line, she tears the paper into tiny pieces. She'll throw it down the privy. Then no one will ever be able to laugh at it again.

೧೧

The next Sunday, coming back from church, Emily's surprised when Charlotte appears at her side.

In a hurried undertone, as if she's pretending to be a spy, Charlotte asks, "How are you?"

Emily eyes her uncertainly. What's happened to being-a-teacher-and-not-a-sister? Is it safe to respond naturally, to tell Charlotte how much she's missed her? She's not sure. She chooses to play it safe and, like a pupil, replies formally, "I am well. Thank you."

"Oh, Emily!"

This would be more affecting if Charlotte didn't immediately look round to see if anyone has heard her using her first name, and Emily's impulse to be spontaneous dies away. She waits to see what will follow.

Charlotte hesitates and then says, "You could try making more of an effort, you know."

"An effort?"

"Well, for a start, you could avoid getting black marks. It's easy enough."

Emily raises her eyebrows. Easy enough for Charlotte, perhaps, who cares for such things, but the thing is, she doesn't care.

"And" — Charlotte looks uncomfortable, but she plows on — "you could make an effort to speak to the others."

"I thought you said I should keep my ideas to myself."

"You know what I mean." Charlotte's tone is exasperated. "You could try to get on with the nicer ones. They're not all like Lydia Marriot."

Emily looks at Charlotte helplessly. She really doesn't understand a thing. "What would be the point?"

"It might help. You might feel better."

Emily stops dead and stares at Charlotte for a long moment. There's so much to be said, but it's so impossible to begin.

She says carefully, "I don't think I would. But thank you for the suggestion." She gestures ahead of them. "I'd better catch up with the others. Before I get another black mark."

And she walks away quickly before Charlotte can say anything else.

❧

One September afternoon their walk takes them to a rise with a good view of the local hills. The heather, Emily sees, with a clutch at her heart, has turned purple. In an instant she's seized with a fierce longing to be at home — she almost doubles up with the pain of it.

It comes to her that she can write to Papa that very evening and ask him to send the carriage for her.

So simple. She feels giddy with joy.

But . . .

If she does that, won't she have let Papa down? He would never say so, but she would feel it. The last thing she wants to do is add to his worries.

There's something else to consider too — her own pride.

If she were to give in to this weakness, it would be such a humiliation, such an admission of failure. She can't do it.

33

Emily sits in her place at the long table in the schoolroom.

Outside, in the mist, everything is still, lifeless. There are no birds flitting about in the trees silhouetted against the grey October sky. Here inside there's silence apart from the drone of Harriet Lister reciting her lesson to Miss Eliza.

Even though the room is quite warm, Emily can't stop shivering. Something's wrong. She can't eat or sleep and she's cold all the time now, especially her hands and feet. The other girls, who wear dainty lace mittens, laughed when she first appeared in her bobbled woolen gloves, but she doesn't care. It doesn't help, though — her hands are still cold.

In front of her the history textbook lies open at the page she's supposed to be learning. But there's something wrong with her brain too — whenever she looks at the sentences, her mind blurs and goes foggy. She can't even write to Mary any more, not even in her head — it's too much effort.

She can't understand it.

Unless this is the brain disease flaring up! A spasm of fear grips her. She'd forgotten about the rabies.

Don't be silly, she tells herself sternly. The dog bite was far too long ago to be affecting you now. You're tired, that's all.

Not surprising, since she spent most of the night staring out of the window again. The view isn't inspiring — across the garden to the road and beyond that to the silhouetted roofs of Mirfield — but sometimes it helps, especially if she can see the stars.

She closes her eyes, just for a minute or two. Actually, she feels so tired she could weep. She won't, of course.

These days, all the time, there's a painful tight feeling in her chest, as if somehow a heavy stone has lodged itself in her heart. It's not unfamiliar — she felt the same after Elizabeth died. But why feel it now? No one's died. But that's what it feels like, like grief.

If Papa were here, he would try to comfort her as he did then by quoting from the psalm: *The Lord is nigh to the broken-hearted.*

But it's not true. God isn't here; she's on her own and she feels displaced, uprooted, wrenched away from everything she knows, everything she loves. She can't get back to that stark treeless land of heath and stone that she longs for.

She whispers to herself, "My heart has lost its home, its true earth."

"Miss Brontë."

Emily jumps. Miss Eliza is summoning her to come and recite her lesson. She doesn't know it, but she stands up anyway and as she does so a peculiar feeling sweeps over her. She feels hot and cold at the same time and something's happening to her eyes — everything's going dark at the edge of her vision. She can hear Miss Eliza's voice in the distance. And then it fades out altogether . . .

 exe

With a sharp smell of ammonia the world suddenly swims into view again.

Unaccountably Emily finds herself staring at the hem of the tablecloth, beneath which she can see the sturdy polished leg of the table. What is she doing lying on the floor? Twisting her head, she sees Miss Eliza with a bottle of smelling salts clutched in her hand.

Emily tries to sit up, but her head swims and she's glad to lie down again.

"Just stay where you are, Miss Brontë." Miss Eliza's tone is crisp, as if she's exasperated by this interruption to her lesson. "Girls, stand back and give her some air. Miss Caris, will you please fetch that cushion and place it under her head, and Miss Upton, open the window."

Julia's face, looking rather alarmed, appears close to hers and her head is lifted and gently replaced on the soft pad.

Emily feels foolish lying there on the carpet. She'd like to get up, but somehow she hasn't got the strength.

After a while Miss Eliza says, "Can you sit up now?"

"I'll try." This time she manages it, although she feels so dizzy she'd quite like to just go on sitting here. But Miss Eliza issues some more instructions and she finds herself being hauled to her feet by Lydia and Harriet, who half-carry her to an easy chair and drop her unceremoniously onto it.

The others take their places round the table. She's half-aware of heads craning in her direction, of muffled whispers, but soon they forget about her and she lies back and shuts her eyes.

Actually, it's quite pleasant to be sitting here by the open window, feeling the cold air on her face and letting her thoughts drift aimlessly.

At dinnertime, though Miss Eliza frowns at her request, she's allowed to stay behind.

She's just starting to relax into the unaccustomed peace when Charlotte appears, her face crumpled with worry.

"It's all right," says Emily. "I only fainted."

Charlotte kneels down by her chair, and to Emily's surprise her sister takes her hand. Giving her a searching look, Charlotte says gently, "It's not all right, is it?"

At this unexpected tenderness Emily is horrified to feel her eyes pricking with tears. She blinks them away, but she knows Charlotte has seen them. "I *can* do this," she says.

For answer, Charlotte squeezes her hand. "I'm sure you can. But . . ."

She stands up with that look in her eye and set of the chin that means she's made up her mind about something and without another word she goes out of the room, leaving Emily to wonder what she means to do.

ↁↂↁ

Two days later, Emily finds out. In the middle of a French lesson with Miss Catherine she's summoned to Miss Wooler's parlor.

Asking her to sit down, the headmistress regards her with such a sorrowful look that Emily's heart turns over. Something terrible has happened at home.

Papa . . . please don't let it be Papa.

"Miss Brontë, your sister has persuaded me, much against my will I must add, to write to your father."

Emily breathes again. Not bad news. But then her hackles rise. Has Charlotte, Miss Goody Two-shoes, asked Miss Wooler to write to Papa to complain of her behavior in an effort to make her care about getting black marks? How dare she?

The headmistress is still talking. "As I said to Charlotte, I think that, given time, these things sort themselves out, and I believe her reaction is rather extreme to what is after all nothing more than homesickness, but she was insistent. So," Miss Wooler taps the piece of paper lying in front of her, "your father writes that he is sending the carriage for you tomorrow."

Emily's heart convulses so violently that for a moment she thinks it has stopped beating.

"Do you mean," she says faintly, "that I am going home?"

"Why, yes," says Miss Wooler, looking puzzled. "Isn't that what you wanted?"

She's saying something about being sorry to lose Emily and the quality of a brain such as hers, but Emily stops listening.

All she can hear is a voice inside her singing in a spirit of joyous release.

And then she remembers that Charlotte has accomplished this for her. Her sister has understood her after all, and has not only given her what she needs, but in a clever way that she can accept. For this is not her doing. *She* has not begged Miss Wooler to send her home; Papa has ordered her to come back.

What else can she do but obey?

When Miss Wooler finally releases her, she flies back to the schoolroom and, rushing past the long table, ignoring the astonished looks of the other girls and Miss Catherine's sour grimace, she goes over to Charlotte, who is sitting with the two little Cook girls, and seizes her hand.

"Thank you," she says simply, giving Charlotte's hand a vigorous shake. "Thank you so much."

Charlotte, looking a little embarrassed, glances at her pupils, who are agog at this startling interruption, but then she looks Emily full in the face and, her mouth curved in a little smile, she nods in acknowledgment.

Then Emily spins away and is sailing out of the room when Miss Catherine's voice pulls her up short. *"Où allez-vous, Mademoiselle Brontë?"*

And Emily turns and announces in a loud voice to the whole room, "I'm going to pack."

34

The minute Emily steps through the front door Grasper hurls himself at her, barking joyfully as she stoops to meet him. It's so good to clasp his solid body in her arms, to bury her face in his rough coat and smell his doggy smell.

"Emily, my dear." There is Papa in the study doorway, patiently waiting to greet her. Emily's heart misses a beat. She's only been away three months, but in that short time, he's aged — he looks more gaunt and frail than ever.

She hugs him tight for a long time. When, eventually, she lets him go, he has a good look at her, and his face changes and she sees fear in his eyes. He should be worrying about himself, not her.

"Papa, there's no need for alarm. I'm not ill."

"But my dear, you look so thin and pale. Are you sure nothing ails you?"

"No, Papa, truly." How can she begin to explain what the trouble was?

Luckily, she's saved from having to try because Anne appears and flings her arms round her. Emily squeezes her sister hard, as if she never wants to let go. Over Anne's head she sees a beaming Tabby, Aunt, looking frosty, and — "Branwell! What are you doing here? I thought you were in London?"

Her brother gives her a sheepish look. "Change of plan, old thing," he mutters.

Emily catches the tail end of a glance passing between Papa and Aunt. Something's going on, clearly, and she and Charlotte have been kept in the dark.

Her brother was due to go to London and present himself at the Royal Academy. By now he should have embarked on his new life as an art student. She gives Branwell a quizzical look, but he won't meet her eyes.

Later she must find out what's happened. Now she just wants to revel in being at home again.

As soon as she's flung off her cloak and bonnet, she strides into the kitchen. Grasper follows at her heels, as if he's afraid to let her out of his sight, and she keeps her hand on his head, reassured by that familiar sensation.

Yes, it's true, she's really here.

She stands there, taking it all in — the scrubbed table, the copper kettle suspended over the fire, the rocking chair with its faded patchwork cushion, oh, and Tiger asleep there! — and then she notices Tabby frowning at her.

"Eh, lass, I don't know what tha's been doing to thiself. Tha's no thicker than a lath. What have they been feeding thee on at yon school?"

"I'm all right, Tabby, really." Emily scoops Tiger up and pushes her face into his fur. "Hello, puss. Have you missed me?"

Tabby is not to be deflected. "Tha looks famished and that's the truth of it. And as for thi face — why, tha looks like a ghost come from the grave. Tha'll put that cat down and sit and eat some oatcake before tha does owt else."

And Emily does just that.

The portion of oatcake isn't very big, but by the time she's halfway through it, she feels as full as if she's eaten an enormous meal. Tabby doesn't let her go, though, until she's finished the last crumb.

She's longing to talk to Anne. She can't tell her about the girls finding her story — it's too humiliating and it's made her feel uncomfortable about Gondal. But Anne will help her get over it. Once they get back into their old way of talking, it will all be right again.

Before she can find her sister, Papa calls her into the study. Oh, there is the piano, its lid open, waiting for her!

She forces herself to attend to Papa. She's puzzled when he begins to question her minutely about the regime at Roe Head: what the food's like, the provision for exercise, hours of study, and so on.

Why does all this matter now? Unless he's worried about Charlotte. But there's no need.

"Papa, I think Roe Head is a very good school. I'm afraid it didn't suit me, but then I don't think any school would — the difficulty lay with me, not the school."

Papa's face clears. "That puts my mind at rest. Your sister will be glad to hear it."

"Charlotte?" Emily feels as though she's missed something.

"No, it's Anne I'm speaking of. Miss Wooler has kindly offered to keep your place for her. Naturally your aunt and I are anxious for her — after all, she's never ventured from home before — so I wanted to speak to you before I agreed to it."

Emily's breath catches in her throat. They can't mean to do it! To send Anne to that dreadful place! "What does Anne say?" she asks bleakly. She has a good idea what the answer will be.

"She seems set on going." Papa sighs. "I am quite surprised to find that our little Anne has so much determination."

Emily is not at all surprised. But as soon as Papa releases her, she rushes to find her sister. She can't do this. It's madness.

Anne listens quietly while Emily enumerates all the reasons she can think of why it's not a good idea for Anne to take her place, beginning with the tedium of the lessons and ending with the stupidity of the other girls. "And," she adds, "they are not nice. They're wealthy, spoiled misses for the most part. You won't fit in."

"I don't suppose I will. But are you sure none of them are nice? Did you talk to them much?" Her wide eyes look innocent as she asks the question, but Emily isn't fooled. Her sister knows her too well.

"Of course I didn't," she mutters. Should she tell Anne about the story? No, she can't. At the very thought of it, her gorge rises and she feels as if she's going to be sick.

"Well, then." Anne gives Emily a direct look. "I'm sorry it hasn't worked out for you, but it might go better for me. You see, I'm tired of being 'little Anne' and being the baby of the family, whom no one expects very much from. You three have had a chance to make your way in the world —"

"I didn't get very far," says Emily drily. "And nor has Branwell, by the looks of it."

Anne nods in acknowledgment, but she says firmly, "I want to see what I can do. This could be a step to making something of myself." She lays her hand on Emily's arm. "You've no need to worry about me. If it turns out to be a trial, I won't be alone."

"You won't see much of Charlotte. Not to speak to anyway. The teachers don't mix with the pupils. I mean, apart from the walking ritual, and you can't talk properly then." She shudders at the memory.

"I wasn't thinking of Charlotte." Anne gives her a seraphic smile. "I was thinking of our Savior."

Emily is silenced. When Anne talks like this, there's nothing more to be said.

She can't bear the thought of her little sister — she can't stop thinking of her in that way — at Roe Head. Anne as the butt of all that teasing. What if it brings on her asthma? If she's ill, how will she cope all on her own there, with no one to look after her?

35

When Emily wakes up in the morning, it takes her a minute to realize that she's not in the school dormitory, but in her own dear room.

She lies there for several minutes in a state of bliss, luxuriating in the silence. But then she remembers — Anne is leaving today — and a wave of misery washes over her. Emily can't imagine what it's going to be like without her.

An air of forced cheerfulness hangs over them all during breakfast and all too soon the carriage is setting off with Anne smiling bravely out at them as she's carried away.

With a heavy heart, Emily stands in the lane, waving good-bye and sending wishes after her sister, as if by an effort of will she could protect her.

Be well . . . be happy . . . be *safe*.

Back indoors, she loiters in the hall, at a loss. What is she supposed to do?

She looks into the parlor. Branwell's in there reading the paper, but he doesn't look up. There's something about his posture and his silence that signals he wants to be left alone. As she hesitates in the doorway, Aunt passes her without a word, her mouth set in a straight line.

Is the old lady being vinegary because she and Branwell have failed to live up to expectations? Or maybe this is Aunt's way of being sad. Since she came into the household all those years ago, she's kept Anne close to her. Of course, she'll miss her too.

Emily sighs. Coming home is nothing like she imagined it would be.

All morning she wanders about the house, unable to settle. In the afternoon she takes Grasper out. It feels so strange to be walking along without Anne by her side. She remembers how Ellen laughingly referred to them as "twins" when she saw them together all the time. It's true — Emily does feel as if a part of her is missing.

As she reaches the top of the first rise she stops.

There they are — the moors stretching ahead of her, harsh and wild, a vast, splendid emptiness, filled only by the soughing of the wind.

Emily stands still, gazing and gazing, letting herself be drawn out into the endless space . . .

Gradually the tight, cramped feeling she had at Roe Head, the invisible cage that closed in on her, dissolves. She can stand tall and breathe freely again. Even her sadness about Anne is soothed as the blessed familiar silence that is the absence of human voices folds itself around her like an embrace.

After a long, long time, she's brought back by Grasper whining and tugging at her dress. She laughs down at him, patting him on the head, and they walk on.

She looks about her, feasting her eyes greedily on all the familiar and beloved things: the red waxcaps nestling like jewels among the grass edging the track; the harebells nodding in the breeze. The faint ghost of the moon is floating between thin vapors of cloud and as she watches it a skein of geese appears from nowhere.

Seeing their effortless passage across the translucent blue sky, she can't help it: She has to run, and she sets off, with Grasper bounding joyfully ahead. But before she's covered any distance, her legs start to tremble and she feels breathless and dizzy.

She comes to a halt, panting and dismayed. What has that place done to her?

Grasper comes back to her and licks her hand, looking at her as if he can't understand what's wrong either.

When she's got her breath back, she continues, but at a walking pace this time. How can she have become so weak? She'd better try to eat whatever Tabby puts in front of her and build up her strength. And she must come out here as often as she can and walk and walk to make her legs sturdy again.

When she arrives home and goes into the kitchen with her hair blown all awry and her boots caked with mud, Tabby looks up from the pastry cases she's filling with jam and a smile spreads over her face.

"Bless thee, lass, there's some color in thi cheeks now."

∞

Within a few weeks, with Tabby's care and plenty of fresh air and exercise, Emily is as physically well as she's ever been. And one day she realizes, with great relief, that she's feeling more like her old self.

She's had a narrow escape, and she must be careful not to let it happen again. In future she'll follow Mary's advice and insist on doing what's best for *her*. She's already written to Mary to tell her she's home again. She'll write another letter and tell Mary what she knows now — that Mary was right.

But days pass and she doesn't write. There's a niggling voice inside her that won't be quiet — it keeps saying that her retreat was cowardly, that she should have been able to stick it out.

And it's so miserable to be back home and yet not have Anne at her side. She worries about her all the time, wondering how she's getting on.

Her days have lost their familiar pattern too. It's all very well for Papa to say that she doesn't have to do any more lessons now, but can please herself about what she studies and how she spends her time — she doesn't know what she wants to do.

She turns to the piano and day after day plays Chopin nocturnes, until Tabby is driven to say, "Can'st tha not play summat a wee bit merrier? All those doleful tunes are very lowering."

Emily is pulled up short by this. Tabby's right. All this sad music isn't doing her any good. What would Anne say? *You'll feel better if you do something helpful.* She remembers that Mary said housework was a good cure for the mopes and she decides to try making herself useful about the house. With Tabby keeping a close eye on her, she learns how to clean the knives, starch collars, and sandstone the hall passage and front steps.

Aunt isn't pleased about this development. While she approves of Emily not wasting her time in idleness, she's not happy that her niece is, as she puts it, demeaning herself by doing the work of a servant. She's horrified when she comes across Emily black-leading the range. "Look at your hands!" she cries. "No lady would let her skin get so rough and dirty."

Emily takes no notice. What's the point of having soft, white skin? And besides, she's found that Mary was right — if she keeps herself busy, she can keep troublesome thoughts at bay.

Also at the back of her mind the thought has been forming that, since she's obviously not fit for earning her living out in the world, perhaps her future lies in making herself indispensable at home, especially with Tabby getting older. As long as Papa and Tabby are grateful for what she does, and they are, it doesn't matter what Aunt thinks. Besides, there's a bonus to housework that she didn't expect — while her hands are busy, her head is free to think.

She's been at home long enough for the horror of having her story exposed to ridicule to have receded. As she goes about the house, working at this and that, she tentatively tries to resurrect Gondal. Sometimes it works. Almost without her realizing it, she stops being aware of her surroundings and her people stand before her as vivid as ever they were. If she's lucky she can lose herself in her beloved world, in the old way.

But it's not as easy as it was. Sometimes she stops and questions herself. Is this childish nonsense? Too melodramatic? She's not sure. And then she rebukes herself. Why is she taking any notice of a philistine like Lydia Marriot? But then it wasn't just Lydia but Julia too, who was more sensible than any of the other girls. But then Julia did say that her story "had something," so perhaps it wasn't so bad . . .

Oh, if only Anne were here. She'd soon tell her if she was taking things too far.

She wonders about Branwell. Though he's obviously aware that Anne and she have been writing away, so far they've kept the details of Gondal secret from him. But it's not much fun having a secret on your own. She'd much rather have someone to share it with. Would Branwell be willing to help her?

One thing that holds her back from asking him is that her brother, unpredictable at the best of times, is in a strange state at the moment, very silent and withdrawn. She's sure he's not happy — he looks so pale and strained — but for once he's not dramatizing his woes, but keeping them to himself. He's stopped going to Mr. Robinson for lessons and he spends most of his time writing, possibly about Angria, but she doesn't know because he never talks about it. She wonders what his plans are. If he has any . . .

No, on the whole it would be better not to ask him. Branwell's very different from Anne. Instead of helping her, he'll criticize her ideas and make her feel inadequate. And she can't forget his rejection of her when Charlotte first went away to school. It still smarts.

The last thing she wants is to be hurt all over again.

36

Emily still has no idea what happened regarding Branwell and the Royal Academy. Since she's been home, no one has said a word about it.

One day when she's in the kitchen with Tabby, getting the dinner ready, she asks casually, "Did Branwell ever go to London in the end?"

Tabby sighs. "Ay, that he did."

"But he didn't stay?"

"After nobbut a few days he was back with his tail between his legs and some story of being set upon by thieves who robbed him of his brass."

Emily's astounded. She looks at Tabby, and there's something in her face that makes Emily say, "You said 'story.' Don't you think it's true?"

Tabby sighs again. "Well, tha knows Maister Branwell and what a talent he has for spinning a yarn. I don't know. Has he not said owt to thee?"

Emily shakes her head. She wonders if Tabby's right. If such a dramatic event had taken place, Branwell would never stop talking about it.

But if that wasn't what happened, then what did?

~∽

That night Branwell still hasn't come home by the time Emily goes to bed.

She's just blown her candle out when she hears the click of the back gate opening and a voice, unmistakably Branwell's, roars, *"We'll drink and we'll never have done, boys,"* under the window.

Oh Lord, he's drunk. And if he carries on like this he'll wake Aunt and Papa.

Emily shoots out of bed, seizes a shawl, and, wrapping it round her shoulders, runs downstairs. There's a red glow from the banked-up fire in the kitchen, where Tiger's lying asleep on the mat, but the back kitchen is in darkness and it takes her a moment to find the latch on the back door. She has to fend off Grasper, who whines with excitement, obviously thinking they're about to go for a midnight walk.

"Sh! Lie down," she commands, finally getting the door open and letting in a blast of icy air.

Branwell is standing out in the yard, bareheaded and coatless, staring at the white snowflakes swirling round him. In the cold blue light the effect is magical, and he looks so entranced that for a moment Emily hesitates to break the spell. But this won't do; his head and shoulders are already covered with a dusting of snow and if he stays out there much longer he'll catch pneumonia.

She hisses, "Branwell!"

His face lights up at the sight of her. "Em! Come out! Have you ever seen anything so bewitching?" He starts to sing: *"Oh snow, how be-oo-tiful art thou . . ."*

For heaven's sake.

"Branny, come in. It's freezing," she entreats, and then see-ing that he isn't budging she goes out and tugs on his arm. "Do come."

He lets her pull him into the house and shut the door. As she helps him through the kitchens he leans his head on her shoul-der and says in a slurred voice, "Em, what a dear you are. My liddel sister — oops — not so liddel — my tall liddel sister . . ."

At the kitchen door she stops and says, "Listen. You must be quiet now and go to bed."

"Bed," he agrees, smiling like a fool.

Though his lurching gait threatens to pull them both over, she manages to get him up the stairs and into his room, where he collapses onto his bed and almost immediately starts snoring.

Nonplussed, Emily wonders what to do. She supposes she should take off his boots. But that's all, she tells herself. He'll have to sleep in his clothes.

She unlaces his boots and tugs them off. She's inclined to leave it at that, but then she relents and puts a blanket over him. Satisfied that he shouldn't come to any harm, she tiptoes out and shuts the door.

On the landing she stops and listens, but all is quiet in the other bedrooms. Emily shivers, suddenly realizing how cold she is, and she's glad to dive back into bed.

Branwell's been drunk before, but never as badly as this. Is it something to do with what happened in London? Is he so unhappy?

She can't let it go on any longer — she must try to find out what's wrong with him.

In the morning Branwell looks ghastly, with a pallid face and bloodshot eyes. And the way he's cradling his head in his hands suggests he's suffering from a headache as well.

When Aunt says, "How are you this morning, Branwell? Are you quite well?" he sits up and tries to look perkier, but Emily can see that he's putting it on.

Later she goes into the parlor, where he's sunk in a chair with his eyes closed. "I thought I'd try for The Meeting of the Waters today. Do you want to come?"

He opens one eye. "Sh, Em, not so loud. And no thanks, I don't want a walk."

"But it's a lovely morning. And have you realized how peaky you look?"

He does raise his head then and says with something like his old spirit, "Not half as pasty as you did when you came home."

"I expect not," says Emily mildly. "But I'm better now, though I'm not sure if I can make it all the way to the falls. That's why it would be nice if you came." She puts on an appealing face.

She's already walked nearly as far without any difficulty, but Branwell doesn't know that. She's counting on his spirit of chivalry, and it seems to work: With a sigh, he pulls himself out of the chair.

"I'd better come, I suppose, but I hope you don't think I'm going to carry you home if you collapse."

"I won't."

37

It's a bright, cold morning and fortunately the snow isn't too deep, so they can walk fairly easily. But Emily's pleasure at being out in the white perfection of the landscape under a blue, blue sky is tempered by her concern for Branwell and an awkwardness about talking to him. It's strange to be alone with him. When she thinks about it, in her whole life she's hardly ever spent time with him without one or both of her sisters present.

Perhaps Branwell's thinking the same, because he breaks the silence by saying, "I expect Charlotte and Anne would rather be here with us than drudging away at that school, don't you think?" and they fall to speculating about how the absentees are getting on.

Suddenly Branwell says, "What was it really like for you there, Em?"

Emily's taken aback. She doesn't know if she can tell him — it feels too private. But if she wants to coax out of him what really happened in London, it's only fair that she shares at least part of the truth with him. So she tells him some of her experiences, concentrating on the more obvious things — the regimentation, the tedium of the lessons, her persecution by the other girls. Not mentioning, of course, the incident involving her story.

To her surprise, he listens with a perfectly serious face and doesn't make any mocking comments at all.

When she's finished, he says, "If you ask me, it sounds bloody awful."

"It was," Emily says feelingly. And then, because she can't think of any subtle way to approach the question, she asks it directly. "What happened to you in London?"

Branwell groans. "I don't want to talk about it. I've had enough sermonizing on the subject from Aunt and Father."

Emily slips her arm through his. "I'm hardly going to judge you, am I? Considering what a success I made of Roe Head."

Branwell comes to a halt and stares up at her. "Is that how you see it? That you failed?"

"Yes," she says simply, meeting his gaze.

"I see." There is a long silence and then Branwell adds, bitterly, "Well, that makes two of us, then."

Emily doesn't say anything but squeezes his arm and they resume their walk. Branwell, deep in thought, is silent, but then he looks up at her and blurts out, "I made a complete hash of it, Em."

She makes a sympathetic face and waits for more.

He sighs. "I don't know, I found London . . . well, it wasn't anything like I expected it to be. There were so many people, you can't imagine; they crowded the pavements, constantly on the move — it made my head spin. And, do you know" — he looks at her as if he's making a confession — "instead of being grand, magnificent, the city was . . . well, dirty . . . and squalid and noisy."

Emily isn't surprised to hear this. It's how she imagined the capital to be, whereas she's always suspected that Branwell and

Charlotte thought of it as being just like Glass Town, with all its dream-like splendor.

Branwell continues, "I had no idea how big it was. I mean, we've been to Leeds and that seems big enough . . . but London! I'd studied the maps and thought I knew my way about, but I found it totally confusing — I had the devil of a job to find my hotel."

He stops walking and stoops to fondle Grasper, hiding his face from her. "You know, Em, it made me feel" — he shakes his head — "as if I was a complete nobody."

He suddenly looks very young and vulnerable, crouching there, and she's tempted to stroke his head. She doesn't, though — he'd only shy away, and she doesn't want him to withdraw from her, not after he's confided so much, come so close.

She does feel for him. For all his life, everyone has spoken to him, of him, in a way that's led him to think of himself as special. London seems to have delivered a terrible shock to his pride.

She says, gently, "But what about the Academy? What did they say about your paintings?"

He stands up, looking abject, his pallor making his freckles stand out. "I never got there, Em."

"What?" She stares at him, shocked.

He shrugs, then indicates with a gesture that they should carry on walking, and this time he takes her arm.

"On the very first day I went to the National Gallery — you know, I've always wanted to see all those wonderful masterpieces. But when I did" — he shakes his head — "I thought, What a fool I am. These are works of genius. What I've done are just worthless daubs."

"But Branny, those paintings in the gallery are by artists at the height of their powers. You can't expect to achieve that straightaway — you're just starting out. But you might one day."

"Hah!" Branwell emits a hollow laugh. "That's a nice theory, Em, but it won't wash. I still hadn't quite given up when I went to the British Museum, because Robinson said I needed some sketches of classical statues for my submission portfolio." He blows the air out of his cheeks. "There was another chap there, sketching away, and we got talking. It turns out he was a student at the Academy, and he showed me some of his drawings. They were brilliant, Em, totally brilliant. I couldn't for the life of me reveal my paltry efforts — I just slunk away. And that was it. I knew I couldn't show my face at the Academy — they'd have laughed me to scorn."

"And that's when you came home?"

"Not right away. I was a fool, Em, a wretched fool. I couldn't face telling them at home that I'd funked it, so I went and found the Castle Tavern, you know, the one I told you about, where the innkeeper, Tom Spring, used to be a prizefighter. It was full of sporting types, fellows who know how to have a good time."

"Is that where your money went?"

"Yes, well, there and . . . other places." Branwell looks sheepish.

Emily gives him a look and he says, "Oh, if you must know, yes, I lost a lot betting at a cockpit. I know it was stupid," he adds hastily as Emily opens her mouth. "You've no need to tell me, but once I'd started, I couldn't seem to stop. I kept going back until the money ran out. Then there was nothing else to do but come home."

"Oh, Branny." Emily can see, all too easily, how all this came about. Her brother is so . . . malleable. Is that the word? He makes her think of a candle flame wavering at every draft . . . bright, vital, but with nothing solid at its center. "Does Papa know what really happened?"

"He got it out of me eventually. Em, it was awful. It would have been better if he was angry. He was just . . . you know . . . disappointed. Aunt, of course, has been very snippy about it. They've both taken the line that it's better to forget it ever happened, say no more about it, you know, that sort of thing. But it's easier said than done. I can't forget it, that's for sure."

Emily squeezes his arm again.

"It hasn't helped that, when I got back, Father knew that I'd been running up a slate at the Bull. I don't know how he found out. I wouldn't have thought John Brown would have blabbed."

"Perhaps Mr. Sugden thought that with you going away, he wasn't going to see his money."

"Oh, I'd have paid him in the end," says Branwell airily, with something of his old spirit. "But the devil of it is that Father keeps trying to get me to promise not to go there again. I mean, what's a fellow to do? I've got to have some amusement. And besides, it's an expression of my artistic nature. Byron was a great tippler, you know."

Emily holds her tongue. On this subject she doesn't feel any sympathy, but there's no point in saying anything — he won't take any notice of her and she doesn't want to alienate him just when they're getting closer.

He looks up at her and says with a slightly embarrassed air, "By the way, thanks for last night. You're a brick."

Emily accepts this compliment with a brief nod. But then she says, "Don't think I'm going to keep putting you to bed, though, if you get into such a state again."

"Oh, I won't," Branwell says earnestly. "I can promise you that."

After a pause, Emily says, "So what are you going to do with yourself now? I mean, now you're not going to be an artist?"

Branwell gives her a grin and with a flash of his old manner says, "I'll be a writer, of course. I've always thought that was more my style than the daubing."

☙

The conversation about London stays with Emily.

She realizes that it's changed the way she feels about Branwell. She no longer resents all the advantages he's been given over the years, the favoritism shown toward him by Aunt. It must be hard to bear all that pressure.

She sees now that she's lucky. Of course, Aunt would prefer that she were proper and ladylike; the old lady would be over-joyed if she suddenly developed a passion for dainty, embroidered handwork, but she can easily shrug all that off. It's not the same as being expected to succeed at everything she does. Poor Branwell — maybe being a boy isn't so wonderful after all.

38

Some days later Branwell comes to find her.

"Did you know that James Hogg has died?"

"Oh no." Emily is sorry to hear the news. The writer is a great favorite with them all, and they've enjoyed his contributions to *Blackwood's Magazine*.

She's surprised that Branwell seems more excited than upset, but he soon explains why. "I've written to the editor of *Blackwood's*. There's a good chance that they'll take me on as his replacement. What do you think?" He thrusts the letter in front of her nose.

Emily reads it, wincing inwardly. "Do you think it's a good idea to sound quite so — well — sure of yourself?"

"What do you mean?"

"This, for instance." She points to a sentence: *I know myself so far as to beleive in my own originality.*

Branwell opens his eyes wide. "But it's true. Don't you think I have originality?"

"Yes, but — oh, never mind. Are you sure that's how you spell 'believe'?"

"Hah." He snatches the letter from her. "What do you know about it? Your spelling's terrible."

He's right about that, so she doesn't argue, but contents herself with wishing him good luck.

"Thanks, Em." He winks. "Here's to the start of my career as a professional writer!"

Emily's glad to see him so cheerful again, though she's not sure that his optimism is well-founded. She's pleased and touched that he's confiding in her, though. Perhaps now that they're getting on so well, it would be all right to show him some of her writing? But she's still not sure. In any case it will soon be the Christmas holidays and Anne will be back. It will be so much better to work with her rather than risk involving Branwell.

She's looking forward to seeing both her sisters. Perhaps, at last, she'll be able to have a proper conversation with Charlotte, and as for Anne — she can't wait to talk to her about all her ideas for Gondal.

ගලු

But when her sisters come home, Emily can see at once that something's wrong — they both look strained and unhappy.

Charlotte must be finding teaching a struggle, but she's wary of asking her about it. Her sister is bound to be prickly and say what she always does — that duty must come before her own feelings — and Emily doesn't want to have a row about it, especially when she's feeling so grateful to Charlotte for rescuing her from Roe Head.

She doesn't get a chance to talk to Anne privately until one afternoon when Charlotte decides not to come for a walk with them, as it's too cold.

Emily and Anne aren't put off by the raw chill in the air and, wrapped up warmly, they set off with Grasper. As soon as she can Emily launches into the subject of Roe Head. But Anne's answers are unexpected. Being at school is tolerable, she says — she likes the work and the teachers aren't so terrifying now that she's used to them.

"What about the other girls? Has Lydia Marriot been bullying you?"

Anne's eyes widen in surprise and she shakes her head. "She doesn't take any notice of *me* — I'm far too insignificant."

Even with more probing, Emily can't get any further.

Giving it up as a bad job, she launches into an account of the latest goings-on in Gondal. In the middle of a dramatic account of the assassination of Julius, she breaks off.

"You're not listening."

"Yes, I am."

But Emily can tell that Anne's mind is elsewhere. Her sister has turned away and is gazing across to the crags, whose tops are white with a dusting of snow.

Deflated, Emily falls silent too. Surely her sister hasn't lost interest in Gondal? Her heart skips a beat at the thought. No, she can't have. It must be something else; it *has* to be.

ᏪᎯ

The next morning, when she and Charlotte happen to be alone in the kitchen getting dinner ready, she asks casually, "Do you know what's troubling Anne?"

Charlotte looks up from the turnip she's peeling. She seems surprised. "Is something troubling Anne?"

"I think so." Emily is irritated. All this time Charlotte's been living in the same place as Anne, seeing her every day, and she hasn't even noticed. She measures some flour into a mixing bowl.

"Well, why don't you ask her? She's more likely to talk to you than to me."

Charlotte's tone is offhand. Doesn't she care how Anne feels?

Exasperated, Emily takes an egg and cracks it with such force on the rim of the bowl that the whole thing collapses into the flour. After patiently picking out the pieces of shell, she adds the second egg with more care and begins to beat the mixture.

"You're good at that," Charlotte observes. "My batter always goes lumpy."

Mollified, Emily shoots a quick smile at her sister and then on an impulse she says, "You know, Charlotte, I'm so glad you made Papa send for me. I . . ." Unable to find the words, she waves her spoon at the kitchen. "This is right, you know, for me."

"Good. I'm pleased for you."

But Charlotte doesn't sound very pleased. Does her sister resent the fact that she's staying at home and able to please herself?

Tentatively, feeling as though she's about to tread on a lapwing's egg, Emily says, "Now that Branwell's not going to the Royal Academy, do you still feel you should keep on at Roe Head?"

Concentrating on another turnip, Charlotte says in a flat voice, "I was talking to Papa last night and he's hoping that Branwell will try for the Academy again next year. Or if not, perhaps he should go on a tour of Europe, studying art in all the great capitals."

"Oh." This is news to Emily — perhaps Branwell himself doesn't know of Papa's plans yet. "Goodness. If he did either of those, it would cost a lot of money."

"Yes." Charlotte's face is grim.

Emily gives her sister a sympathetic glance. How she would love to go on such a tour herself. But Charlotte isn't looking — with fierce concentration and rapid movements of the knife, she's chopping the turnips into small pieces. "And then there's Anne to think of — oh, damn it."

"Charlotte!" Emily is shocked. Not so much at the sight of blood spurting from Charlotte's thumb where the knife caught her, but because her sister never swears.

Scooping up a basin of water from the pail, she catches hold of Charlotte's injured hand and plunges it in. "You must keep it in till it stops bleeding." She looks at her sister and is surprised to see that Charlotte's eyes are brimming with tears.

"Does it hurt a lot?"

Charlotte shakes her head. "It's only a scratch."

She draws her hand away from Emily's to dry it on her apron, but she takes her time about it, as if she doesn't want to look Emily in the face.

Emily touches her sleeve. "Charles, what is it?"

Charlotte opens her arms in a gesture of despair. "I don't know what to do." She looks directly at Emily. "I feel as if I must keep on at Roe Head because it saves the expense of two of us and it's giving Anne an education. It helps Papa too, if he knows that I can support myself — it's one less thing for him to worry about. But, you know . . . I was right — I'm not cut out for teaching."

Emily doesn't know what to say. It's true, of course, but it doesn't seem tactful to say so. "You didn't do too badly."

Charlotte gives her a look. "Don't be silly, Emily. You saw what I was like. But that's not the point. I wouldn't mind not being brilliant at it if I enjoyed it, but I don't. The truth is, I hate it."

"Oh, Charles." Emily would like to give her sister a hug, but she knows that Charlotte's struggling to maintain her self-control.

"And . . ." Charlotte pauses and then says in a rush, "Don't mock, but what I really want to do is try to earn my living as a writer. You know, with Branwell approaching *Blackwood's* — I had no idea it was that simple. I'd love to try something like that too." She looks at Emily half-beseechingly, as if she's desperate for her approval.

But Emily is already beaming. If Charlotte devotes herself to writing it will mean she'll stay at home. When Anne finishes at school, they'll all be together again, just like they were in the old days. "Charlotte, that's a marvelous idea."

Charlotte adds, flushing slightly, "I know it's unlikely, but I would love it if my work was published. Just think, it might be known about and talked about, perhaps even after I am dead. Don't you think that would be a fine thing?"

Emily doesn't see it at all. She has no desire to be famous. For her the whole delight of writing lies in the doing of it, in the living in her imaginary world. What does it matter if no one ever reads it? She does it for herself. She can see, though, that it matters to Charlotte.

She says encouragingly, "You never know, perhaps it *will* happen. Your writing's brilliant, just as good as Branwell's, no, better sometimes."

But Charlotte shakes her head and sighs. "No, it's just a foolish dream. I'm not going to be able to be a writer, am I? I mean, a published one."

"You must speak to Papa," says Emily decisively. "If he knows how unhappy you are teaching, he won't want you to carry on."

"What about Anne?"

"Papa can ask Aunt to pay Anne's fees. You're always saying that Anne is her little pet — she's sure to say yes."

Charlotte still looks doubtful. But Emily's determined to convince her.

"Listen, Charlotte. You missed out on your chance to be an artist because you wouldn't speak out. Don't make the same mistake again. Once Papa knows how important this is to you, he'll do everything he can to support you. I think he'll be thrilled. You know how much he values literature. And he had his own poems published, didn't he? And *The Maid of Killarney?*"

As Emily speaks, Charlotte's expression changes to one of dawning hope. "Oh, Emily, you might be right. I *will* speak to Papa."

"Do it now. I think he's in his study."

Charlotte shakes her head, laughing. "No. I won't interrupt him when he's working. I'll wait for a better moment."

39

Emily feels very pleased with herself for cheering Charlotte up and this emboldens her to try the same with Anne. The problem is she's not sure where to begin, since she has no idea what's troubling her little sister.

She's given a clue on Sunday morning in church, when, happening to glance at Anne during the sermon, she's alarmed to see her staring at Papa with a stricken look on her face. What can be the matter? Papa's theme today is cheerful, about God's mercy being shown to those who repent. There's nothing distressing there as far as Emily can see, but Anne has such awkward notions sometimes, there's no telling what might be going through her mind.

The last thing Emily wants is a conversation about religion with her sister.

As far as she's concerned, a person's relationship with God is a private matter. And her sister can always talk to Aunt or Papa. They'd be much better at sorting out any spiritual questions that might be plaguing her.

Emily's sorry that Anne's unhappy, but she can't help feeling relieved. At least it means Anne hasn't lost interest in Gondal.

ৎৎ

The next day is wild and squally, but in the afternoon the weather brightens up. Though it's still windy, Emily persuades Anne to come out and as soon as they're away from the house she plunges straight in.

"Going back to Julius's assassination . . . I thought that one of the assassins could be slain himself, but that Douglas could escape. I imagine him riding up the glen and the soldiers trapping him on a mountain ledge with a chasm below. But he manages to escape by starting an avalanche, which kills his pursuers. What do you think?"

Anne shrugs.

"Come on, you must have an opinion."

Biting her lip, Anne is silent, but then she bursts out, "I can't . . . you know . . . I can't feel very interested at the moment in these made-up people."

"Made-up people! What do you mean? You make it sound as if they don't matter."

"Well, they don't, really, do they? Not compared to real life."

Emily comes to a dead stop. At once the wind drives against her as if it's determined to beat her down.

Did Anne really just say that? Did she really say that their heroes and heroines didn't matter?

A kind of panic seizes her, making her want to lash out. If she stays where she is, she'll say something unforgivable.

Setting her mouth in a grim line, she strides off, splashing through the mud and yanking Grasper's lead to make him follow.

What's happened to Anne in the space of a few short months? How can she say such a thing? The people of Gondal are *more* real than anything in ordinary life. They are her friends, her companions. How can Anne say that they don't matter?

Grasper stops to sniff at something.

"Come on!" In turning to speak to him, she catches sight of Anne.

Her sister is standing where she left her and from the shaking of her shoulders Emily can tell that she's sobbing.

Sighing, Emily goes back to her and silently passes her a handkerchief.

Eventually Anne lifts her tear-stained face and gives Emily a wobbly smile. "Sorry."

Her sister's shivering and her teeth are chattering. They should go home, but as Emily starts forward, Anne puts a hand on her arm. "The thing is — I just — oh, I don't know how to put it into words."

Emily waits. Anne takes a deep breath. "If you want to know, I'm frightened that I'm going to go to hell."

Emily gapes at her. "What! Whatever gave you that idea?"

"Well, I try so hard to be good, but I'm always failing. I'm sure I can't possibly be one of the Elect and Mr. Allbutt says —"

"Mr. Allbutt is a fool!" Emily's suffered many of the clergyman's tedious homilies at school. "You surely don't believe all that Calvinistic nonsense?"

"I . . ." Anne falters. "I don't know. All the ministers at Mirfield speak of it with such certainty, it makes me think . . . well, there has to be something in it, hasn't there?"

Emily stares at Anne, feeling completely at a loss. She can't understand the tangles both her sisters seem to get themselves into about these things. For her it's simple — for some time now she's felt fairly certain that if God is the Creator of all things, then He has made her as she is, and so she must accept herself.

But Emily can't just dismiss Anne's ideas for the claptrap she thinks they are — it would only upset her more. "Listen." She takes hold of Anne's cold hands. "You must speak to Papa. I don't know how to make you feel better about this, but he'll know what to say."

In fact, Emily's not so sure about that. Lately she's been finding it harder to accept that God, if He's good, could bring Himself to condemn sinners to everlasting punishment, but Papa, she knows, truly believes in the Last Judgment and the separation of humankind into sheep and goats, the saved and the damned. But Anne isn't an unrepentant sinner. Perhaps Papa will be able to convince her of that.

Anne is looking doubtful. "I don't like to bother Papa — it's not that important."

"Of course it is. Promise me that you'll talk to him before you go back to school."

Anne nods. "All right, I will."

"We must go home. You're freezing."

They walk back in silence, each deep in thought.

Emily feels shaken. She would like to get hold of those wretched clergymen at Mirfield and give them a piece of her mind. And it's not just Anne who's affected — it feels as if there's a huge barrier between Emily and her sister now. Anne has moved away from her to a place where she can't reach her.

As for Gondal . . . Emily has a bitter taste like ashes in her mouth. She can hardly bear to think about it, it hurts so much.

ॐ

When they return to the parsonage, Emily goes up to her bedroom to change her damp stockings and she finds Charlotte there, staring out of the window.

"Charles? What are you doing up here in the cold?"

Charlotte turns and Emily can see that she's been crying. "I spoke to Papa."

"Oh." Emily's heart sinks. It doesn't look good. "What did he say?"

"He said . . ." Charlotte stops and her mouth twists into a grimace. She takes a deep breath and goes on, "He said that writing wasn't a suitable profession for a woman and, even if I was determined to pursue that path, I was very unlikely to make any money. And he said writing was all very well as a leisure activity, but I shouldn't let it interfere with real life."

"Oh, Charlotte." Emily sinks onto the bed, at a loss for words. She can't believe that Papa is *so* conventional. But then, thinking about it, of course it's all of a piece with Papa approving of them sewing because Mama was a fine needlewoman and he thinks it's appropriate for girls, and with Branwell always being the favored one just because he's a boy.

Even so, she's dismayed by Papa's attitude to writing. He's let them read whatever they wanted and he's never stopped them from writing. Why, it was Papa who, as each of them turned twelve, gave them their precious writing desks. She thought he approved of all their literary activity and took it seriously.

"How can Papa think that what we do is just a nice hobby?"

Charlotte shrugs. "Well, apparently he does. And he said that if I let myself dwell too much in imaginary worlds I would probably make myself unhappy."

"He said that?" Emily is astounded.

It has never occurred to her that she shouldn't immerse herself in Gondal — to do so is as natural as breathing.

Charlotte continues, "And he said that I should look to God for support rather than my imagination."

"But that's ridiculous!" This time Emily can't help herself. "I don't agree with Papa. After all, God has given us our imagination, hasn't He? He must want us to use it. Why does it have to be a choice between God and writing? Why can't we have both?"

Charlotte looks shocked. "You shouldn't say such things. And Papa must be right, mustn't he? He knows far more about these things than we do."

Emily presses her lips together. Papa is wrong about this, she's sure he is. But there's no point in arguing with Charlotte. She'll never get her sister to agree. She changes the subject. "So what are you going to do now? Do as Papa says?"

"Of course. What else can I do?" Charlotte's voice rises into a wail. "I'll go back to Roe Head and try to love teaching and sewing and all those other things a woman is supposed to devote herself to as much as I love reading and writing. And forget about earning my living as a writer."

She rushes out of the room, banging the door shut behind her.

Emily puts her head in her hands. She'd like to crawl under the bedcovers and hide from it all — her sisters' misery, and her own heartache.

৩৯৩

Just when things seem at their bleakest, Charlotte announces that Mary is coming to stay for a few days.

Emily's so glad to hear this. She can't wait to see Mary again. Apart from anything else, she's been worried because Mary never answered her last letter telling her she had returned home. Perhaps she hadn't received it? In any case, Mary's bound to cheer them all up.

When she arrives it's obvious that Mary's in good form, and their first evening is just as jolly as Emily hoped it would be. Mary entertains them by telling them about her youngest brother, who has recently decided to wear blue clothes. "Just imagine, everything blue — trousers, coat, even his waistcoat!"

"Why on earth would he do that?" Branwell tugs at the sleeve of his green coat, carefully chosen to contrast with his fawn trousers.

"I've no idea — it's some silly notion he's got into his head that it's more dignified to wear one color. His schoolmates tease him no end, saying he's turned into a sailor, but he doesn't care."

"He sounds brave," says Emily. "Not giving in to public opinion."

Mary flashes her a smile. "Yes, indeed. I think he is." Clasping her hands together, she leans forward. "But enough of that. Come on, I want to hear all about Roe Head."

Emily stiffens. But it's all right. Mary's looking at Charlotte. "Do tell, what are the inestimable Wooler sisters really like?"

Charlotte laughs. "You mean you want to know whether they have any secret vices. Miss Catherine, an opium addict? Miss Eliza, a secret gambler? I'm sorry to disappoint you, but no, they're just as they seem."

Mary looks crestfallen. "Well, what about the girls? What are they like?"

"Oh, the girls." Charlotte rolls her eyes. With a wicked grin, she launches into satirical character assassinations of her pupils.

Emily, laughing along with the rest, is delighted to see her sister in this mood. It's like having the old Charlotte back. Branwell's grinning his head off and even Anne, flushed pink with amusement, looks less haunted.

What a blessing that Mary's come. It's doing them all a power of good.

෨෬

Later, Emily lies in her camp bed, listening to Charlotte and Mary talking. Actually, they're arguing, in a good-humored way, about novels. Charlotte earlier claimed that all writers since Scott were worthless and Mary is taking her to task.

"Who do you mean? What have you read since we last met?"

Charlotte has to admit that she hasn't read any current fiction.

"Oh, Charlotte! Then your assertion is nonsense. Shame on you! I've just read Balzac's *Le Père Goriot*. It's a splendid book. You should try it."

"You read it in French!"

"Yes, slowly, of course, and with my dictionary at my elbow. But it was worth it. He says right at the beginning that it's not a romance, and he's right. I mean, Scott's good in his way, if you want an adventurous romp, but in Balzac everything seems just like real life, it's so believable."

Charlotte snorts. "I experience real life every day. When I read I want something different, you know, to take me away from it."

"Well, I enjoy that too, but this is something new — I feel as if he shows you the truth of what people are really feeling. It's very affecting."

At Mary's words, a thrill shoots through Emily, like a flame sparking into life. She would never desert her beloved Scott, but Mary has a point. Aiming to be real, to examine the human heart in your writing . . . What a fine thing that would be, if you could achieve it.

Lying there in the dark, she's filled with a sense of excitement, of anticipation. Since the conversation with Anne, she's hasn't wanted to think about Gondal, but Mary's words have inspired her. She can't wait to try out this new idea in her writing.

40

Two days later, when Emily's in the kitchen making bread, Mary comes in and flops onto a chair. "Hello, my dear. I've come to see what you're doing. Gosh, it's nice and warm in here."

Emily gives her a shy smile. Normally she'd hate being observed by anyone who wasn't one of the family, but she doesn't mind Mary watching her. Anyway, she's glad to have a chance to talk to Mary by herself.

Mary seems content to sit quietly, though, until Emily's in the middle of kneading the dough, when she suddenly says, "Do you enjoy doing that?"

Emily looks up, surprised. "Yes, I do."

"Hmm." Mary ponders this and then says, "Well, I like to be active, but I shouldn't want to spend my whole life bound to housework."

Emily's not sure what to say. She doesn't feel that housework is bondage — she enjoys it and finds it liberating, as she can think about her writing while she's doing it. But she still doesn't feel able to confide in Mary about her stories. What if Mary wanted to see them? After what happened at Roe Head, Emily never wants anyone outside the family to read her efforts. And now that she knows what Mary thinks of Scott, what would she say about Gondal?

In the lengthening silence, Emily blurts out awkwardly, "Is there something you *would* like to do?"

Mary looks at her and grins. "Indeed. I mean to earn my own living and be beholden to no one."

Emily sighs inwardly. This wretched subject again — earning one's own living.

Why is everyone so obsessed with it?

Mary has picked up a wooden spoon and is twirling it between her hands. "But I wouldn't like to be doing what Charlotte does." She pulls a face. "Certainly not under the terms she's agreed to. She told me that after paying Anne's fees and putting something by for their clothes, she's nothing left."

This is news to Emily. It makes Charlotte's self-sacrifice even more pointless and awful. She fixes Mary with her eyes. "Oh, would you speak to her about it? And get her to see how stupid it is? Because she won't listen to me. She's afflicted with this ridiculous sense of duty and she's going to make herself ill if she carries on."

Mary puts down the spoon and lays a hand on Emily's arm. "I'll try. But you know Charlotte. Once she's set her mind on something . . ." She sighs. "Oh, let's hope, my dear, that we don't have to be teachers or bonnet makers."

Emily's amused by Mary's vehemence. Of course *she* has no intention of being any such thing. Remembering the conversation they had last time Mary was here, she says mischievously, "You don't fancy a life of trimming bonnets with hand-worked roses, then?"

"No, indeed." Mary laughs. "I want to travel if I can and see as much of this world as possible . . . and I hope I might find a better means of earning my livelihood in another country, where they don't have such narrow ideas of what women are capable of."

Suddenly it's not so funny. Mary means to go far away? Emily didn't know. Perhaps they could still go on writing to each other? But then, Mary didn't reply to her last letter. She's screwing up her courage to mention it when Mary stretches and says, "Anyway, whatever happens, I will not stay at home." Her mouth twists with distaste as she says the word.

Emily almost gasps. Tentatively she says, "Why not? What's wrong with home?"

"Oh, I couldn't bear it. To be trapped in the same daily routine, to see the same small group of people all the time . . ." She shudders. "I know myself too well. Without variety and a wider circle of social contacts, I should never survive. Anyway" — jumping to her feet, she gives Emily one of her dazzling smiles — "I'd better leave you to your bread making or your dough might not rise."

She bounces out of the kitchen, leaving Emily staring after her.

Something inside her has shriveled. She thought that she and Mary were so alike and had similar ideas about things. But she was wrong. To her, home means . . . oh, everything. She can't put it into words and, even if she could, she can see now that Mary would never understand.

ᐁᐁᐁ

By the next morning Emily's recovered somewhat. After all, just because she and Mary don't agree about everything, it doesn't mean they can't be friends. She's looking forward to more conversations, especially if they manage to have another walk together, just the two of them.

But over the next day or two it becomes obvious that this isn't likely to happen, and it's all because of Branwell. Whatever they're doing, whether they stay in or go out, he insists on being with them.

At first Emily doesn't think anything of it — she's just waiting for him to go away and leave them to it. But he doesn't. And it gradually dawns on Emily that it's Mary who's keeping him there.

She'd noticed on Mary's last visit that Branwell seemed to like their guest's company; now she can see that he's definitely interested in her. It's frustrating — it means there's no chance for any of the rest of them to take Mary off for a private chat.

As Emily hangs back, scowling and watching Branwell lavish attention on Mary, it dawns on her that Mary herself doesn't seem to mind. In fact, she's positively encouraging him, making a point of sitting next to him at mealtimes and walking with him when they go out.

With a sickening jolt she sees that Mary might be becoming fond of Branwell. Surely not! Mary's just being polite, that's all.

But she can't deceive herself for long. Mary isn't polite — she behaves as she wants and says what she feels. She begins to watch Mary carefully. Everything about her behavior suggests that she's only interested in Branwell; her eyes are always on him.

Emily is astonished. Mary seemed such a strong, self-reliant person — someone she could really admire — and now it appears she's just like other women Emily's read about, letting themselves become infatuated and behaving foolishly.

After a while Emily can't bear it any longer. She takes herself off to the kitchen and starts peeling the potatoes for dinner, relieved that Tabby's still out shopping so she won't have to talk.

She'd been so looking forward to this visit, to seeing more of Mary and getting to know her better, and now *this* had to happen.

Oh, this love! If that's even what it is. Emily pulls a face and stabs her knife into a potato. It won't do you any good, Mary.

She's fond of her brother, of course, but she's amazed that Mary has fixed on him. He's so unsuitable for her. He's not likely to be careful of Mary's feelings, and she's bound to end up dissatisfied and unhappy.

What a nuisance Branwell is. Why couldn't he have left Mary alone? Savagely Emily chops the potatoes in half. But then she pauses, and putting down the knife, she presses her hands against her chest, against her heart.

She can't really blame Branwell. Mary knows her own mind. And it's obvious to Emily now why Mary didn't answer her letter. Apart from that one time in the kitchen, not once has Mary sought her out, not once has she tried to have a personal conversation with Emily.

Emily lets her hands fall.

She can't avoid the truth any longer — Mary isn't really interested in her at all.

41

When Mary leaves them, Emily tells herself she's glad she doesn't have to see Mary making a fool of herself over Branwell anymore.

But deep down, she feels wretched.

Mary's not the only one to behave idiotically. She herself has been a fool too, believing there was more to their relationship than there was. She let herself get carried away by the idea of who she thought Mary was, when really, she hardly knew her. On the basis of a few conversations and letters she had let herself believe that she and Mary were alike, no, more than that, were soul mates. In reality, they didn't have all that much in common. Look at how Mary flirted with Branwell. Even more distressing, look at what she feels about home!

Emily winces. She doesn't just feel wounded, she feels annoyed with herself for being such an idiot. And she shouldn't have gone so far — revealed so much of herself to Mary. She feels ashamed, as if she's violated what is most precious to her — her inner private self.

Ruefully she rubs her scar. When the dog bit her, she coped by herself.

This has been a useful lesson, she thinks grimly. She won't

fall into that trap again. Never again will she put her trust in someone she doesn't know.

享

After the diversion of Mary's visit, Charlotte and Anne lapse back into gloom too. And then they have to go back to school.

Emily feels terribly sorry for both of them. Charlotte's so unhappy, and as for Anne, well, she talked to Papa and it seemed to help a bit, but Emily's not convinced that she won't succumb to the same doubts once she's back at Roe Head, at the mercy of those frightful clergymen. What if she agonizes so much over this she becomes ill?

Emily can't help feeling guilty. It's as if both her sisters are going into battle while she stays safe at home.

"But it's no good," she tells herself. "I can't do it. I've tried and I've failed."

This dismal thought does little to raise her spirits. Altogether this last month has been horrible. She feels just as miserable as she did when Anne went off to Roe Head last term, no, worse, because her hope of a friendship with Mary has died and her treasured collaboration with Anne on Gondal has ended.

But she resolves that this time she won't mope: It doesn't achieve anything. Instead, she grits her teeth and does her best to comfort herself with Grasper's company; she starts to learn a new and challenging sonata by Beethoven; and she attacks the housework with vigor, launching into the spring-cleaning even though it's only January and causing Tabby to declare, "Bless the lass, she's been spirited away by the fairy folk and they've left a whirlwind in her stead!"

Even though the thought of Mary makes her feel sad, Emily hasn't forgotten the electrifying effect of Mary's comments about Balzac and her desire to see if she can attempt something more real in her own writing. She keeps putting it off, not wanting to reawaken the memory of that awful scene with Anne, but one afternoon, feeling at a loose end, she thinks she might just have a look at an old Gondal story.

If she finds it upsetting, she can always stop.

Within minutes, she's pulling a face. There's romance by the cartload, but insight into the human heart? The adventure proceeds at such a pace that the characters scarcely have time to breathe, let alone feel. Maybe Julia Caris was right — it is rather exaggerated. And she can see now that she was so eager to get the tale told that she's not given enough thought to the way she was telling it. In places her language is far too elaborate. What an idiot! Just showing off that she knows all these clever words. And then sometimes the style's so clumsy that she's not even saying what she meant to.

With a snort of disgust Emily tosses the story aside. Call herself a writer! She'd be better sticking to making bread — at least her loaves are nothing to be ashamed of.

She stands up and paces about the room.

Does this mean that she'd better give up the attempt? But if she enjoys doing it, what does it matter how *good* her stories are? It's not as if she has any desire to be published. She's not like Charlotte and Branwell, wanting "to be forever known," as Charlotte puts it.

But it does matter. It matters to her. She wants her stories to be the best she can make them.

Sitting down, she picks up the story and looks at it again. Yes, she can see now. She needs to slow it down, not everywhere, but here, for instance, and here. At these points she needs to show in more depth what the characters are feeling. And she needs to write more plainly, more directly, and think more carefully about choosing words that say exactly what she means. Yes, that's it.

Throwing back the lid of her writing desk, she fetches out a sheet of paper. Such a familiar action and yet how long it's been since she last did this! She can feel her pulse racing in anticipation.

Taking a deep breath, she dips her pen into the ink, and begins a new version of the story.

Within minutes she's absorbed and she only realizes it's time for tea when Branwell comes to fetch her.

"Didn't you hear me? I've been calling you for ages. What are you doing?"

Called back from far away, Emily lifts her head and gives him a dazed look.

"Nothing. Just writing."

∞

"Just writing," that is, rewriting, becomes a new, engrossing interest. It's not the same as creating new stories — it doesn't engage her deeper self in the same way — but, without Anne, she doesn't feel like doing that anyway. Reworking old material doesn't salve her heartache, but it helps — while she's doing it, she can't think about anything else.

It drives Emily back to the library at Ponden Hall in search of books, not her old favorites, but new books that she reads in a new way — instead of just letting herself be carried away by the story, she's alert to what the writers are doing and how they're doing it, and then she tries to apply what she's discovered to her own writing.

She spends as much time as possible on it, scribbling away on a corner of the kitchen table while Tabby bustles round her, or sitting in her bedroom by the window so she can see the moors when she looks up. After tea, she takes her work into the parlor and joins Branwell at the table.

One evening after they've both been writing for some time, Branwell throws down his pen with a sigh of satisfaction. "Listen to this, Em!" he exclaims and he proceeds to read her a stirring passage in which his hero, Alexander Rogue, now the Earl of Northangerland, declares his love for his wife, saying he would rather spend an hour in her arms than an eternity in heaven.

He reads well, his eyes flashing and his voice trembling with passion.

Emily finds it thrilling. "Branny, that's marvelous," she says when he's finished, and she means it. Used to his depictions of wars and endless political wrangling, she had no idea he was capable of writing like this. She feels a glow of pleasure that at long last he's shared this with her.

She can't help being envious, though. How is it that Branwell can write about feelings so easily? But then again, she's not so sure about his style — it's very ornate in places, definitely showing off.

"It's not bad, is it?" He grins at her.

On an impulse, she says, "Can I read you something?"

"Of course."

She flicks back a few pages in her notebook, looking for a particular passage. It's a scene from a story she's been reworking in which Fernando, leaving his home for Gondal, bids farewell to his sweetheart, who is also his foster sister, and she's tried hard to bring out the complexity of his emotions. As she reads it her voice trembles slightly.

"Do you think I've got him right?" she asks. "Is that how a man would feel?"

She braces herself as she waits for his reaction. Has she made a mistake in sharing this with him? Is he going to humiliate her again?

But to her amazement, Branwell says, "I'd say you've got him to a T. By gosh, Em, you've come on a bit since those little tales you used to write."

Heat rushes to Emily's cheeks. She feels absurdly pleased at his unexpected praise.

"Read me some more." Branwell's tone is peremptory.

"Really?"

He nods, leaning forward in anticipation.

Somewhat self-conscious at first, Emily reads on, but soon she is caught up in the tale and forgets her audience.

"Stop!"

Emily blinks in surprise.

"I don't think that's right. Fernando wouldn't kill himself."

"He would. That's exactly what he'd do."

And they are off, arguing fast and furiously.

They're still at it when Papa looks in on his way to bed to say good night. As soon as he's gone, Branwell gathers his papers, saying it's time he was off — to the inn, she guesses.

Left alone, Emily feels suddenly bereft.

This is the time for their nightly walk round the table, she, Anne, and Charlotte. If only Branwell had stayed in, she might have persuaded him to join her. It was so much fun to be working together again.

ᎧᎧ

One morning a few weeks later Branwell seems particularly gloomy, and Emily fears he's received a rejection from the editor of *Blackwood's Magazine*. Casually she asks, "Have you heard anything from Mr. Blackwood?"

"No, and I don't understand why. I'm surprised people like him can't see genius when it's under their noses." Branwell heaves a deep sigh. "Father thinks I'd be better concentrating on the painting than expecting anything to come of the writing. And he thinks it's time I was earning some money . . ."

"He said that?" Emily is surprised. Though Papa seems happy for Charlotte to earn her living, no one has ever suggested that Branwell should be doing the same.

"Not in so many words, no. He suggested I should paint some portraits — local dignitaries and so on. He thought it would be good practice for me and then he said he couldn't quite see his way to financing the Europe tour just yet, so putting two and two together, I think it was a hint that I should stir myself." He blows the air out of his cheeks. "It's not a bad idea, I suppose, since I'm not getting anywhere with the writing at present."

He doesn't sound very keen and Emily can't blame him. Painting portraits doesn't sound like a lot of fun.

She regrets it for herself too. What if his painting puts an end to their writing conversations? Branwell's far more dogmatic than Anne, of course, and he always believes he's right, which can be exasperating. And it irritates her that he doesn't seem to care if his writing's slapdash. Though she's suggested that he might try to improve pieces, he never does — whatever pours out is left, unedited.

But sometimes working with him is nearly as good as working with Anne and he's even helped her to come up with ideas that could turn into new stories, because his suggestions make her realize she wants to do just the opposite.

Emily smiles to herself, thinking of how he complains that her female characters have too much to say for themselves. Little does he know that comments like, "Your Augusta is more like a man," only serve to confirm that Augusta is just as she wishes her to be.

42

The first sitter to present himself at the front door of the parsonage, looking rather awkward, is John Brown, the sexton. As Emily takes him upstairs she wonders whether Branwell has persuaded his friend to have his portrait painted to hoodwink Papa, but Branwell later assures her that it's a proper commission, paid for by the Freemasons.

John Brown is followed in due course by other sitters, and while Emily is glad that Branwell seems to be having some success, she's annoyed that he seems to expect her to play the part of a maid, answering the door and showing up the visitors while he grandly waits in his studio.

One afternoon the doorbell rings while they're both in the parlor and Branwell immediately rushes from the room, saying, "I expect that's for me. Open the door, will you, Em?"

She calls after his retreating back, "I will not. I'm not your servant, you know." After a few minutes she hears the front door open and close and smiles to herself. Branwell has been forced to give in.

The next moment she hears a cough and a voice says, "Excuse me." Startled, she looks up to see a young man standing in the doorway.

Emily is taken aback. Before she can gather her wits and send him upstairs, he's in the room.

"I beg your pardon. Your servant let me in — she said she had to get back to her stewpan and that I was to wait in here."

Silently cursing Tabby, Emily stares coldly at the visitor. She was in the middle of revising a critical passage — Augusta is faced with the choice between revealing the existence of her illegitimate child or killing it. Emily was struggling to convey the anguish of Augusta's inner conflict and the intrusion of this young man has broken the spell.

He doesn't seem put off in the slightest by his chilly reception, instead saying, "Might I introduce myself? I'm Robert Taylor."

She knows him by sight from church — his father is a trustee and an acquaintance of Papa's — but she's never spoken to him. She doesn't intend to start now. Countless tea parties with the curates have taught her that not replying is the quickest way of preventing further unwelcome attentions. But Robert Taylor seems impervious to this tactic.

Advancing to the table, he continues, "And you, I believe, are Miss Emily? I'm sorry I've interrupted you — writing to your sisters, are you?" He nods at the papers scattered in front of her.

She immediately sweeps them together. In doing so one of the pages falls to the floor and the visitor moves to pick it up. "I can get it," Emily snaps and, plucking up the sheet of paper, she dashes it down on the pile and puts her arms over it protectively.

She's affronted. How dare he speak about her writing? It's private. And how does he know Charlotte and Anne are away from home? Branwell's obviously been tittle-tattling. She wonders briefly whether Robert Taylor is one of Branwell's cronies from the Black Bull. If he's one of the young men encouraging Branwell to drink far more than is good for him, then she dislikes him even more.

She's certainly not going to ask him to sit down, but nor will she demean herself by showing him upstairs. Branwell must come and fetch him. "You *are* expected, I take it?" she asks. If not, she can send him packing.

"Oh yes. Your brother is going to paint me."

Emily doesn't comment. What's keeping Branwell? She doesn't like the way this young man keeps looking at her.

At last she hears Branwell running down the stairs. Thank heavens for that.

Her brother hastens in, full of apologies. "Taylor, my dear fellow. I'm sorry you've been left down here." He glowers at Emily.

"Not at all. I have been delighted to make the acquaintance of your charming sister."

Emily gives Robert Taylor a Medusan glare. If only she *could* turn him to stone.

But he's smiling broadly at her. "I said to your brother here, I hope he's going to cast me in a flattering light. If he creates a true likeness of my ugly face, it'll frighten anyone who looks at it."

What a vain fellow. He obviously doesn't believe a word of what he's saying, but if he's expecting her to contradict him, he'll be disappointed. Why on earth doesn't Branwell take him away? She frowns at her brother, who finally takes the hint.

"Come on, Taylor. We'd better get started." Branwell takes his friend's arm.

"Very glad to meet you at last, Miss Emily."

She acknowledges this with a stiff nod. And praise be, the two of them are finally going.

Out in the hallway, Robert Taylor says something that makes Branwell laugh.

Emily grits her teeth. They'd better not be talking about her.

ᘒ

When Branwell comes down for tea, late and with his hands stained with paint, Emily says, "I'm not opening the door for that young man when he comes for his sittings. You must let him in yourself."

Branwell laughs. "I don't know why you've taken against him. He's a perfectly pleasant fellow."

Emily doesn't deign to respond.

"Anyway, he's taken a shine to you."

"How could he? He doesn't know anything about me."

"Well, he's seen you often enough at church and been admiring you from a distance, so I now hear."

Emily snorts.

"As for not knowing anything about you, I think he's worked you out pretty well."

"What do you mean?"

"He says you've got fiery eyes. And he seems to find that rather appealing, for some strange reason. I said he was right — you are a firebrand, but that he didn't have to live with you and he wouldn't find your temper so appealing if he did."

Emily throws a bread roll at Branwell's head, but he just ducks and laughs.

Grasper, whose eyes have never left the table, immediately wolfs down the unexpected treat. When he's done, Emily calls him over and he snoozles his nose into her face. Fondling his head and not looking at Branwell, she says, "I'd rather the two of you didn't talk about me."

Branwell shrugs. "I've no desire to discuss you — can't think of anything more boring. Don't!" he adds as she picks up another roll. "You'll give the poor dog indigestion. But I can't help it if Taylor wants to talk about you, can I?" And he gives her an angelic smile.

࿊

When Robert Taylor comes for further sittings, Emily makes sure she keeps out of his way. She can hear the two of them talking and laughing upstairs and if she finds this too disturbing she takes herself out for a walk.

One afternoon on her way to her bedroom she notices that the studio door is ajar. Branwell's not about and, suddenly curious to see how he's been getting on, she slips in.

The room, which still smells slightly of the malt and grain that used to be stored there, is in a fine old state of disorder, with half-finished canvases stacked anyhow against the wall, dried-up brushes sitting in jars, and splashes of paint on the floor. The easel is over by the window and she goes across to look.

She has to admit that her brother has caught his friend's likeness rather well. Robert Taylor does look pleasant enough, with his wavy brown hair and open expression, but it's a bland, rather ordinary-looking face. There's nothing about it to hold the onlooker's attention or suggest that this person would be interesting to know.

She remembers what he's supposed to have said about her and she grimaces.

Silly nonsense.

Then she pauses. Supposing that it was true? Supposing he did admire her? Emily Jane, beloved object of someone's affections . . .

She shakes her head with a wry laugh.

Remembering the way that Mary behaved with Branwell, surely it would be tedious to be someone's beloved object, to have them following you around all the time, hanging off your every word, never leaving you alone. It would be suffocating.

Unless her lover was someone extraordinary, someone with a proud, passionate soul who felt things deeply and understood her need for freedom. In other words, someone like one of her Gondal characters.

But such people only existed in books. In real life you were saddled with someone like Robert Taylor, someone about as exciting as a dishcloth.

With a sigh she leaves the studio, closing the door on his smiling painted face.

43

Eventually the portrait is finished, the carrier takes it off to Stanbury, where the Taylor family are reportedly "very satisfied" with it, according to Branwell, and Emily doesn't give Robert Taylor another thought. She occasionally catches sight of him at church gazing in her direction, but she simply turns her head away.

The chilly spring turns into a miserable summer — day after day of rain — but one afternoon it eases off and a watery sun comes out. It's a good opportunity to return a book to the library at Ponden Hall.

Just as Emily's leaving the house with Grasper, Papa catches her.

"Will you take this note to Mr. Taylor? It's about the church rate meeting, so I'd like you to wait for his reply, if you don't mind."

She can easily make a detour to the Taylors' farm on her way home and with luck she won't have to speak to Mr. Taylor. Then she remembers, with a frown, that that foolish young man, Robert Taylor, might be there.

But she only has to hand the note to a servant and wait on the doorstep. She's not likely to bump into him. Smiling at Papa, she takes the note.

It's quite late by the time she reaches the Manor House. The servant who opens the door tells her that "the maister" is in the barn, if she just wants to step across and speak to him. The woman points to the large stone building adjoining the house.

Skirting the puddles, Emily crosses the muck-bespattered yard and hovers uncertainly on the threshold of the barn. When her eyes have adjusted to the gloom, she spies Mr. Taylor at the far end talking to one of his hands. They seem to be discussing a cow that, penned in by straw bales, is lowing mournfully.

Emily hesitates; she doesn't want to interrupt them. But just then Grasper catches sight of the cow and gives a sharp bark.

Mr. Taylor looks round and, seeing her, comes forward. "Miss Emily! What can I do for you?"

Silently, Emily proffers the note.

"From your father, is it? Now let me see."

As he reads the missive, Emily gives him a covert glance. He's not as tall as his son, but he has the same wavy brown hair, although his is greying at the temples, and the same round face, albeit with a ruddier complexion.

"This needs an answer, but it won't take a minute. Will you come into the house while I write it? It looks as if it might rain again."

Emily shakes her head and then, remembering that Mr. Taylor has the power to affect Papa's income, she adds, more politely, "No, thank you. I'd rather stay out here."

"As you wish. Go through the barn if you like and have a look round. You'll find my horses stabled out at the back there, if you're interested."

Emily's eyes widen. Of course she's interested. "Should I tie up my dog?"

"There's no need. Shep and Nell are chained up in the side yard and my Jessie's in the house — she's due to whelp soon."

He goes off and Emily follows Grasper into the barn, glad to see that the farmhand has gone as well. Grasper thrusts his nose at the cow and growls.

"No, Grasper. Leave it," Emily orders, shooing him out the rear door.

She spends a few minutes with the cow, which licks her with its big, slobbery tongue, and then she wanders out into the yard.

After the shadowiness of the barn, even the weak sunshine seems bright. There's no sign of Grasper, but the horses — a chestnut and a grey — are peering over their stable doors. She goes over and strokes their necks, letting them nuzzle her and breathing in their warm, malty smell.

She's laughing because the grey is trying to nibble her sleeve when she hears quick footsteps behind her and Mr. Taylor appears at her side.

"I'm sorry I took so long. My wife seemed to feel the need of my opinion on some brocades, though I couldn't for the life of me see much difference between 'em."

He laughs and Emily smiles politely. She's hoping he won't keep her talking for long because she has no idea what to say to him, but to her relief he hands her the note, saying, "Tell your father I'd be glad to see him any time he cares to drop by."

Emily nods and calls Grasper, but he doesn't reappear.

"He might be in the end stable." Mr. Taylor nods at an open door. "I'll look in the washhouse, though I can't think he'd find anything interesting in there."

Emily looks in at the door of the empty stable and there's Grasper in the corner, head down, intently eating something.

"What have you got there, Grasper?" she asks, approaching him.

The bloody mangled remains are barely identifiable, but then she sees the long tail. "Oh, a rat!"

"What's that? A rat, you say?" Mr. Taylor comes up behind her.

"Yes, he must have caught it. Papa thought he'd be a good ratter, but I've never seen him do it before." Emily feels quite proud. It looks as if it was a big rat, and as far as she can see Grasper is unscathed.

"Mm, well, I hope he did catch it." Mr. Taylor's cheery geniality has disappeared and he looks worried.

"What do you mean?" asks Emily.

Mr. Taylor attempts a rather strained smile. "Oh, it doesn't matter. I'm sure it will be all right."

୧୦୨

Emily's not been back home five minutes when Tabby, who's been listening to her account of her visit to the farm, interrupts her, drawing her attention to Grasper.

"By heck, yon lad's got a thirst on him."

Grasper, having emptied his water bowl, is licking at it desperately.

"Do you want some more?" Emily fills his bowl again and Grasper laps away.

"Has he been running all over?" asks Tabby, watching him.

"Not more than usual. He . . . Oh, Tabby, look!" Emily breaks off in alarm as Grasper's back legs give way.

He tries to get up, but he can't — and then he begins to retch, his sides heaving, saliva dripping from his mouth.

Emily rushes over to him and, throwing herself down onto the floor, she cradles his head. "There, there, Grasper, it's all right, boy." She looks up at Tabby, her eyes wide. "What's wrong with him?"

Tabby shakes her head. "I don't know, lass. Mebbe it's summat he ate?"

"But he hasn't — oh!" Emily's hand flies to her mouth. "The rat! He was eating a rat in Mr. Taylor's stable."

They both turn to look at Grasper, who now manages to get up and stagger a few steps. He's shivering and then he suddenly squats and Emily watches, horrified, as he releases a stream of bloody diarrhea onto the stone floor before collapsing again.

Emily gives Tabby an agonized look.

Tabby's face is grim. "I'll fetch maister. Happen he'll know what to do."

Left alone in the kitchen, Emily goes on stroking Grasper and murmuring endearments in his ear, as if by the sheer force of her love she can will him to recover.

But he just lies there in her arms with his eyes half-closed and every now and then a spasm shakes him.

Emily's relieved when Papa comes. Surely it will be all right now.

While Tabby hovers in the background, her father squats down and studies Grasper, who doesn't seem aware of his presence, not even when he touches Grasper's ears.

"Hmm. They're cold," Papa murmurs to himself, as if he half-expected it.

"Do you know what's wrong, Papa?"

Papa's face is grave as he gazes at her. "I fear it looks as if he's been poisoned."

"Poisoned? You mean, the rat . . . ?"

Papa nods. "It seems very likely."

"What can we do?"

Her father lays his hand on her head and the look he gives her makes her heart turn over. "Nothing, my love."

"What do you mean? Surely there's something we can do!"

But Papa shakes his head.

Emily swallows hard. "How long has he got?"

"Not long."

She doesn't utter a sound.

Turning back to Grasper, she caresses his rough coat, his dear, dear head, and then she just holds him. Her throat and chest are tight, but she remains dry-eyed as she sits there, watching, holding, as Grasper's eyes glaze over and he slips into unconsciousness.

After a while, Papa touches her arm. "Emily? He's gone."

She gives the briefest of nods, but still she goes on holding him, and it's a long time before she'll allow Papa to lift him out of her arms and take him away.

44

"This'll cheer you up, Em."

"What is it?" says Emily wearily, putting down the book she's been trying and failing to read. Several weeks have passed since Grasper died, but she's still in a low state. Since she lost her dearest friend, she has no interest in anything. But there's no ignoring Branwell when he's in this mood — bouncing into the parlor and pushing his eager face into hers. It's better to respond and hope he'll go away soon.

"Mr. Taylor —"

"Don't." Emily covers her ears. "I don't want to hear anything about that man."

"No, listen." Branwell pulls her hands away. "You'll like this, honestly. He caught me after church this morning and said I was to tell you that his Jessie has had her pups and you're welcome to have one, if you like."

Emily screws up her face. "I don't want a pup."

"But it's a good idea, isn't it? To help you get over . . ."

"It's too soon." She turns her head away, caught by a fresh wave of loss. She would rather experience the physical pain of the dog bite again than suffer this — and it just goes on and on.

"Em?" Branwell is still here, looking at her hopefully.

Exasperated, she sucks air in through her teeth. He's impossible. But then she relents — after all, he's only trying to help.

"Look," she says, "one day I might be able to think about having another dog, but I couldn't have one of Mr. Taylor's, not after what happened."

"But it wasn't his fault."

Emily gives him a stony look. "He said it was all right for Grasper to run about the yard."

"Maybe it had slipped his mind that the groom had put down the poison. He can't possibly remember every detail about what goes on at the farm."

"Why are you so keen to defend him?"

"Because it was an accident, Em. Robert says —"

"What has this to do with *him*?" She can't keep the irritation out of her voice.

He hesitates. "Oh, it doesn't matter. The point is, Mr. Taylor feels sorry for what happened and he wants to make it up to you. Can't you do the poor fellow a favor and accept his offer?" Branwell's face is shining with earnestness.

Emily clenches her teeth. "Why should I do Mr. Taylor a favor?"

Branwell tugs at his hair in exasperation. "Hang it, Em! I'm only saying all this because I think a puppy would make *you* feel better."

Emily doesn't deign to respond.

Sighing, Branwell gets up and goes to the door, where he delivers a parting shot. "At least think about it."

৩৩

Despite herself, Emily does. She can't help it. The house is so dismal without Grasper.

She tries to console herself with Tiger, encouraging him to sit on her lap and spoiling him with scraps, but it's no good. The cat, like all cats, is independent and once he's eaten his treat, he's ready to go off on his own business.

Grasper was quite different — he really seemed to seek out her company. She misses the weight of his head on her foot when she's playing the piano. She misses his warm body pressed against hers when she lies on the rug reading and the way he'd push his nose into her book when he was bored. And there's such a gaping void at her side when she goes out walking.

Of course, she'll never feel the same about another dog, but it might be worth a look. Still, she hesitates. It seems disloyal to be thinking about a puppy so soon.

But a few days later she says to Branwell, "Next time you see Mr. Taylor, tell him I'd like to have a look at the pups."

The thought of the puppies has proved irresistible. She adds hastily, "Just a look, mind. I've not decided definitely to have one. And you realize, of course, that I'm not doing this to oblige Mr. Taylor."

"No, of course not." Branwell nods gravely. "I understand completely. I'll pass the message on."

He duly reports back that Emily is welcome to go to the farm the next afternoon to see the puppies.

"I won't have to meet Mr. Taylor, will I?"

"Oh no, I made sure of that." There's a gleam in Branwell's eye that suddenly makes Emily suspicious. Is he up to something?

She almost changes her mind about going. But if Mr. Taylor appears, she'll just march straight out of there without saying a word.

ᏯᎧ

The farm servant who opens the door says, "You're expected, miss. Come in."

Emily enters the house warily — she'd imagined she'd be directed to the barn. "Is your master at home?"

"No, miss. He's taken missis to Halifax to buy some stuff for new dresses."

Emily relaxes. "I've come to see the puppies."

"Yes, miss, I know. They're in here." The woman shows her into what is obviously the family's sitting room. Emily doesn't waste any time looking around — she's spotted the mother sheepdog and her litter in a large box next to the fireplace.

Throwing off her bonnet, she crouches down in front of them, entranced.

The puppies are wide awake and full of life, tumbling over one another and fighting. In a corner two of them are tussling over an old glove, playing at tug-of-war, and she can't help smiling at their antics.

She notices that the mother is watching her suspiciously, so she puts her hand out and lets the dog sniff her fingers. When the slow thump of the dog's tail signals that she's been accepted, she lets her hand dangle in the box. Within seconds one of the pups starts chewing at it, its little teeth as sharp as needles.

"Ow, you little rascal." Emily scoops up the squirming bundle. "Let me have a good look at you."

Like its mother and siblings, the puppy is black with white markings, but its eye patches aren't symmetrical, which gives it a comical look.

"Aren't you a funny one!" she exclaims, but then she almost drops the pup as a voice at her shoulder says, "He's jolly, isn't he?"

She spins round. Robert Taylor is standing there, smiling down at her. She thrusts the puppy back in the box and scrambles to her feet.

"Forgive me if I startled you. You were so absorbed I didn't want to intrude." The young man puts out his hand as if to shake hers, but Emily doesn't take it.

How long has he been watching her? And how dare he? She feels exposed, vulnerable. And she can't think of a single thing to say.

"Miss Emily, I'm so sorry about what happened to your dog. Branwell tells me you were very fond of it."

They've been talking about her. Branwell really is the limit.

Her eyes flick toward the door, but the young man is rattling on. "I lost my dog last year. It was to be expected — old age, you know — but even so I miss her. I can imagine how upset you must be feeling about yours. I'm glad you're going to have one of these little ones. It's the least we can do."

Emily finds her voice at last. "But I'm not . . . that is . . . I haven't decided yet."

Robert Taylor gestures toward the puppies. "Please. Carry on, and take your time."

Oh Lord, he's misunderstood. Why doesn't he go away and leave her alone?

But he doesn't. Instead, he squats by the box and gestures for her to join him.

Emily finds herself sinking onto her knees beside him. What *is* she doing? She should just get up and leave, now.

But he's off again. "Now, I know you fancied that odd-looking fellow, but have you seen this little girl here? She's very pretty, and has a more placid temperament, I'd say." He holds out one of the pups for her inspection. "Wouldn't she suit you better? She'd make a lovely pet."

Mutely, Emily shakes her head. A pet! That's the last thing she would want.

"All right, the boy it is. He's yours." He puts the puppy in her arms. But instead of drawing back, he stays where he is, stroking the puppy's head.

This is terrible. He's so close to her she can smell the soapy scent of his skin. But she's trapped and can't get up without making a spectacle of herself or squashing the puppy.

Mesmerized, she watches his hand move back and forth across the puppy's head, noticing how clean his nails are as his fingers come perilously close to hers.

And then his hand stops moving, he lifts his head, and, looking right into her eyes, he says quietly, "Miss Emily, you can't imagine how happy you've made me by coming to see me today."

Emily widens her eyes. "But —" That's all she manages to say, because suddenly he kisses her on the lips. Frozen with shock, she lets it happen, inwardly recoiling from the warm moistness of his mouth pressed against hers.

She's brought back to her senses by the puppy suddenly whimpering and wriggling. She jerks her head back and, by shuffling away from him, she manages to scramble up.

"How dare you?"

He blinks at her, stupefied, and then he looks embarrassed and rises awkwardly to his feet.

"I — I'm sorry. You're so absolutely lovely, I forgot myself."

Emily screws up her face. What nonsense is this?

"Please." He takes a step toward her and she moves back out of his reach. "Please don't think badly of me. It won't happen again, I promise."

She manages to find her voice. "You can be sure of that, because I'll never come near you again." Unceremoniously, she dumps the puppy into his arms and retreats to the door.

Her hand is on the latch when he cries out, "Oh, don't say that. Don't let one moment of rash impulse affect your feelings for me."

Emily turns back. "My feelings? But I don't have any feelings for you."

Robert's face falls and he looks confused. "But Branwell said —"

"Branwell!"

Suddenly she sees it all.

Branwell and his friend have devised this ridiculous charade in order to amuse themselves at her expense. She can just imagine how heartily they'll laugh when Robert gives his account of the scene.

Lifting her chin, she says as coldly as she can, "I won't endure another moment of your mockery. And I wouldn't take one of your pups if you paid me to. Good day!"

She turns on her heels and makes her exit. She hears him bleating after her down the lane, but she splashes on without looking back or slowing her pace.

45

When she gets home, she marches straight into Branwell's studio, where he's dabbing at a canvas on his easel.

He looks up, surprised. "You're back early." Then he turns his attention back to the painting, saying casually, "Did you choose a puppy?"

Emily glares at him. "How could you!"

"How could I what?" His look is wide-eyed.

"Don't pretend you don't know what I'm talking about. How could you trick me like that? Sending me up to Stanbury to choose a puppy, when all the time you were plotting with Robert Taylor to make a fool of me."

"But I —"

"Oh, stop acting. It's not convincing, you know. Your friend did a better job of it, though he overdid the spooniness. Ugh!" Emily shudders at the memory of that kiss. "The pair of you should be thoroughly ashamed of yourselves."

He goes to speak, but she cuts him off. "And I don't understand how you could have done that, Branwell . . . playing on my feelings about Grasper. It's . . . it's *despicable*."

At least he has the grace to look shamefaced. Putting down his brush and palette, he wipes his hands on a rag and tries to take her hands in his, but she pulls away.

"Listen, Em, we weren't trying to make a fool of you. And Robert wasn't acting."

Emily darts a withering look at him. "Oh, come on, you don't expect me to believe that."

"No, honestly. He wasn't. I told you before. He's really smitten with you, you know. Truly."

He looks so earnest that she's taken aback. Remembering Robert's manner, it seems there might be some truth in what Branwell's saying.

Falteringly, she mutters, "But he doesn't know me."

"What's that got to do with it?"

"Everything."

Branwell sighs and scratches his head.

She can tell he hasn't got a clue what she's talking about. But there's no point in trying to explain — she's not even sure she can explain it to herself.

Branwell says, "Look. All I know is that Robert believes he's in love with you."

She stares at him and the truth dawns on her. In a quiet but deadly voice, she says, "So you sent me up there to oblige your friend?"

"What?" He opens his eyes wide in amazement. Or a good pretense of it. "No, Em, you've got it all wrong." He takes a deep breath. "The puppy business was genuine. I was really sorry about what happened to Grasper and Robert was too. I mean, his father felt bad about it, but it was Robert's idea to offer you a puppy. He wanted to make it up to you."

"I see." She narrows her eyes. "So why couldn't I have just gone and looked at the puppies by myself? Why did he have to be there?"

There's a silence in which Branwell shifts from foot to foot. Finally he admits, "That was my idea."

Emily draws her breath in with a hiss.

"No, listen." Branwell puts on a beseeching look. "I thought that if you had a chance to talk to him properly, you'd realize what a decent fellow he is. I think you'd like him, you know, if you let yourself."

She feels completely bewildered. What on earth is he playing at? "Why do you want me to like him? He's nothing to me." And then she remembers what Robert said and her anger surges back again. "You told him that I returned his feelings, didn't you?"

"Yes, but —"

"In heaven's name, why did you do that? What were you thinking of?"

"I thought he could do with some encouragement." He grins. "You can be pretty scary sometimes, you know."

Speechless, Emily clenches her fists. She'd like to smack that stupid smile from his stupid face. "Do you know what, Branwell? I could hate you for this. It's the worst thing you've ever done to me."

His face reddens and then goes pale again. "But you don't understand. I didn't do it for Robert's sake, I did it for yours," he says in aggrieved tones.

"Mine? How could it possibly benefit me?"

"Because . . . I thought . . . I thought that if you grew close to him, it would make you happy."

Emily blinks. What's he talking about? "But how could Robert Taylor possibly make me happy? It was bad enough before, but Grasper dying . . ." She stops, unable to go on.

"That's my point." Branwell's agitated now. "I don't think you know what's best for you. I mean, a dog's all very well, Em, but it's not a person, is it?"

"What do you mean?"

"You know, pouring all that emotion out . . . after all, it's just an animal."

She can't believe he just said that. Swallowing down all the bitter things she could retort, she says quietly, "Dogs are better than people. At least they don't betray you."

"I didn't betray you!" he shouts. "I was trying to help you. Hang it all, if you go on like this, you're going to end up an old maid! Is that what you want?"

She is utterly confounded. She stares at him and can't speak — there's something rising in her chest that threatens to choke her. She turns and scrabbles blindly for the door handle and at last she's out of there.

In two paces she's across the landing and in her room with the door firmly shut. She leans against it, heaving deep breaths as though she's been running and swallowing the sobs thickening in her throat.

Why does she want to cry? She should be angry with him — a fierce burst of fury that would make her feel better — not this feeble weakness.

But somehow Branwell, clumsy stupid Branwell, has blundered his way in, past her defenses, and pierced her.

She doesn't understand it, not really. It's partly to do with what he said about Grasper, his words striking her with the same force as if he'd attacked her beloved companion with physical cruelty. But it's more to do with her self, her inner self — she feels a sense of violation, as if Branwell has burst in where he has no right to be.

She presses her hand on her eyes in an attempt to blot out what's just happened and in an instant the scene of her humiliation at the Manor House rises up.

She cringes at the memory.

She knows that people experience feelings for others based on the most superficial things . . . for heaven's sake, look at the way Mary was attracted to Branwell . . .

But she doesn't want to be the object of such an infatuation. It's all so silly, and nothing to do with love. That's what she was trying to tell Branwell.

Love is two people being as close as she was with Elizabeth, as she has been at times with Charlotte and then Anne when they shared the same vision of Gondal; it is knowing each other utterly, seeing each other's souls and knowing that they are indissolubly linked.

Whatever that foolish young man thinks he feels for her, it isn't love.

She sighs. She must try not to think of him. Though he offended her, he did it unwittingly, whereas Branwell . . .

How could he fail so badly to understand her? And just when they were getting on so well and becoming so close? When she thought that once again she'd found a soul mate to share her writing?

She can't think about what he's done, what he's said, without feeling raw.

෨෬

Emily stays in her room for the rest of the afternoon, and by teatime she has decided on her course of action. She doesn't join Branwell at the kitchen table — she doesn't want to eat anything and she can't yet trust herself to be with him in Tabby's presence. Later, when he's alone in the parlor, she goes in and takes up a position just inside the door.

When Branwell looks up, she says, "There's something I want you to know. What I feel and who I choose to care for are nothing to do with you. So there's no need to busy yourself with plans for me or my future. Whatever happens, it will be me who decides. Do you understand?"

Branwell looks at her mutinously, as if there's a lot he'd like to say, but after a moment he nods.

"Good."

She spins on her heel and goes out, shutting the door quietly behind her.

46

The next day, when she comes in from her walk, Emily retreats to her bedroom. She doesn't want to have to see Branwell, but she's too restless to read.

After pacing about and staring out of the window, she's suddenly moved to sit down with her writing desk and write a story, her first new story for ages, which turns out to be about Angelica, who, having been wronged, doesn't rest until she has gained revenge. Emily pours her heart into describing Angelica's feelings and takes a savage satisfaction in the bloody outcome. She's never written anything so fast — it's as if it's been ripped out of her whole, leaving her shaken.

Afterward, she feels drained, but more at peace. She's still wary of Branwell, though. For days she'll only speak to him when she has to and even then she keeps to practical everyday matters. Luckily, Branwell seems to want to avoid her too.

Tabby notices, of course, and one day when they're clearing the table, she says to Emily, "Hast tha had a falling out with Maister Branwell?"

Emily ducks her head, half-acknowledging that this is the case.

Tabby sighs. "Well, tha knows our lad — if tha's looking for him to change, tha's in for a long wait." She pats Emily's hand. "If tha'll take my advice, even if it's thee who's been wronged, don't bear a grudge, lass. Tha'll only regret it in the long run."

Afterward, Emily thinks about what Tabby said.

She hasn't been waiting for Branwell to change — she hasn't actually been looking for anything from him. She's just been going on and struggling to cope with the sense of being injured.

But perhaps Branwell wasn't being malicious — perhaps he did think he was helping her. And maybe she was expecting too much from him, wanting him to understand her inner, hidden self. Her brother is probably the last person to look to for profound insight — it's like trying to swim in a shallow brook when really what you need is a deep pool.

The prospect of their being estranged forever seems utterly dismal.

That evening she joins him in the parlor, where he's sitting at the table with a book. He barely acknowledges her, but after a few minutes, determined to put an end to this, she asks, "What are you reading?"

Branwell looks up, surprised. "Oh, this article in *Blackwood's* about the National Gallery and how it could be improved. Quite interesting, actually."

"Would you read it to me?"

He raises his eyebrows. "Really?"

"Yes."

He looks at her for a moment and then nods, as if accepting that this is a truce.

The next evening, he asks rather tentatively if he might read to her from his latest writing; Emily agrees and even has some comments to make about his work.

But when he says, "Do *you* want to read something?" she

shakes her head. They might be talking to each other again, but this is as far as she wants it to go.

She never wants to share her inner world with him again.

⚬⚭⚬

Gradually, Emily picks up some of her usual pursuits, because after all, what else is there to do? She walks as often as she can; she practices the piano and goes to Ponden Hall to borrow some new books. But when she takes out an old story, intending to revise it, she soon gives up — the savor has gone from that activity. And since the Angelica story she's lost the desire to attempt anything new.

She feels hollowed out, hopeless, and quite alone.

Even the weather seems to be mocking her. Rather than being dull and grey, which would suit her mood, it brightens up: Sunshine succeeds all those days of rain and it becomes unseasonably warm.

Late one sultry afternoon, she's setting out on her walk when a sudden impulse takes her into the church.

It's cool inside and quiet. Emily drifts down the aisle, trailing her fingers along the rough wood of the pew doors.

She's not sure what's she's doing here.

Is she expecting some kind of message, from God, perhaps? Or, if He's too busy to come Himself, from an angelic messenger bringing comfort?

She smiles wryly.

By now she has reached the front of the church and the familiar plaque. Emily traces the lettering: *Here lie the remains* . . . Then she rests her forehead on the cold stone.

"Elizabeth."

She calls the name silently. Just for a moment she wants to be small again, snuggling up to her big sister; she wants to be cuddled.

Isn't there an ancient ballad about a dead mother roused from her sleep by her children's weeping, who rises from her grave to comfort them?

But no answering call comes, no warm arms embrace her.

The church remains still and empty.

Emily gives herself a shake. Stupid! What did she expect?

She turns and marches swiftly to the door, her footsteps echoing on the stone flags.

ᏜᏯ

She takes her usual path, ascending the moor at a steady pace. It's muggy and close, not a breath of air stirring, and before long she's perspiring and wishing she'd left her shawl at home. But she still keeps on — it helps, this regular beat of her feet on the stony path, it helps to assuage the ache in her heart.

By the time she reaches Ponden Beck the light has changed — the sky has turned an ominous yellow and, above the horizon, a black band is growing broader by the minute. On the other side of the stream she comes across Martha Brown, the sexton's daughter, picking whinberries with her little sister.

"Look," says Martha, showing Emily their pail. "We've got some right beauties." Both children's mouths are stained purple with juice.

"You've done well. But see," Emily indicates the dark curtain sweeping toward them, "there's a storm brewing. Isn't it time you were setting off home?" As she speaks, a white flash streaks across the sky.

A stubborn look comes over Martha's face. "We'll go in a minute. Ma won't be pleased unless we take a full pail home. And I'm not scared of a drop of rain, are you, Alice?"

"No," says the little one stoutly.

Emily is amused. "Well, you mind yourselves." And she continues on her way.

There's a deep rumble of thunder, overhead now. She quickens her pace, hoping she's got time to reach the shelter of the Grey Stones before the storm breaks.

The next moment a wind springs up from nowhere, whipping her hair against her face and threatening to whirl her shawl away, and fat drops of rain begin to splash down onto her.

Clutching her shawl, she makes for the rocks, where she huddles under the great slab, the rocking stone, balanced on two boulders. Within minutes the gale is driving the rain into her refuge, soaking her. Praying that the rocking stone won't come crashing down on her, she peers out over the wide sweep of the moors.

By now the storm is directly overhead, the dark clouds swirling and seething, thunder following lightning in quick succession and, as she watches the play of electricity flickering wildly across the sky, Emily feels an answering blaze flare up inside her. On an impulse she dashes out from her hiding place, and, holding out her arms and lifting her face to the heavens, she exposes herself to the full impact of the storm.

The rain beats down on her, the thunder deafens her, and the lightning dazzles her eyes. Buffeted by the wind, she feels delirious, giddy, and all the small meanness of her self and her unhappiness vanish as she's absorbed into this fierce and powerful force.

At the height of her exaltation, there's a loud explosion.

The ground shakes and across the moor, on Crow Hill, the ground erupts in a fountain of stones and peat from which a long black serpent uncurls and begins to slither down the slope.

Emily stares. She can't understand what she's looking at. And then she suddenly realizes that the serpent is the bog itself. It's come alive and is advancing down the hill, intent on smothering the valley below.

Suddenly she remembers with a stab of horror — the little girls! If they're still where she left them, they're right in the path of the landslide.

She hesitates. It's too dangerous.

But then the horror of what might happen to them seizes her and with a wild cry she sets off down the hillside at full tilt, leaping from tussock to tussock. At one point she stumbles and falls to her knees, but she rights herself and carries on. Her heart is hammering, she's struggling for breath, but as the black snake picks up speed, she pushes herself on.

Will she be in time?

She reaches Ponden Crag, perched on the lip of the valley, and there below are the Brown girls. Oblivious of the danger they're in, they're trying to shelter from the rain in the lee of a boulder. If they can get up here, to Ponden Crag, they might be safe. Emily waves her arms and shrieks, but the wind carries her voice away and they don't look up.

She'll have to go down to them.

She skids and slides down the steep incline, calling as she goes, and at last Martha turns round and sees her.

Emily beckons frantically and shouts, "Martha! Alice! Come here."

The little girl waves but stays where she is.

Desperate, Emily pants on until she reaches them. Pointing up the hill, she gasps, "The bog!"

The girls look at her as if she's mad. She scoops up Alice and, seizing Martha's arm, she hurries them back the way she came, ignoring Martha's protests and Alice's screams. Reaching the Crag, she thrusts them into the small cave at its base and flings herself down so that her body covers the entrance.

A second later the torrent arrives with a deafening roar. She struggles to keep her footing as the mud swirls round her, pummeling her with stones and threatening to suck her away. There's nothing to cling on to, but, closing her eyes, she presses herself against the rock face and waits to die.

The next moment the mudslide has swept past her and on down the valley, leaving behind an eerie silence.

It's stopped raining, Emily realizes. And she's alive.

She opens her eyes.

Yes, she's alive and miraculously unhurt, apart from some bruising to her back. She waits until her breath slows, then, rising unsteadily to her feet, she looks down at the two shocked little faces peering up at her.

"You can come out now," she says. "It's safe."

47

The three of them walk home without speaking. Emily guesses that the little girls must feel as stunned as she does. Everything seems slightly unreal — after what's happened, it feels odd to be walking along as though it's just a normal day.

When they've nearly reached the village they see a man hurrying toward them across the common, shouting and waving.

As he comes closer Emily recognizes him. It's Papa! And he's come out without his hat and stick.

Rushing up to them, he seizes her hands. "You're safe. Thank God for that."

When she feels his warm grip, the reality of what might have happened suddenly washes over her and she starts to shake. She'd like to hold on to Papa's hands, but he's already turning away from her.

"And these little ones are safe too, thank the Lord. We heard the explosion at the house and feared the worst."

"Miss Em'ly saved us. Otherwise we'd have been drownded," announces Martha in a quavery voice, as if she hasn't yet got over their narrow escape.

"Did you? Well done, my dear." But Papa says this in a distracted way, as if his thoughts are elsewhere. He's wild-eyed and excited. Perhaps it's because of the fright he must have had about her. He says, "Come, we must hurry home," and he sets off back along the path, shepherding them in front of him.

At the parsonage gate he suddenly says, "To think this day has come at last. This earthquake —"

"Earthquake?" Emily's surprised. "It didn't seem like that to me. It —"

"Oh yes, almost certainly, and we must prepare ourselves."

"For what, Papa?"

"Why, for the end of the world, of course."

She stares at him in utter amazement. Has he gone mad?

She notices the little girls gazing at him with eyes as round as saucers. She must get him into the house — Tabby will know what to do.

"Run on home, now, girls," she says. "Your mother will be worried."

"Oh!" Martha puts a hand to her mouth. "We left the pail behind. Ma will give us what for."

"I don't think she'll be cross," says Emily. "I think she'll just be glad you've come to no harm."

As the two little girls trot away down the lane, she turns to her father. "What do you mean, Papa? About the end of the world?"

"Do you not recall the book of Revelation?" Standing there in the lane, with his arms outstretched and his white hair all awry, he proclaims in a loud voice, "'And lo, there was a great earthquake; and the sun became black as sackcloth of hair, and the moon became as blood.'"

Suddenly he doesn't seem mad, but rather splendid, like an Old Testament prophet.

" 'For the great day of His wrath is come; and who shall be able to stand?' "

At his words Emily experiences a thrill that runs right through her, from the top of her head to her toes.

What if Papa's right? What if this really is the end of everything? Of everyone? All of them swept up together in one final apocalyptic convulsion.

Strangely, she doesn't feel at all afraid. Rather, she's elated. This feels like the right and proper climax to the tumultuous events of the day.

"What should we do, Papa?"

"We await His judgment, of course."

⌀

"We have just seen something of the mighty power of God: He has unsheathed His sword, and brandished it over our heads, but still the blow is suspended in mercy — it has not yet fallen on us."

Listening to Papa's voice ringing from the pulpit, it's all Emily can do not to leap up from her pew and challenge him.

Papa was wrong about the end of the world, for here they all are still, three days later.

And she's pretty sure he's wrong about this too — she can't believe that the eruption of the bog was an earthquake sent by God as a warning to sinners to repent before it's too late.

It *was* terribly destructive. She's been back to Crow Hill to see for herself, and the vast crater in the moor is amazing. And it caused a lot of damage — all those bridges and walls demolished, mud pouring into people's homes.

But was it a message from God? She doesn't think so. She's inclined to agree with those who think the eruption was caused by all that rain earlier in the summer. In other words, extraordinary as it was, it was a natural phenomenon.

She can't help feeling just a tiny bit disappointed that the mudslide didn't herald the end of the world. It would have been so exciting to witness it, so satisfying to know once and for all exactly what was to happen. And there was something comforting in the idea of dying at the same time as everyone else — better than having to leave knowing that the world would be going on without you.

But even that — dying on your own — doesn't seem as frightening now. She hasn't been able to shake off the notion that the earth almost claimed her. But if it had, would it have been such a bad thing? To be swept up in the cataclysmic eruption and buried out there on the moor with the wind and the rain and the sun, her body dissolving into the soil, her spirit staying and haunting forever the place she loves best . . .

It would truly be a homecoming, her heart finally at rest in the earth.

But she wasn't swept away — the earth spared her. Like the thorns at that isolated farmhouse, Top Withens, she has been bent by the fierce force of the wind, but not broken.

She remembers how bereft she felt in here, alone on the day of the storm, and how she called out to Elizabeth. It was not her beloved sister who answered, or Mama, as in the old ballad, but out of the heart of the storm the earth itself arose, coming, not to comfort her, but to energize her with its song. For witnessing that great power of nature and coming within a hairsbreadth of death has shaken her awake and made her aware that the same vital force that flowed through the moor and changed it utterly also flows through her.

The earth has granted her more time and she resolves not to waste another moment. How silly she's been, squandering so much time moping about, being unhappy because she couldn't have what she wanted, when she could have been experiencing so much. From now on when she walks on the moors, she will be alert, attentive to every detail; she will lay herself open to all the changing moods of the natural world.

Dear, dear nature — even at its most threatening it's not something to be feared, as Papa believes, but something to celebrate.

Normally she sings quietly into her hymnbook, but today the chorus seems to express exactly how she feels — not grateful to have been spared the wrath of God, but glad to be alive. "Rejoice! Rejoice!" the congregation sings and Emily, for once, joins in with gusto.

〰️

That night, unable to sleep because she's in such a state of simmering excitement, Emily throws open the window and the freshness of the breeze blowing down from the moors fills her lungs and floods her veins. She stares up at the stars and the full, round moon.

What would it have been like if, instead of experiencing the storm on Crow Hill when she did, in the daytime, it had been now, in the middle of the night?

She can just imagine it — being out there in the middle of that vast dark space in the moonlight, and then the storm coming: the sky alive with lightning, the heather bending as the wind rushes over it, everything vital and in motion, including the very earth itself . . .

All at once she's impelled to relight her candle and, seizing a piece of paper and a pencil from her writing desk, she begins to scribble, trying to recapture exactly how it felt to be caught up in the midst of the storm and the tumult of the landslide that day.

When she's done, she looks at what she's written. It's not like anything she's ever written before. She can see that it's not perfect yet and needs some polishing. But nevertheless, here it is — a poem, vital and true.

She feels enormously satisfied. She feels as if she could do anything, as if she's as potent and fearless as her heroine Augusta Geraldine Almeda. And those gifts she has been granted — the power of her own imagination and her ability to experience that amazing, fearful connection with the natural world — will endure and can be relied on in a way that people can't. She can go forward, secure in the knowledge that, as long as she has herself, she will survive.

There will be more poems, she's sure. And maybe more stories too, stories that she creates by herself, for herself, in which she explores her own deepest passions.

She reads through her poem once more. Then she picks up the pencil and signs her name at the bottom: Emily Jane Brontë.

To Imagination

When weary with the long day's care,
And earthly change from pain to pain,
And lost, and ready to despair,
Thy kind voice calls me back again
O my true friend, I am not lone
While thou canst speak with such a tone!

So hopeless is the world without,
The world within I doubly prize;
Thy world where guile and hate and doubt
And cold suspicion never rise;
Where thou and I and Liberty
Have undisputed sovereignty.

What matters it that all around
Danger and grief and darkness lie,
If but within our bosom's bound
We hold a bright unsullied sky,
Warm with ten thousand mingled rays
Of suns that know no winter days?

Reason indeed may oft complain
For Nature's sad reality,
And tell the suffering heart how vain
Its cherished dreams must always be;
And Truth may rudely trample down
The flowers of Fancy newly blown.

But thou art ever there to bring
The hovering visions back and breathe
New glories o'er the blighted spring
And call a lovelier life from death,
And whisper with a voice divine
Of real worlds as bright as thine.

I trust not to thy phantom bliss,
Yet still in evening's quiet hour
With never-failing thankfulness
I welcome thee, benignant power,
Sure solacer of human cares
And brighter hope when hope despairs.

— Emily Brontë

AUTHOR'S NOTE & ACKNOWLEDGMENTS

I am aware that in presuming to write about the Brontës, and Emily in particular, I am treading on dangerous ground, so highly are they revered by generations of avid readers.

But I must point out that *The World Within* is a work of fiction, not a historical account of this period in the Brontës' lives. Many of the events depicted in these pages did happen, but not always in the order or at the time I've chosen to put them. Other events are invented.

I have taken these liberties partly because there is frustratingly little in the historical record to inform us about the inner world of that enigmatic person, Emily Brontë. We know more about Charlotte because some of her letters and early writings have survived, but no trace of the Gondal stories has been found — the only existing material written by Emily consists of a few documents, her poems, and, of course, *Wuthering Heights*.

For a novelist such a state of affairs is not necessarily to be regretted. I did not set out to write an accurate history, but to explore my version, my vision of Emily Brontë. As such, this is, appropriately I feel, a work of the imagination, and I apologize to any reader who is disappointed because my Emily is not theirs.

Having said that, for factual information about the family, I have made extensive use of Juliet Barker's rigorously detailed biography: *The Brontës*.

Of the two attempts I know of to piece together the Gondal saga from Emily's poems, I have relied on the Appendix of *The Brontës: Charlotte and Emily* by Laura L. Hinkley.

And I have been utterly inspired by Stevie Davies's brilliant interpretations of Emily and her writing in *Emily Brontë: The Artist as a Free Woman*; *Emily Brontë: Heretic*; and "Emily Brontë & The Vikings."

I am indebted to Ann Dinsdale, Collections Manager of the Brontë Parsonage Musuem, for suggesting relevant material and for her patience in answering numerous queries.

Of the many friends who have helped me in the writing of this book, I would particularly like to thank Anne Farmer, for giving me a refuge from workmen; Melissa Laird, for deepening my understanding of what it means to love a dog; and Sarah Hymas and Elizabeth Burns, for their insights into the writing process.

I am more than grateful to my editors, Cheryl Klein and Emily Clement, for their commitment to this project.

And finally, my greatest thanks to Sheila Wynn and to my agent, Lindsey Fraser. Without their unfailing support and encouragement, I would never have succeeded in completing this book!

This book was edited by Cheryl Klein and Emily Clement. It was designed by Jeannine Riske. The text was set in Berling LT Roman and the display type was set in Pastonchi MT. The book was printed and bound at RR Donnelley in Crawfordsville, Indiana. Production was supervised by Starr Baer, and manufacturing was supervised by Shannon Rice.